...ERS

Missing...

"There is a confidence to Coben's writing that carries the reader along on this literary journey. He knows his subject matter; he knows his characters; he knows his plot. He is supremely confident in all he puts down on paper and this confidence enhances the reader's pleasure. *Missing You* is another winner in Coben's stack of winners. If you are smart, you will grab it up as quickly as possible and start letting the pieces fit." —The Huffington Post

"Harlan Coben, master of the suburban thriller, delivers another outstanding look at the truth behind the facade with *Missing You*.... This is a dive-in, lose-sleep and miss-your-bus-stop reading experience."

—The Associated Press Online

"*Missing You* delivers twists aplenty, including—mercifully briefly—a chilling, horrific, and completely deserved revenge scene that makes the recent spate of zombie movies and television episodes pale significantly in comparison."

—The Boston Globe

"Warning: Under no circumstances do you skip to the ending of this superbly crafted novel. Yes, there is a twist—several of them, in fact. And you have to work your way through all of them to relish the stinger on the final page ... one of Coben's best ever."—*The Globe and Mail* (Canada)

"Continues to mine the truly terrifying from everyday life.... This as the book masterfully explores the costs of our techno-crazed existence in which the emotional costs of these Twitter-age relationships can be shattering and, in this case, dangerous. That's the power of Coben's uncannily prescient ability to guess where the darkness is going to settle next, making the brilliantly staged *Missing You* not to be missed."

—The Providence Journal

continued ...

"A dandy story . . . fun to read." — *St. Louis Post-Dispatch*

"The finale is epic, as all these story lines slam together in a thunder of meshing subplots." — *The Charlotte Observer*

"Once again, Coben has brilliantly used a current trend, in this case Internet dating, to create a can't-put-it-down thriller."
— *Publishers Weekly* (starred review)

"Coben has expertly constructed and then dismantled a time bomb of a plot." — *Booklist*

Six Years

"The beauty of Coben's craftsmanship here is how often he can lure us into not perceiving what's right in front of our eyes . . . furious plot twists." — *The Washington Post*

Stay Close

"Funnier and darker than many Coben thrillers, and packs a lot of surprises. It's the beach read of the pre–beach season." — *People* (4 stars)

Live Wire

"A master of the page-turner crime novel . . . one of Coben's most exciting and multidimensional tales yet . . . gripping." — *The Columbus Dispatch*

Caught

"The thrill-a-minute action zooms on sharp, slippery twists and turns in a white-knuckle race from start to finish."
—#1 *New York Times* bestselling author Nora Roberts

Long Lost

"The action unfolds with the intensity of TV's *24*. . . . Nobody writes them better than Coben."
— The Associated Press

Hold Tight

"A thriller for the Google era." —*The New York Times*

The Woods

"A lively, fast-moving entertainment, jam-packed with the bizarre plot twists that are his stock-in-trade."
—*The Washington Post*

Promise Me

"Truly surprising." —*Entertainment Weekly*

The Innocent

"Another twist-filled triumph." —*Life*

Just One Look

"The only plausible reason for setting down this book is to make sure your front door is locked and double-bolted."
—*People*

No Second Chance
**THE FIRST INTERNATIONAL
BOOK-OF-THE-MONTH CLUB® SELECTION**

"Every time you think Harlan Coben couldn't get any better at uncoiling a whip snake of a page-turner, he comes along with a new novel that somehow surpasses its predecessor." —*San Francisco Chronicle*

Gone for Good

"This killer thriller has more twists and turns than an amusement park ride. . . . *Gone for Good* is great." —*USA Today*

Tell No One

"Pulse-pounding. . . . Coben layers secret upon secret, crisscrossing years and crime scenes." —*People*

HARLAN
COBEN
THE
STRANGER

A SIGNET BOOK

SIGNET
Published by New American Library,
an imprint of Penguin Random House LLC
375 Hudson Street, New York, New York 10014

This book is a publication of New American Library. Previously published in a
Dutton edition.

Signet International Edition, October 2015

For more information about Penguin Random House, visit penguin.com.

ISBN 978-0-451-47752-1

Printed in the United States of America
10 9 8 7 6 5 4 3 2

Penguin
Random
House

*In loving memory of my cousin
Stephen Reiter*

*And in celebration of his children,
David, Samantha, and Jason*

Oh my soul, be prepared for the coming of the Stranger.
Be prepared for him who knows how to ask questions.
There is one who remembers the way to your door:
Life you may evade, but Death you shall not.

—T. S. Eliot

CHAPTER 1

THE stranger didn't shatter Adam's world all at once.

That was what Adam Price would tell himself later, but that was a lie. Adam somehow knew right away, right from the very first sentence, that the life he had known as a content suburban married father of two was forever gone. It was a simple sentence on the face of it, but there was something in the tone, something knowing and even caring, that let Adam know that nothing would ever be the same.

"You didn't have to stay with her," the stranger said.

They were in the American Legion Hall in Cedarfield, New Jersey. Cedarfield was a town loaded up with wealthy hedge fund managers and bankers and other financial masters-of-the-universe types. They liked to drink beer in the American Legion Hall because it was comfortable slumming, a way to pretend that they were salt-of-the-earth good ol' boys, like something in a Dodge Ram commercial, when they were anything but.

Adam stood by the sticky bar. There was a dartboard behind him. Neon signs advertised Miller Lite, but Adam had a bottle of Budweiser in his right hand. He turned to the man, who had just sidled up to him, and even though

Adam already knew the answer, he asked the man, "Are you talking to me?"

The guy was younger than most of the fathers, thinner, almost gaunt, with big, piercing blue eyes. His arms were white and reedy with a hint of a tattoo showing beneath one of the short sleeves. He was wearing a baseball cap. He wasn't quite a hipster, but there was something of a wonk attitude coming off him, like some guy who ran a tech department and never saw the sun.

The piercing blue eyes held Adam's with an earnestness that made him want to turn away. "She told you she was pregnant, right?"

Adam felt his grip on the bottle tighten.

"That's why you stayed. Corinne told you she was pregnant."

It was right then that Adam felt some kind of switch go off in his chest, as if someone had tripped the red digital timer on some movie bomb and now it had started to tick down. Tick, tick, tick, tick.

"Do I know you?" Adam asked.

"She told you she was pregnant," the stranger continued. "Corinne, I mean. She told you she was pregnant and then she lost the baby."

The American Legion Hall was loaded up with town dads sporting those white baseball T-shirts with the three-quarter sleeves and either baggy cargo shorts or perfectly no-assed Dad jeans. Lots of them wore baseball caps. Tonight was the fourth-, fifth-, and sixth-grade boys' lacrosse draft and A-team selections. If you ever wanted to witness type As behaving as such in their natural habitat, Adam thought, watch when parents get involved in their own offsprings' team selections. The Discovery Channel should film this.

"You felt obligated to stay, am I right?" the man asked.

"I don't know who the hell—"

"She lied, Adam." The younger man spoke with such conviction, not just as though he knew for certain but as though, at the end of the day, he had Adam's best interest at heart. "Corinne made it all up. She was never pregnant."

The words kept landing like punches, dazing Adam, sapping his resistance, leaving him shaken and confused and ready to take a standing eight count. He wanted to fight back, grab the guy by the shirt, toss him across the room for insulting his wife like this. But he didn't for two reasons.

One, there was the whole dazed-like-taking-punches, sapped-resistance thing.

Two, something about the way the man spoke, something about the guy's confident tone, the damn conviction in his voice, made Adam start thinking it might be smartest to listen.

"Who are you?" Adam asked.

"Does it matter?"

"Yeah, it does."

"I'm the stranger," he said. "The stranger with important knowledge. She lied to you, Adam. Corinne. She was never pregnant. It was all a ruse to get you back."

Adam shook his head. He swam through, tried to stay rational and calm. "I saw the pregnancy test."

"Fake."

"I saw the sonogram."

"Again fake." He held up a hand before Adam could say more. "And yes, so was the stomach. Or should I say stomachs? Once Corinne started to show, you never saw her naked, right? What did she do, claim some kind of late-night sickness so you wouldn't have sex? That's what happens most times. So when the miscarriage occurs, you can kinda look back on the whole thing and realize the pregnancy was difficult right from the start."

A booming voice from the other side of the hall called out, "Okay, guys, grab a fresh beer and let's get this show on the road."

The voice belonged to Tripp Evans, the president of the lacrosse league, a former Madison Avenue ad exec and a pretty good guy. The other dads started to grab aluminum chairs, the kind you use for your kid's school concert, from a rack and placed them in a circle around the room. Tripp Evans looked over at Adam, spotted the undoubtedly pale expression on his face, and frowned his concern. Adam shook him off and turned back to the stranger.

"Who the hell are you?"

"Think of me as your savior. Or like the friend who just released you from prison."

"You're full of crap."

All conversation had pretty much ended. The voices were hushed now, the sounds of scraping chairs echoing in the still hall. The fathers were getting their game faces on for the draft. Adam hated this. He wasn't even supposed to be here—Corinne was. She was the treasurer of the lacrosse board, but her school had changed the scheduling of her teachers' conference in Atlantic City, and even though this was the biggest day of the year for Cedarfield lacrosse—indeed the main reason Corinne had become so active—Adam had been forced to step in for her.

"You should be thanking me," the man said.

"What are you talking about?"

For the first time, the man smiled. It was, Adam couldn't help but notice, a kind smile, the smile of a healer, of a man who just wants to do the right thing.

"You're free," the stranger said.

"You're a liar."

"You know better, don't you, Adam?"

From across the room, Tripp Evans called, "Adam?"

He turned toward them. Everyone was seated now except Adam and the stranger.

"I have to go now," the stranger whispered. "But if you really need proof, check your Visa card. Look for a charge to Novelty Funsy."

"Wait—"

"One more thing." The man leaned in close. "If I were you, I'd probably run DNA tests on your two boys."

Tick, tick, tick ... ka-boom. "What?"

"I have no evidence on that, but when a woman is willing to lie about something like this, well, it's a pretty good bet it isn't her first time."

And then, with Adam dazed anew by this final accusation, the stranger hurried out the door.

CHAPTER 2

WHEN Adam managed to get his legs back, he ran after the stranger.

Too late.

The stranger was sliding into the passenger seat of a gray Honda Accord. The car pulled out. Adam ran to get a closer look, maybe see the license plate, but he could tell only that it was from his home state of New Jersey. As the car made the turn toward the exit, he noticed something else.

There was a woman driving the car.

She was young, with long blond hair. When the streetlight hit her face, he could see that she was looking at him. Their eyes met for a brief moment. There was a look of concern on her face, of pity.

For him.

The car roared away. Someone called his name. Adam turned around and headed back inside.

THEY started with house team drafts.

Adam tried to pay attention, but it was like all sound

was traveling through the auditory equivalent of a blurry shower door. Corinne had made Adam's job simple. She had ranked every boy who had tried out for the sixth-grade team, so he could simply select based on who was left. The real key—the real reason he was here—was to ensure that Ryan, their sixth grader, made the all-star travel team. Their older son, Thomas, who was now a sophomore in high school, had been shut out from the all-stars when he was Ryan's age because, at least Corinne thought and Adam tended to agree, his parents weren't involved enough. Too many of the fathers were here tonight not so much out of love of the game as to protect their own kids' interests.

Including Adam. Pathetic, but there you go.

Adam tried to push past what he just heard—who the hell was that guy anyway?—but that wasn't happening. His vision blurred as he stared down at Corinne's "scouting reports." His wife was so orderly, almost anal, listing the boys in order from best to worst. When one of the boys was drafted, Adam numbly crossed out his name. He studied his wife's perfect cursive, practically the template for those sample letter examples your third-grade teacher pinned atop the blackboard. That was Corinne. She was that girl who came into class, complained that she was going to fail, finished the test first, and got an A. She was smart, driven, beautiful, and . . .

A liar?

"Let's break it down to the travel teams, fellas," Tripp said.

The sound of scraping chairs again echoed through the hall. Still in a fog, Adam joined the circle of four men who would round out the A and B travel teams. This was where it really counted. The house league stayed in town. The best players made A and B and got to travel to play in tournaments across the state.

Novelty Funsy. Why did that name ring a bell?

The grade's head coach was named Bob Baime, but Adam always thought of him as Gaston, the animated character from Disney's *Beauty and the Beast* movie. Bob was a big puff pastry of a man with the kind of bright smile you find only on the dim. He was loud and proud and stupid and mean, and whenever he strutted by, chest out, arms swaying, it was as though he was accompanied by a sound track singing, *"No one's slick/fights/shoots like Gaston . . ."*

Push it away, Adam told himself. *The stranger was just playing with you. . . .*

Picking the teams should take seconds. Each kid was scored between one and ten in various categories—stick handling, speed, strength, passing, stuff like that. The numbers were totaled and an average was determined. In theory, you should just go down the list, put the top eighteen boys on A, the next eighteen boys on B, and the rest don't make it. Simple. But first, everyone had to be assured that their own sons were on the teams that they were coaching.

Okay, fine, done.

Then you start down those rankings. Things were moving along swiftly until they got down to the very last pick for the B team.

"Jimmy Hoch should be on it," Gaston pronounced. Bob Baime rarely just spoke. He mostly made pronouncements.

One of his mousy assistant coaches—Adam didn't know his name—said, "But Jack and Logan are both ranked ahead of him."

"Yes, true," Gaston pronounced. "But I know this boy. Jimmy Hoch. He's a better player than those two. He just had a bad tryout." He coughed into his fist before continuing. "Jimmy's also had a tough year. His parents got divorced. We should give him a break and put him on the team. So if no one has a problem with that . . ."

He started to write down Jimmy's name.

Adam heard himself say, "I do."

All eyes turned toward him.

Gaston pointed his dimpled chin toward Adam. "Sorry?"

"I have a problem with it," Adam said. "Jack and Logan have higher scores. Who has the higher score of the two?"

"Logan," one of the assistants said.

Adam skimmed down the list and saw the scores. "Right, okay, so Logan should be on the team. He's the kid with the better evaluation and higher ranking."

The assistants didn't gasp out loud, but they might as well have. Gaston was unused to being questioned. He leaned forward, baring his big teeth. "No offense, but you're just here to sit in for your wife."

He said the word *wife* with a little attitude, as though having to sit in for one meant you weren't a real man.

"You're not even an assistant coach," Gaston continued.

"True," Adam said. "But I can read numbers, Bob. Logan's overall score was a six-point-seven. Jimmy only has a score of six-point-four. Even with today's new math, six-point-seven is greater than six-point-four. I can show you with a graph if that would help."

Gaston was not digging the sarcasm. "But as I just explained, there are extenuating circumstances."

"The divorce?"

"Exactly."

Adam looked to the assistant coaches. The assistant coaches suddenly found something fascinating on the ground in front of them. "Well, then, do you know what Jack's or Logan's home situations are?"

"I know their parents are together."

"So that's now our deciding factor?" Adam asked. "You have a really good marriage, don't you, Ga—" He had almost called him Gaston. "Bob?"

"What?"

"You and Melanie. You guys are the happiest couple I know, right?"

Melanie was small and blond and perky and blinked as though someone had just slapped her across the face. Gaston liked to touch her ass a lot in public, not so much to show affection, or even lust, as to illustrate that she was his property. He leaned back now and tried to weigh his words carefully. "We have a good marriage, yes, but—"

"Well, that should deduct at least half a point off your own son's score, right? So that knocks Bob Junior down to, let me see here, a six-point-three. The B team. I mean, if we are going to raise Jimmy's score because his parents are having problems, shouldn't we also lower your son's because you guys are so gosh-darn perfect?"

One of the other assistant coaches said, "Adam, are you okay?"

Adam snapped his head toward the voice. "Fine."

Gaston started flexing his fists.

"Corinne made it all up. She was never pregnant."

Adam met the bigger man's eye and held it. *Bring it, big boy*, Adam thought. Bring it tonight of all nights.

Gaston was the kind of big and muscular guy you knew was all show. Over Gaston's shoulder, Adam could see that Tripp Evans was looking on, surprise on his face.

"This isn't a courtroom," Gaston said, flashing his teeth. "You're out of line."

Adam hadn't seen the inside of a courtroom in four months, but he didn't bother to correct him. He lifted the sheets in the air. "The evaluations are here for a reason, Bob."

"And so are we," Gaston said, running his hand through his black mane. "As coaches. As guys who've watched these kids for years. We make the final call. I, as a head coach, make the final call. Jimmy has a good attitude. That matters too. We aren't computers. We use all the tools at our disposal to select the most deserving kids." He spread his giant hands, trying to win Adam back into the fold. "And come on, we are talking about the last kid on the B team. It's not really that big a deal."

"I bet it's a big deal to Logan."

"I'm the head coach. The final call is mine."

The room was starting to break up. Guys were leaving. Adam opened his mouth to say more, but what was the point? He wouldn't win this argument, and what was he making it for anyway? He didn't even know who the hell Logan was. It was a distraction from the mess the stranger had left behind. Nothing more. He knew that. He got up from the chair.

"Where are you going?" Gaston asked, chin stuck out long enough to invite a punch.

"Ryan is on the A team, right?"

"Right."

That was why Adam was there—to advocate, if need

be, for his son. Done. The rest was flotsam. "Have a good night, guys."

Adam made his way back to the bar. He nodded at Len Gilman, the police chief in town, who liked to work behind the bar because it kept down the DUIs. Len nodded back and slid Adam a bottle of Bud. Adam twisted off the cap with a little too much gusto. Tripp Evans sidled up to him. Len slid him a Bud too. Tripp held it up and clinked bottles with Adam. The two men drank in silence while the meeting broke up. Guys called out their good-byes. Gaston rose dramatically—he was big on dramatically— and shot a glare at Adam. Adam lifted the bottle toward him in a "cheers" response. Gaston stormed out.

"Making friends?" Tripp asked.

"I'm a people person," Adam said.

"You know he's the VP of the board, right?"

"I must remember to genuflect next time I see him," Adam said.

"I'm president."

"In that case, I better get some kneepads."

Tripp nodded, liking that line. "Bob's going through a lot right now."

"Bob's an ass waffle."

"Well, yes. Do you know why I stay on as president?"

"Helps you score chicks?"

"Yes, that. And because if I resign, Bob's next in line."

"Shiver." Adam started to put down his beer. "I better go."

"He's out of work."

"Who?"

"Bob. Lost his job over a year ago."

"I'm sorry to hear that," Adam said. "But that's no excuse."

"I didn't say it was. I just wanted you to know."

"Got it."

"So," Tripp Evans continued, "Bob has this head-hunter helping him find a job—a big-time, very important headhunter."

Adam put down the beer. "And?"

"So this big-time headhunter is trying to find Bob a new job."

"So you said."

"So the headhunter's name is Jim Hoch."

Adam stopped. "As in Jimmy Hoch's father?"

Tripp said nothing.

"That's why he wants the kid on the team?"

"What, you think Bob cares that the parents are divorced?"

Adam just shook his head. "And you're okay with it?"

Tripp shrugged. "Nothing here is pure. You get a parent involved in their own kids' sports, well, you know it's like a mother lion around a cub. Sometimes they pick a kid because he lives next door. Sometimes they pick a kid because he's got a hot mom who dresses provocatively at the games. . . ."

"You know that from personal experience?"

"Guilty. And sometimes they pick a kid because his daddy can help them get a job. Seems a better reason than most."

"Man, you're so cynical for an ad exec."

Tripp smiled. "Yeah, I know. But it's like we always talk about. How far would you go to protect your family? You'd never hurt anyone; I'd never hurt anyone. But if someone threatens your family, if it means saving your child . . ."

"We'd kill?"

"Look around you, my friend." Tripp spread his arms. "This town, these schools, these programs, these kids, these families—I sometimes sit back and can't believe how lucky we all are. We're living the dream, you know."

Adam did know. Sort of. He had gone from underpaid public defender to overpaid eminent domain attorney in order to pay for the dream. He wondered whether it was worth it. "And if Logan has to pay the price?"

"Since when is life fair? Look, I had these clients from a major car company. Yeah, you know the name. And yeah, you read in the paper recently how they covered up a problem with their steering columns. A lot of people got hurt or killed. These car guys, they're really nice. Normal. So how do they let it happen? How do they work out some cost-benefit crap and let people die?"

Adam could see where he was going with this, but the ride was always a good one with Tripp. "Because they're corrupt bastards?"

Tripp frowned. "You know that isn't true. They're like tobacco company employees. Are they all evil too? Or how about all the pious folks who covered up church scandals or, I don't know, pollute the rivers? Are they all just corrupt bastards, Adam?"

Tripp was like this—a suburban-dad philosopher. "You tell me."

"It's perspective, Adam." Tripp smiled at him. He took off his cap, smoothed down the receding wisps of hair, put it back on his head. "We humans can't see straight. We are always biased. We always protect our own interests."

"One thing I notice about all those examples . . . ," Adam said.

"What?"

"Money."

"It's the root of all evil, my friend."

Adam thought about the stranger. He thought about his two sons at home right now, probably doing homework or playing a video game. He thought about his wife at some teachers' conference down in Atlantic City.

"Not all evil," he said.

CHAPTER 3

THE American Legion parking lot was dark. Only the flashes of light from opened car doors or the smaller bursts from checked smartphones broke the black curtain. Adam got into his car and sat in the driver's seat. For a few moments he did nothing. He just sat there. Car doors were being slammed shut. Engines were starting. Adam didn't move.

"You didn't have to stay with her. . . ."

He could feel his phone vibrate in his pocket. It would be, he figured, a text from Corinne. She'd be anxious to know about team selections. Adam took out the phone and checked the message. Yep, from Corinne:

How did it go tonight??

As he thought.

Adam was staring at the text as though it might contain a hidden message when the rapping of knuckles against the glass made him jump. Gaston's pumpkin-size head filled the passenger-side window. He grinned at Adam and made a rolling-down motion. Adam put the key in the ignition, pressed the button, and watched the window slide open.

"Hey, man," Gaston said, "no hard feelings. Just an honest difference of opinion, right?"

"Right."

Gaston stuck his hand in the window to shake. Adam returned the grip.

"Good luck this season," Gaston said.

"Yeah. And good luck with the job hunt."

Gaston froze for a second. The two men stayed there, Gaston looming large in the window, Adam sitting in the car but not looking away. Eventually, Gaston pulled his mitt free and stalked away.

Buffoon.

The phone buzzed again. Again it was Corinne:

Hello?!?

Adam could see her staring down at the screen, dying for an answer. Head games had never been his style—he saw no reason not to give it to her:

Ryan's on A.

Her reply was immediate:

Yay!!! Will call u in half an hour.

He put away the phone, started up the car, and headed home. The ride was exactly 2.6 miles—Corinne had measured it with her car's odometer when she first got into running. He drove past the new Dunkin' Donuts/Baskin-

Robbins combo store on South Maple and made a left at the Sunoco station on the corner. It was late when he got home, but as usual, every light in the house was still switched on. A lot of school time nowadays was spent on conservation and renewable energy, but his two boys hadn't learned yet how to depart a room without leaving on the lights.

He could hear their border collie, Jersey, barking as he approached the door. When he unlocked the door with his key, Jersey greeted him as though he were a returning POW. Adam noticed that the dog's water bowl was empty.

"Hello?"

No answer. Ryan could be asleep by now. Thomas would either be finishing up homework or claiming the same. He was never in the middle or end of playing video games or messing around on his laptop—Adam always managed to interrupt him *just* as he was finishing his homework and *starting* to play video games or mess around on his laptop.

He filled the water bowl.

"Hello?"

Thomas appeared at the top of the stairs. "Hey."

"Did you walk Jersey?"

"Not yet."

Teen code for: No.

"Do it now."

"I just need to finish this one homework thing first."

Teen code for: No.

Adam was about to tell him "Now"—this was a familiar teen-parent dance—but he stopped and stared up at the boy. Tears pushed their way into his eyes, but he fought them down. Thomas looked like Adam. Everyone said so.

He had the same walk, the same laugh, the same second toe bigger than the first toe.

No way. No way he wasn't Adam's. Even though the stranger had said that . . .

Now you're listening to a stranger?

He thought about all the times he and Corinne had warned the boys about strangers, about so-called stranger danger, all the lessons about not being too helpful, about drawing attention to yourself if an adult approached, about creating a safe code word. Thomas had gotten it right away. Ryan was more naturally trusting. Corinne had been wary of those men who hung around the Little League fields, the lifers who had an almost pathological need to coach even when their kids were long out of the program or, worse, when they had no kids at all. Adam had always been a little more lax about all that—or maybe it was something darker. Maybe it was the fact that he trusted no one when it came to his kids, not just those who might normally arouse suspicion.

It was just easier that way, wasn't it?

Thomas spotted something in his father's face. He made a face of his own and did that teenage tumble-walk-clump down the stairs, as though some invisible hand had pushed him from behind and his feet were trying to catch up.

"Might as well take Jersey out now," Thomas said.

He stumbled past his father and grabbed the leash. Jersey was huddled up against the door, ready to go. Jersey was, like all dogs, always ready to go. She displayed her intense desire to go outside by standing in front of the door so you couldn't open it and let her out. Dogs.

"Where's Ryan?" Adam asked.

"In bed."

Adam checked the clock on the microwave. Ten fifteen. Ryan's bedtime was ten, though he was allowed to stay up and read until lights-out at ten thirty. Ryan, like Corinne, was a rule follower. They never had to remind him that it was nine forty-five or any of that. In the morning, Ryan got out of bed the moment his alarm went off, showered, dressed, made his own breakfast. Thomas was different. Adam often considered investing in a cattle prod to get his older son moving in the mornings.

Novelty Funsy . . .

Adam heard the screen door shut as Thomas and Jersey started out. He headed upstairs and looked in on Ryan. He had fallen asleep with the light on, a copy of the latest Rick Riordan novel resting on his chest. Adam tiptoed in, picked up the book, found a bookmark, put it away. He was reaching for the lamp's switch when Ryan stirred.

"Dad?"

"Hey."

"Did I make A?"

"The e-mail goes out tomorrow, pal."

A white lie. Adam wasn't supposed to officially know yet. The coaches were not supposed to tell their kids until the official e-mail in the morning so everyone learned at the same time.

"Okay."

Ryan closed his eyes and fell asleep before his head actually touched down. Adam watched his son for a moment. Lookswise, Ryan favored his mother. That never meant much to Adam before tonight—it had in fact always been a plus—but now, tonight, it was making him wonder. Stupid, but there you go. The bell you can't unring. The niggling in the back of the brain wouldn't leave him alone, but then again, so the hell what? Let's take a complete theoretical. He stared at Ryan and felt that overwhelming feeling he sometimes got when he looked at his boys—part pure joy, part fear of what could happen to them in this cruel world, part wishes and hopes, all blended together in the only thing in this entire planet that felt completely pure. Corny, yes, but there you go. Purity. That was what hit you when you get lost looking at your own child—a purity that could be derived only from true, unconditional love.

He loved Ryan so damned much.

And if he found out that Ryan wasn't his, would he just lose all that? Does all that go away? Does it even matter?

He shook his head and turned away. Enough philosophizing on fatherhood for one evening. So far, nothing had changed. Some weirdo had handed him some nonsense about a fake pregnancy. That was all. Adam had been involved in the legal system long enough to know that you take nothing for granted. You do the work. You do the research. People lie. You investigate because too often your preconceived notions will get blown out of the water.

Sure, Adam's gut was telling him that the stranger's words had a ring of truth to them, but that was the problem. When you listen to your gut, you are often just fooled with greater certainty.

Do the work. Do the research.

So how?

Simple. Start with Novelty Funsy.

The family shared a desktop computer that used to be kept in the family room. This had been Corinne's idea. There would be no secret Web browsing (read: porn watching) in their home. Adam and Corinne would know all, the theory went, and be mature, responsible parents. But Adam quickly realized that this sort of policing was either superfluous or nonsense. The boys could look things up, including porn, on their phones. They could go to a friend's house. They could grab one of the laptops or tablets lying around the house.

It was also lazy parenting, he thought. Teach them to do the right thing because it's the right thing—not because Mom and Dad are looking over your shoulder. Of course, all parents start off believing stuff like that, but quickly, you realize that parenting shortcuts are there for a reason.

The other problem was more obvious: If you wanted to use the computer for its intended use—to study or do homework—the noise from the kitchen and the television would be certain to distract. So Adam had moved the desktop into the small nook that they'd generously dubbed a "home office"—a room that was too many things to too many people. Corinne's students' papers, ready to be graded, were stacked on the right. The boys' homework was always in disarray, a rough draft of some essay left behind in the printer like a wounded soldier on a battlefield. The bills were piled on the chair, waiting for Adam to pay them online.

The Internet browser was up and on a museum site. One of the boys must be studying ancient Greece. Adam checked the browser's history, seeing what sites had been visited, though the boys had grown too savvy to leave anything incriminating behind. But you never knew. Thomas once accidentally left his Facebook up and logged in. Adam had sat at the computer and stared at the front page, trying like hell to fight off the desire to take a peek in his son's message file.

He'd lost that fight.

A few messages in and Adam stopped. His son was safe—that was the important thing—but it had been a disturbing invasion of his son's privacy. He had learned things that he wasn't supposed to know. Nothing heavy. Nothing earth-shattering. But things that a father should perhaps talk to his son about. But what was he now supposed to do with this information? If he confronted Thomas, Adam would have had to admit going through his private things. Was that worth it? He'd debated telling Corinne about it, but once he relaxed and gave it some time, he realized that, really, the communications he'd read were not abnormal, that he himself had done some stuff when he was a teenager he wouldn't have wanted his parents to know about, that he had simply outgrown it and moved on, and if his parents had spied on him and confronted him about it, he probably would have been worse off.

So Adam let it go.

Parenting. It ain't for sissies.

You're stalling, Adam.

Yeah, he knew that. So back to it.

Tonight there was nothing spectacular in the recent history. One of the boys—probably Ryan—was indeed studying ancient Greece or just getting really into his Riordan book. There were links to Zeus, Hades, Hera, and Icarus. So more specifically, Greek mythology. He moved down the history and clicked for yesterday. He saw a search for driving directions to the Borgata Hotel and Casino in Atlantic City. Made sense. That was where Corinne was staying. She had also searched for the convention's schedule and clicked on that.

That was about it.

Enough stalling.

He brought up his bank's Web page. He and Corinne had two Visa accounts. They unofficially called one personal, the other business. It was for their own bookkeeping records. They used the "business" card for what they might deem a business expense—like, for example, the teachers' con in Atlantic City. For everything else, they used the personal card.

He brought up the personal card account first. They had a universal search feature. He put in the word *novelty*. Nothing showed up. Okay, fine. He logged out and made the same search through the business Visa.

And there it was.

A little more than two years ago, there was a charge to a company called Novelty Funsy for $387.83. Adam could hear the low hum of the computer.

How? How had the stranger known about this charge?

No idea.

Adam had seen the charge way back when, hadn't he? Yes, he was sure of it. He racked his brain and scraped together the flimsy remnants of a memory. He had been sitting right here, checking the Visa charges. He had asked Corinne about it. She had made light of the charges. She'd said something about decorations for the classroom. He'd wondered about the price, he thought. Seemed high. Corinne had said the school was going to reimburse her.

Novelty Funsy. That didn't sound like anything nefarious, did it?

Adam opened up another window and Googled *Novelty Funsy*. Google spit back:

Showing results for Novelty *Fancy*

No results found for Novelty Funsy

Whoa. That was odd. Everything was on Google. Adam sat back and considered his options. Why wouldn't there be even one hit for Novelty Funsy? The company was real. He could see it on his Visa charge. He assumed that they sold some kind of decorations or, uh, fun novelty items.

Adam chewed on his lower lip. He didn't get it. A stranger comes up to him and tells him that his wife lied to him—elaborately, it seemed—about being pregnant. Who was he? Why would he do it?

Okay, forget those two questions for now and let's get to the one that matters most: Is it true?

Adam wanted to simply say no and move on. Whatever their problems, whatever scars were left from eighteen years of marriage, he trusted her. Many things slipped away with time, broke down and dissolved or, more optimistically, altered and changed, but the one thing that seems to remain and grow more cohesive is the protective family bond—you are a team, you and your spouse. You are on the same side, in this together, you have each other's backs. Your victories are hers. So are your failures.

Adam trusted Corinne with his life. And yet . . .

He had seen it a million times in his line of work. Put simply, people fool you. He and Corinne might be a cohesive unit, but they were also individuals. It would be nice to trust unconditionally and forget the stranger ever appeared—Adam was tempted to do just that—but that felt a tad too much like the proverbial sticking your head in the sand. The voice of doubt in the back of his head might one day quiet, but it would never go away.

Not until he knew for sure.

The stranger had claimed that the proof was in this seemingly harmless Visa charge. He owed it to himself and, yep, Corinne (she wouldn't want the voice around either, would she?) to follow up, so Adam called the Visa's toll-free number. The recorded voice made him dial in the card number, the expiration date, and the CVV code number on the back. It tried to give him the information via a machine, but eventually the recorded voice asked whether he'd like to speak to a representative. Representative. Like he was calling Congress. He said, "Yes," and heard the phone ring through.

When the representative came on, she made him repeat the exact same information—why do they always do that?—along with the last four numbers of his social security and his address.

"What can I help you with today, Mr. Price?"

"There's a charge on my Visa card from a company called Novelty Funsy."

She asked him to spell *funsy*. Then: "Do you have the amount and date of the transaction?"

Adam gave her the information. He expected some pushback when he said the date—the charge was more than two years old—but the representative didn't comment on that.

"What information do you need, Mr. Price?"

"I don't recall buying anything from a company called Novelty Funsy."

"Um," the representative said.

"Um?"

"Um, some companies don't bill under their real name. You know, to be discreet. Like when you go to a hotel and they tell you the name of the movie won't be on your phone bill."

She was talking about pornography or something involving sex. "That's not the case here."

"Well, let's see what's what, then." The clacking of her keyboard came over the phone line. "Novelty Funsy is listed as an online retailer. That usually indicates that it is a company that values privacy. Does that help?"

Yes and no. "Is there any way to ask them for a detailed receipt?"

"Certainly. It may take a few hours."

"I guess that's okay."

"We have an e-mail for you on file." She read off his address. "Should we send it there?"

"That would be great."

The representative asked whether she could assist him with any other matter. He said no, thanks. She wished him a good evening. He hung up the phone and stared at the charge screen. Novelty Funsy. Now that he thought about it, the name did sound like a discreet name for a sex shop.

"Dad?"

It was Thomas. Adam quickly reached for the screen's off switch like, well, one of his sons watching porn.

"Hey," Adam said, the very essence of casual. "What's up?"

If his son found his father's behavior bizarre, he didn't show it. Teens were ridiculously clueless and self-involved. Right now, Adam appreciated that. What Thomas's father did on the Internet couldn't be the least bit interesting to him.

"Can you give me a ride to Justin's?"

"Now?"

"He has my shorts."

"What shorts?"

"My practice shorts. For practice tomorrow."

"Can't you wear other shorts?"

Thomas looked at his father as though a horn had sprung out of his forehead. "Coach says we have to wear the practice shorts to practice."

"Can't Justin just bring them to school tomorrow?"

"He was supposed to bring them today. He forgets."

"So what did you use today?"

"Kevin had an extra pair. His brother's. They were too big on me."

"Can't you tell Justin to put them in his backpack right now?"

"I could, yeah, but he won't do it. It's only like four blocks. I could use the practice driving anyway."

Thomas had gotten his learner's permit a week ago— the parental equivalent of a stress test without using an actual EKG machine. "Okay, I'll be down in a sec." Adam cleared the history on the browser and headed downstairs. Jersey was hoping for another walk and gave them the pitiful "I can't believe you're not taking me with you" eyes as they hurried past her. Thomas grabbed the keys and got behind the wheel.

Adam was now able to let go when he sat in the passenger seat. Corinne was too much of a control freak. She would keep shouting out instructions and cautions. She almost put her foot through the imaginary passenger-side brake. As Thomas pulled onto the street, Adam turned and studied his son's profile. Some acne was forming on his cheeks. There was faint hair growing down the side of his face, Abe Lincoln's lines if not thickness, but his son had to shave now. Not every day. Not more than once a week, but it was there. Thomas wore cargo shorts. His legs were hairy. He had beautiful blue eyes, his son. Everyone commented on them. They had the sparkling blue of ice.

Thomas pulled into the driveway, drifting a little close to the right curb.

"I'll be two seconds," he said.

"Okay."

Thomas put the car in park and sprinted toward the front door. Justin's mom, Kristin Hoy, opened it—Adam could see the bright shock of blond hair—and that surprised him. Kristin taught at the same high school as Corinne. The two women had grown pretty close. Adam had figured that she'd be down in Atlantic City, but then he remembered that this conference was for history and languages. Kristin taught math.

Kristin smiled and waved. He waved back. Thomas vanished into the house as Kristin started down the path toward the car. Politically incorrect as it sounded, Kristin Hoy was a MILF. Adam had overheard a bunch of Thomas's friends saying that, though he could have figured it out on his own. Right now, she was sashaying toward him in painted-on jeans and a tight white top. She was some sort of competitive bodybuilder. Adam wasn't sure what kind. Her name had a bunch of letters after it, and she had earned the distinction of being a "pro," whatever exactly that entailed. Adam had never been a fan of the muscular weight lifting women of old, and in some of her competitive pictures, Kristin did indeed look a little corded and cut. The hair was a little too blond, the smile a little too white, the tan a little too orange, but the look worked pretty damn well in person.

"Hey, Adam."

He wasn't sure whether he should get out of the car. He settled for staying in his seat. "Hey, Kristin."

"Corinne still away?"

"Yep."

"But she's back tomorrow, right?"

"Right."

"Okay, I'll touch base with her. We have to train. I've got the states in two weeks."

On her Facebook page, she claimed to be a "fitness model" and "WBFF Pro." Corinne envied her body. They had started working out together recently. Like most things that were good or bad for you, you reach a stage where what started as a happy habit turns into something of an obsession.

Thomas was back with the shorts.

"'Bye, Thomas."

"'Bye, Mrs. Hoy."

"Have a good night, boys. Don't have too much fun with Mom away."

She sashayed back toward the house.

Thomas said, "She's kind of annoying."

"That's not nice."

"You oughta see their kitchen."

"Why? What's wrong with their kitchen?"

"She has bikini pictures of herself on the fridge," Thomas said. "It's gross."

Hard to argue. As Thomas pulled out, a small smile tugged at his lips.

"What?" Adam said.

"Kyle calls her a butterface," Thomas said.

"Who?"

"Mrs. Hoy."

Adam wondered if that was a new term for MILF or something. "What's a butterface?"

"It's what you call someone who's not pretty—but she has a good body."

"I'm not following," Adam said.

"Butterface." Then Thomas spoke slowly. "But. Her. Face."

Adam tried not to smile as he shook his head in disapproval. He was about to admonish his son—wondering exactly how to do so and keep a straight face—when his cell phone rang. He looked down at the caller ID.

It was Corinne.

He hit the ignore button. He should pay attention to his son's driving. Corinne would understand. He was about to put his phone in his pocket when he felt it vibrate. Fast for a voice mail, he thought, but no, it was an e-mail from his bank. He opened it. There were links to see the detailed purchases, but Adam barely noticed them.

"Dad? You okay?"

"Keep your eyes on the road, Thomas."

He would go through it in detail when he got home, but right now, the top line of the e-mail said more than he wanted to know.

Novelty Funsy is a billing name for the following online retailer:

Fake-A-Pregnancy.com

CHAPTER 4

WHEN he was back home and in his office nook, Adam hit the link in the e-mail and watched the website come up.

Fake-A-Pregnancy.com.

Adam tried not to react. He knew that the Internet catered to every peccadillo and taste, even ones that defied the imagination, but the fact that there was an entire website based on faking a pregnancy was yet another one of the moments when a rational human being just wants to surrender and cry and admit that our worst instincts have won.

Underneath the large pink lettering, in a slightly smaller font, was the tagline: FUNNIEST GAGS EVER!

Gags?

He clicked on the link for the "featured products you purchased!" The top item was for a "SUPER NEW Fake Pregnancy Test!" Adam just shook his head. The normal price of $34.95 had a red slash through it in favor of the sale price $19.99, and then, in black italics underneath that, *"You save $15!"*

Well, great, thanks for the savings. I sure hope my wife didn't pay retail!

The item shipped in twenty-four hours with "discreet packaging." He read farther down the page:

Use it the same way you would a real pregnancy test!

Urinate on the strip and read the results!

They show up positive every time!

Adam's mouth felt dry.

Scare the bejesus out of your boyfriend or your in-laws or your cousin or your professor!

Cousin and professor? Who the hell wants to scare a cousin or professor into thinking . . . Adam didn't even want to go there.

There was a warning in small print on the bottom.

CAUTION: This item has the potential to be used irresponsibly. By completing and submitting the form below, you agree not to use this product for purposes that may be illegal, immoral, fraudulent, or hurtful to others.

Incredible. He clicked the item image and zoomed in on the packaging. The test was a white strip with a red cross indicating pregnancy. Adam racked his brain. Was that the test Corinne had used? He didn't remember. Had he even bothered looking? He couldn't be sure. They all looked the same anyway, didn't they?

But he did recall now that Corinne had done the test while he was home.

That was new for her. With Thomas and Ryan, Corinne had greeted him at the door with a big smile and told him the news. But this last time, she had wanted him there. He remembered that. He had been lying in bed, flipping stations on the television. She had gone into the bathroom. He thought the test might take a few minutes, but that wasn't the case. She had come running out of the bathroom with the strip.

"Adam, look! I'm pregnant!"

Had the strip looked like this?

He didn't know.

Adam clicked the second link and just dropped his head into his hands.

FAKE SILICONE BELLIES!

These came in various sizes: First trimester (1–12 weeks), second trimester (13–27 weeks), third trimester (28–40 weeks). There was also an extra-large size and one for twins, triplets, and even quadruplets. There was a photograph of a beautiful woman gazing lovingly at her "pregnant" belly. She wore wedding-gown white and held lilies in her hand.

The sales pitch on the top read:

Nothing throws you in the spotlight like being pregnant!

And underneath that, a less subtle pitch:

Get better presents!

The product was made of "medical-grade silicone" that the site described as "the closest thing to skin invented so far!" On the bottom, there were video testimonials from "real Fake-A-Pregnancy clients." Adam clicked on one. A pretty brunette smiled into the camera and said, "Hi! I love my silicone belly. It's so natural!" She went on to explain that it had arrived in just two business days (not quite as fast as the pregnancy test, but you wouldn't need it as fast, would you?) and that she and her husband were adopting and didn't want their friends to know. The second woman—this time a thin redhead—explained that she and her husband were using a surrogate and didn't want their friends to know (Adam hoped, then, for their sakes that their friends were not creepy enough to frequent this website and out them). The final testimonial was from a woman who used the fake belly to play "the funniest joke ever" on her friends.

She must have some pretty strange friends.

Adam clicked back to the cart page. The last item listed was . . . oh man . . . fake ultrasound sonograms.

2-D or 3-D! Your choice!

The fake sonograms were on sale for $29.99. Glossy, matte, or even a transparency. There were fields so you could type in a doctor's name, a hospital's or clinic's name, and the date of the ultrasound. You could choose your fetus's gender or just the odds ("Male—80% certainty"), not to mention their ages, twins, you name it. For an extra $4.99, you could "add a hologram to your fake sonogram to make it appear more authentic."

He felt sick. Had Corinne splurged for the hologram? Adam couldn't remember.

Again the website tried to make it seem like people would buy this for laughs. **"Perfect for Bachelor Parties!"** Yeah, what a knee-slapper. **"Perfect for Birthday Parties and even Christmas Gags!"** Christmas gag? Wrap up a fake pregnancy test and leave it under the tree for Mom and Dad. Laughs galore.

Of course, the "gag" talk was a cover for lawsuit protection. There was no way this site didn't know that people were using it for purposes of deception.

That's it, Adam. Keep showing outrage. Keep ignoring the obvious.

That dazed feeling was back. There was nothing more to be done tonight. He would go to bed. He would lie down and think about it. Don't do anything rash. Too much was at stake. Stay calm. Block, if you have to.

He walked past both of his sons' bedrooms as he headed toward his own. Their rooms, this whole house, suddenly seemed so fragile, made of eggshells, and if he wasn't careful, what the stranger had told him could crush them all.

He entered the bedroom that he shared with his wife. A trade paperback of some debut literary novel by a Pakistani woman sat on Corinne's night table. A copy of *Real Simple* magazine with folded pages for bookmarks lay next to it. There was an extra set of reading glasses. The prescription was pretty light, and Corinne didn't like wearing them in public. The clock radio was also a charging dock for her iPhone. Adam and Corinne had similar tastes in music. Springsteen was a favorite. They'd seen a dozen live shows. Adam always lost it at some point, getting so caught up in the music that he lost control. Corinne focused and concentrated. She stood and she might move a little, but mostly her eyes were on the stage.

Adam, meanwhile, danced around like an idiot.

He headed into the bathroom and brushed his teeth. Corinne used some newfangled sonic boom electric toothbrush that looked like something from NASA. Adam stayed old-school. A box of L'Oréal sat out. He could still get a whiff of the chemical smell from the hair dye. Corinne had probably touched up the gray before heading down to Atlantic City. The gray seemed to come in one long strand at a time. For a while, she would pull them out and study them. Then she'd frown, hold up the hair, and say, "It has the texture and color of steel wool."

His mobile rang. He checked the caller ID, but he already knew who it was. He spit out the toothpaste, quickly rinsed, and picked it up.

"Hey," he said.

"Adam?"

It was, of course, Corinne.

"Yep."

"I called before," she said. He could hear the slight panic in her voice. "Why didn't you answer?"

"Thomas was driving. I wanted to focus."

"Oh."

In the background, he could hear music and laughter. She was probably still at the bar with her colleagues.

"So how did it go tonight?" she asked.

"Fine. He's on the team."

"How was Bob?"

"What do you mean, how was Bob? He was a buffoon. As always."

"You have to be nice to him, Adam."

"No, I don't."

"He wants to move Ryan to middie so he doesn't compete with Bob Junior. Don't give him an excuse."

"Corinne?"

"Yeah?"

"It's late and I got a big day tomorrow. Can we talk tomorrow?"

Someone in the background—a male someone—broke into guffaws of laughter.

"Everything okay?" she asked.

"Fine," he said before he hung up.

He rinsed off the toothbrush and washed his face. Two years ago, when Thomas was fourteen and Ryan ten, Corinne had gotten pregnant. It had been a surprise. Adam had some issues with a low sperm count as he got older, so their birth control had been closest to the silent-prayer method. This was, of course, irresponsible on their part. At the time, he and Corinne had never discussed the fact that they wouldn't have more children. It just seemed—up to that point anyway—to be an unspoken agreement between them.

Adam caught his reflection in the mirror. The voice in the back of his head was starting up again. He quietly padded back down the hall. He brought up the Web browser and searched for *DNA test*. The first one was sold at Walgreens. He was about to hit the order button and then thought better of it. Someone might open the box. He'd pick it up tomorrow.

Adam headed back to his room and sat on the bed. Corinne's scent, still a powerful pheromone after all these years, lingered, or maybe that was just his imagination working overtime.

The stranger's voice came back to him.

"You didn't have to stay with her."

Adam laid his head on the pillow, blinked up at the ceiling, and just let the gentle sounds of his still home overwhelm him.

CHAPTER 5

ADAM woke up at 7:00 A.M. Ryan was waiting by the bedroom door. "Dad . . . ?"

"Yeah."

"Can you check the e-mail and see if Coach Baime sent out the results yet?"

"Already done. You made the A team."

Ryan didn't outwardly celebrate. That wasn't his way. He nodded and tried to hold back his smile. "Can I go to Max's after school?"

"What are you guys going to do on such a beautiful day?"

"Sit in the dark and play video games," Ryan said.

Adam frowned, but he knew that Ryan was pulling his leg.

"Jack and Colin are coming over too. We're going to play lacrosse."

"Sure." Adam swung his legs out of the bed. "Did you eat breakfast?"

"Not yet."

"You want me to make you Daddy eggs?"

"Only if you promise not to call them Daddy eggs."

Adam smiled. "Deal."

For a moment, Adam forgot about the night before and the stranger and Novelty Funsy and Fake-A-Pregnancy.com. It had, as such things do, taken on a dreamlike quality, where you nearly question whether you had imagined the whole thing. He knew better, of course. He was blocking. He had, in fact, managed to sleep pretty well last night. If there had been dreams, Adam didn't remember them now. Adam slept well most nights. Corinne was the one who stayed up and worried. Somewhere along the way, Adam had learned to not worry about what he couldn't control, to let go. This had been a healthy thing, this ability to compartmentalize. Now he wondered whether it was an ability to let go or simply to block.

He headed downstairs and made breakfast. "Daddy eggs" were scrambled up with milk, mustard, and Parmesan cheese. When Ryan was six, he loved Daddy eggs, but like most things with little kids, he outgrew them, labeling them "lame" one day and vowing never to touch them again. Recently, his new coach had told Ryan that he should always start the day with a high-protein breakfast, and so Daddy eggs had been revived like a nostalgic musical.

As Adam watched his son attack the plate as though it had offended him, he again tried to picture the six-year-old Ryan eating this same dish in this same room. The image wouldn't come to him.

Thomas had a ride, so Ryan and Adam drove to school in comfortable silence, father and son. They passed a Baby Gap and a Tiger Schulmann's karate school. A Subway had opened up in that "dead" spot on the corner, that one storefront in every town where nothing seems to work. It'd already housed a bagel shop, a jewelry store, an upscale mattress chain, and a Blimpie, which Adam had always thought was the same thing as Subway anyway.

"'Bye, Dad. Thanks."

Ryan hopped out of the car without a cheek kiss. When did Ryan stop kissing him? He couldn't remember.

He circled across Oak Street, headed past the 7-Eleven, and saw the Walgreens. He sighed. He parked in the lot and sat in the car for several minutes. An old man hobbled by, his prescription bag death-gripped between his gnarly hand and the top of his walker. He glared at Adam, or maybe that was just the way he looked at the world now.

Adam headed inside. He grabbed a small shopping basket. They needed toothpaste and antibacterial soap, but that was all for show. He flashed back to his youth when he'd throw a bunch of toiletries into a similar container so it wouldn't look as though he was just buying condoms, which would remain unused in his wallet until they started cracking from age.

The DNA tests were located near the pharmacist. Adam walked over, doing his best to look casual. He looked left. He looked right. He picked up the box and read the back:

THIRTY PERCENT OF "FATHERS" WHO TAKE THIS TEST WILL DISCOVER THAT THE CHILD THEY ARE RAISING IS NOT THEIRS.

He dropped the box onto the shelf. He hurried away as though the box might beckon him back. No. He would not go there. Not today, anyway.

He brought the other toiletries up to the counter,

grabbed a pack of gum, and paid. He hit Route 17, passed a few more mattress chains (what was it with northern New Jersey and all the mattress stores?), and pulled into the gym. He changed and worked out with weights. Throughout his adult life, Adam had cycled through a potpourri of workout programs—yoga (not flexible), Pilates (confused), boot camp (why not just join the military?), Zumba (don't ask), aquatics (near drown), spin (sore butt)—but in the end, he always returned to simple weights. Some days he loved the strain on his muscles and couldn't imagine not doing it. Other days he dreaded every moment, and the only thing he wanted to lift was the postworkout peanut butter protein shake to his lips.

He went through the motions, trying to remember to contract the muscle and hold at the end. This was, he'd learned, the key to results. Don't just curl. Curl up, hold it a second while squeezing the bicep, curl down. He showered, changed into his work clothes, and headed into his office on Midland Avenue in Paramus. The office building was four floors and sleek glass and the architecture stood out only in the sense that it was stereotypically an office building, indistinguishable from every other. You would never mistake it for anything else.

"Yo, Adam, got a second?"

It was Andy Gribbel, Adam's best paralegal. When he first started here, everyone called him the Dude because of his scruffy looks similar to the Jeff Bridges character. He was older than most paralegals—older, in fact, than Adam—and could easily have gone to law school and passed the bar, but as Gribbel once put it, "That ain't my bag, man."

Yes, he had said it just like that.

"What's up?" Adam asked.

"Old Man Rinsky."

Adam's legal expertise was in the field of eminent domain, which involved the government trying to take away your land to build a highway or school or something like that. In this case, the township of Kasselton was trying to take away Rinsky's house for the purpose of gentrification. In short, that area of town was politely labeled "undesirable" or, in layman's terms, "a dump," and the powers that be had found a developer who wanted to level all the houses and build shiny new homes, stores, and restaurants.

"What about him?"

"We're seeing him at his place."

"Okay, good."

"Should I bring the, uh, big guns?"

Part of Adam's nuclear option. "Not yet," Adam said. "Anything else?"

Gribbel leaned back. He threw his work boots up on the desk. "I got a gig tonight. You coming?"

Adam shook his head. Andy Gribbel played in a seventies cover band that played in some of the most prestigious dives in northern New Jersey. "Can't."

"No Eagles songs, I promise."

"You never play the Eagles."

"I ain't a fan," Gribbel said. "But we are debuting 'Please Come to Boston.' You remember that song?"

"Sure."

"What do you think of it?"

"I ain't a fan," Adam said.

"Really? It's a heartbreaker, man. You love the heartbreakers."

"It isn't a heartbreaker," Adam said.

Gribbel sang: *"Hey, ramblin' boy, why don't you settle down?"*

"Probably because his girlfriend is annoying," Adam said. "The guy keeps asking her to go with him to a new city. She keeps saying no over and over and starts whining about him staying in Tennessee."

"That's because she's the number one fan of the man from Tennessee."

"Maybe he doesn't need a fan. Maybe he needs a life partner and a lover."

Gribbel stroked his beard. "I see your point."

"And all he says is 'Please come to Boston for the springtime.' The springtime. It's not like he's asking her to leave Tennessee forever. What's her response? 'She said no, boy.' What kind of attitude is that? No discussion, no hearing him out—just no. So then he gently suggests Denver or even L.A. Same response. No, no, no. I mean, spread your wings, sister. Live a little."

Gribbel smiled. "You're nuts, man."

"And," Adam continued, feeling the rant rising up, "then she claims that in these massive cities—Boston, Denver, Los Angeles—that there ain't nobody like her. Full of yourself much?"

"Adam?"

"What?"

"You may be overthinking it, my brother."

Adam nodded. "True."

"You overthink a lot of stuff, Adam."

"That I do."

"It's why you're the best attorney I know."

"Thanks," Adam said. "And no, you can't leave work early for your gig."

"Aw, come on. Don't be that guy."

"Sorry."

"Adam?"

"What?"

"The guy in that song. The rambling boy who asks her to come to Boston?"

"What about him?"

"You got to be fair to the girl."

"How so?"

"He tells his girl that she could sell her paintings on the sidewalk, outside the café where he hopes to be working soon." Gribbel spread his hands. "I mean, what kind of financial planning is that?"

"Touché," Adam said with a small smile. "Sounds like maybe they should just break up."

"Nah. They got a good thing. You can hear it in his voice."

Adam shrugged and headed into his office. The rant had been a welcome distraction. Now he was back in his own head again. Bad place to be. He made some calls, had two client meetings, checked in with the paralegals, made sure the right briefs had been followed. The world moves on, which is an outrage. Adam had learned that when he was fourteen years old and his father died of a sudden heart attack. He had sat in the big black car next to his mom and stared out the window and watched everyone else in the world living their lives. Kids still went to school. Parents still went to work. Cars honked their horns. The sun still shone. His dad was gone. And nothing changed.

Today he was being reminded yet again of the obvious: The world doesn't give even the slightest damn about us or our petty problems. We never quite get that, do we? Our lives have been shattered—shouldn't the rest of us take notice? But no. To the outside world, Adam looked the same, acted the same, felt the same. We get mad at someone for cutting us off in traffic or for taking too long to order at Starbucks or for not responding exactly as we see fit, and we have no idea that behind their facade, they may be dealing with some industrial-strength shit. Their lives may be in pieces. They may be in the midst of incalculable tragedy and turmoil, and they may be hanging on to their sanity by a thread.

But we don't care. We don't see. We just keep pushing.

He flipped radio stations on the way home, finally settling on mindless arguments on sports radio. The world was divisive and always fighting, so it was nice when people fought over something as meaningless as professional basketball.

When he reached his street, Adam was a little surprised to see Corinne's Honda Odyssey in the driveway. The car dealer had called the color Dark Cherry Pearl with a straight face. On the back cargo door, there was an oval magnetic decal with the name of their town written in black, a seemingly requisite automotive tribal tattoo in suburbia nowadays. There was also a round sticker with crossed lacrosse sticks that read PANTHER LACROSSE, the town's mascot, and one with a giant green *W* for Willard Middle School, Ryan's.

Corinne had gotten home from Atlantic City earlier than expected.

That threw off his timing a bit. He had rehearsed the upcoming confrontation in his head nonstop all day. It had been on a loop for hours now. He had tested out several approaches, but none had felt exactly right. He knew that there was no point in planning. Talking about what the stranger had told him—confronting her with what he now believed was the truth—would be pulling the proverbial pin from the proverbial grenade. You had no idea how anyone would react.

Would she deny it?

Maybe. There was still the possibility that there was an innocent explanation for all this. Adam was trying to remain open-minded, though it felt more like false hope than anything in the "don't prejudge" camp. He parked next to her car in the driveway. They had a two-car garage, but there was old furniture and sports equipment and other trappings of consumption that had taken precedence. So he and Corinne parked in the driveway instead.

Adam got out of the car and started up the walk. The grass had a few too many brown spots. Corinne would notice and complain about that. She had trouble simply enjoying and letting be. She liked to correct and make right. Adam considered himself more live-and-let-live, but others might confuse the attitude with laziness. The Bauer family, who lived next door, had a front yard that looked ready to host a PGA event. Corinne couldn't help but compare. Adam didn't give a rat's ass.

The front door opened. Thomas came out with his lacrosse bag over his shoulder. He was wearing his "away" uniform. He smiled at his father, his mouthpiece dangling out of his mouth. A familiar warmth rushed through Adam's chest.

"Hey, Dad."

"Hey, what's up?"

"I got a game, remember?"

Understandably enough, Adam had indeed forgotten, though this explained why Corinne had made it a point to be home early. "Right. Who are you playing?"

"Glen Rock. Mom is going to drive me over. You coming later?"

"Of course."

When Corinne appeared at the door, Adam felt his heart fall into his shoes. She was still a beautiful woman. If Adam had trouble visualizing his two sons at younger ages, something close to the opposite was happening with Corinne. He still saw her only as the twenty-three-year-old stunner he fell in love with. Sure, if he looked hard enough, there were the lines around her eyes and some softening with age, but maybe it was love or maybe it was because he saw her every day and so the changes were too gradual, but she never looked any older to him.

Corinne's hair was still wet from a recent shower. "Hey, hon."

He just stood there. "Hey."

She leaned in and kissed his cheek. Her hair smelled wonderfully of lilacs. "Will you be able to get Ryan?"

"Where is he?"

"A playdate at Max's."

Thomas winced. "Don't call it that, Mom."

"What?"

"A playdate. He's in middle school. You have a play-date when you're six."

Corinne sighed but with a smile. "Fine, whatever, he's having a mature gathering at Max's." Her eyes met Adam's. "Could you get him before you come to the game?"

Adam knew that he was nodding, but he didn't re-member consciously telling himself to do so. "Sure. We'll meet you at the game. How was Atlantic City?"

"Nice."

"Uh, guys?" Thomas interrupted. "Can you chitchat later? Coach gets pissed if we aren't there at least an hour before game time."

"Right," Adam said. Then, turning back to Corinne, he tried to keep it light. "We can, uh, chitchat later."

But Corinne hesitated for half a second—long enough. "Okay, no problem."

He stood on the stoop and watched them walk down the path. Corinne hit the minivan's remote, and the back yawned open like a giant mouth. Thomas tossed his bag into the back and took the front passenger seat. The mouth closed, swallowing the equipment whole. Corinne gave him a wave. He waved back.

He and Corinne had met in Atlanta during their five-week precorp training for LitWorld, a charitable enterprise that sent teachers to needy parts of the world to teach reading. This was before the days when every kid took a trip to Zambia to build a hut so they could put it on their college applications. For one thing, all of the volunteers had already graduated college. The trainees were sincere, maybe too sincere, but their hearts were in the right place.

He and Corinne didn't meet on the Emory University campus where the training took place but in a bar nearby, where students over twenty-one could drink and hit on one another in peace over bad country music. She had been with a group of her female friends, he with a group of males. Adam had been looking for a one-nighter. Corinne had been looking for something more. The two groups met slowly, the guys coming over to the girls like some clichéd dance scene in a bad movie. Adam asked Corinne if he could buy her a drink. She said sure but that wasn't going to get him anywhere. He bought her the drink anyway with the awesomely clever line that the night was young.

The drinks came. They started talking. It went well. Somewhere late into the night, not long before closing time, Corinne told him that she had lost her father at a young age, and then Adam, who had never talked about it with anyone, told her the story of his father's death and how the world hadn't cared.

They bonded over their paternal tragedies. And so it began.

When they were first married, they lived in a quiet condo off Interstate 78. He was still trying to help people as a public defender. She was teaching in the roughest neighborhoods of Newark, New Jersey. When Thomas was born, it was time to move into a proper house. That, it seemed, was just the way it went. Adam hadn't cared much where they lived. He didn't care if the house they chose was contemporary or something more classic like this one. He wanted Corinne happy, not so much because he was a great guy but because it didn't matter to him much. So Corinne had picked this town for obvious reasons.

Maybe he should have stopped it then, but as a young man, he hadn't seen the point. He had let her pick this specific house too, because it was what she wanted. The town. The house. The garage. The cars. The boys.

And what had Adam wanted?

He didn't know, but this house—this neighborhood— had been a financial stretch. Adam ended up leaving his job as a public defender for the far higher pay at the Bachmann Simpson Feagles law firm. It hadn't been what he wanted so much as the smooth, well-paved path that men like him simply ended up taking: a safe place to raise his children, a lovely home with four bedrooms, a two-car garage, a basketball hoop in the driveway, a gas grill on the wooden deck overlooking the backyard.

Nice, right?

Tripp Evans had wistfully called it "living the dream." The American dream. Corinne would have concurred.

"You didn't have to stay with her. . . ."

But of course, that wasn't true. The dream is made of delicate yet invaluable stuff. You don't casually destroy it. How ungrateful, selfish, and warped to not realize how lucky you are.

He opened the door and headed into the kitchen. The kitchen table was a mess, done up in Early American Homework. Thomas's algebra textbook was open to a problem that asked him to complete the square in the quadratic function f given by $f(x) = 2x2 - 6x = 4$. A number two pencil lay snuggled in the book's crevice. Sheets of white-with-light-blue-squares graph paper were strewn everywhere. Some of the sheets had fallen to the floor.

Adam bent down, picked them up, and put them back on the table. He stared down at the homework for a moment.

Tread gently, Adam reminded himself. This wasn't just his and Corinne's dream at stake here.

CHAPTER 6

THOMAS'S game was just starting when Adam and Ryan arrived.

With a quiet "Later, Dad," Ryan immediately peeled off to hang with fellow younger siblings and not risk being seen with a real-live parent. Adam headed to the left side of the field, the "away team" section, where the other Cedarfield parents would be.

There were no metallic stands, but some parents brought folding chairs so as to have a place to sit. Corinne kept four mesh ones in her minivan, all with cup holders on both arms (did anyone really need two for one chair?) and a shade for above the head. Most of the time—like right now—she preferred to stand. Kristin Hoy was next to her, wearing a sleeveless top with shorts so tiny that they had Daddy issues.

Adam nodded to a few parents as he strolled toward his wife. Tripp Evans stood in the corner with several other fathers, all with arms crossed and sunglasses, looking more like the Secret Service than spectators. To the right, a smirking Gaston hung with his cousin Daz (yes, everyone called him that), who owned CBW Inc., a high-end corporate investigation firm that specialized in employee background checks. Cousin Daz also ran less extensive background checks on every coach in the league to make sure that none had a criminal record or anything like that. Gaston had insisted the lacrosse board hire the high-priced CBW Inc. for this seemingly simple task, one that could be done far more cheaply online, because, hey, what are families for?

Corinne spotted Adam approaching and moved a few feet away from Kristin. When Adam got close, she whispered in near panic, "Thomas isn't starting."

"The coach is always rotating the lines," Adam said. "I wouldn't worry about it."

But she would and she was. "Pete Baime started over him." Son of Gaston. That explained the smirk. "He's not even cleared from his concussion yet. How can he be back already?"

"Do I look like his doctor, Corinne?"

"Come on, Tony!" a woman shouted. "Make the clear!"

Adam didn't have to be told that the woman shouting was Tony's mother. Had to be. When a parent calls out to her own child, you can always tell. There is that harsh ping of disappointment and exasperation in their voice. No parent believes they sound this way. Every parent does. We all hear it. We all think that only other parents do it but that magically we are immune.

An old Croatian proverb Adam had learned in college applied here: "The hunchback sees the hump of others—never his own."

Three minutes passed. Thomas still hadn't gotten in. Adam sneaked a glance at Corinne. Her jaw was set. She was staring at the far sideline, at the coach, as though willing him through the power of her glare to put Thomas into the game.

"It'll be okay," Adam said.

"He's always in the game by now. What do you think happened?"

"I don't know."

"Pete shouldn't be playing."

Adam didn't bother responding. Pete caught the ball and threw it to a teammate in the most routine play imaginable. From across the field, Gaston shouted, "Wow, helluva play, Pete!" and high-fived cousin Daz.

"What kind of grown man calls himself Daz?" Adam muttered.

"What?"

"Nothing."

Corinne gnawed on her lower lip. "We were a minute or two late, I guess. I mean, we were here fifty-five minutes before game time, but the coach said an hour."

"I doubt it's that."

"I should have left the house sooner."

Adam felt like saying that they had bigger problems, but maybe for now, this distraction would be helpful. The other team scored. The parents moaned and dissected what their defensemen had done wrong to cause the goal.

Thomas ran onto the field.

Adam could feel the relief coming off his wife in waves. Corinne's face went smooth. She smiled at him and said, "How was work?"

"Now you want to know?"

"Sorry. You know how I get."

"I do."

"It's kinda why you love me."

"Kinda."

"That," she said, "and my ass."

"Now you're talking."

"I still have a great ass, don't I?"

"World class, prime Grade A, one hundred percent top sirloin with no fillers."

"Well," she said with that sly smile she broke out far too little. "Maybe one filler."

God, he loved the too-rare moments when she let go and was even a little naughty. For a split second, he forgot about the stranger. A split second, no more. Why now? he wondered. She made remarks like that twice, thrice a year. Why now?

He glanced back toward her. Corinne wore the diamond studs he'd bought her at that place on Forty-Seventh Street. Adam had given them to her on their fifteenth anniversary at the Bamboo House Chinese restaurant. His original idea had been to stick them in a fortune cookie somehow—Corinne loved opening, though not eating, fortune cookies—but that idea never really panned out. In the end, the waiter simply delivered them to her on one of those plates with a steel covering. Corny, cliché, unoriginal, and Corinne loved it. She cried and threw her arms around him and squeezed him so hard that he wondered whether any man in the world had ever been hugged like that.

Now she only took them off at night and to swim because she worried the chlorine might eat away at the setting. Her other earrings sat untouched in that small jewelry box in her closet, as if wearing them in lieu of the diamond studs would be some kind of betrayal. They meant something to her. They meant commitment and love and honor and, really, was that the kind of woman who would fake a pregnancy?

Corinne had her eyes on the field. The ball was down at the offensive end, where Thomas played. He could feel her stiffen whenever the ball came anywhere near their son.

Then Thomas made a beautiful play, knocking the ball out of a defender's stick, picking it up, and heading for the goal.

We pretend otherwise, but we watch only our own child. When Adam was a newer father, he found this parental focus somewhat poignant. You would go to a game or a concert or whatever and, sure, you'd look at everyone and everything, but you'd really only see your own child. Everyone and everything else would become background noise, scenery. You'd stare at your own child and it would be like there were a spotlight on your kid, only your kid, and the rest of the stage or field or court was darkening and you'd feel that warmth, the same one Adam had felt in his chest when his son smiled at him, and even in an environment loaded up with other parents and other kids, Adam would realize that every parent felt the exact same way, that every parent had their own spotlight directed at their own kid and that that was somehow comforting and how it should be.

Now the child-centricity didn't feel quite as uplifting. Now it felt as though that concentrated focus wasn't so much love as obsession, that the single-lens single-mindedness was unhealthy and unrealistic and even damaging.

Thomas ran down on the fast break and dumped a pass off to Paul Williams. Terry Zobel was open to score, but before he could shoot, the referee blew the whistle and threw the yellow flag. Freddie Friednash, a middie on Thomas's team, was sent off for a one-minute slashing penalty. The fathers in the corner had a group conniption: "Are you kidding me, ref?" "Bad call!" "You gotta be blind!" "That's BS!" "Call them both ways, ref!"

The coaches caught on and started in too. Even Freddie, who had been jogging off at a brisk pace, slowed and shook his head at the referee. More parents joined the chorus of complaints—the herd mentality in action.

"Did you see the slash?" Corinne asked.

"I wasn't looking over there."

Becky Evans, Tripp's wife, came over and said, "Hi, Adam. Hi, Corinne."

Because of the penalty, the ball was in the defensive zone now, far away from Thomas, so they both glanced toward her, returning the smile. Becky Evans, mother of five, was almost supernaturally cheerful, always with a smile and a kind word. Adam was usually suspicious of the type. He liked to watch these happy moms for the unguarded moment, when the smile would falter or grow wooden, and for the most part, he always found it. But not with Becky. You constantly saw her cruising the kids around in her Dodge Durango, the smile alight, the backseats loaded up with kids and gear, and while these mundane tasks eventually wore down most in her maternal order, Becky Evans seemed to feed off it, to gain strength even.

Corinne said, "Hi, Becky."

"Great weather for a game, isn't it?"

"Sure is," Adam said, because that was what you said.

The whistle blew again—another slashing call on the away team. The fathers went nuts anew, even swearing. Adam frowned at their behavior but stayed silent. Did that make him part of the problem? He was surprised to see that the jeers were being led by the bespectacled Cal Gottesman. Cal, whose son Eric was a quickly improving defenseman, worked as an insurance salesman in Parsippany. Adam had always found him to be mild-mannered and well-meaning, if not somewhat didactic and dull, but Adam had also noticed of late that Cal Gottesman's behavior had grown increasingly odd in direct proportion to his son's improvement. Eric had grown six inches in the last year and was now a starting defender. Colleges were buzzing around him, and now Cal, who had been so reserved on the sidelines, could often be seen pacing and talking to himself.

Becky leaned in closer. "Did you hear about Richard Fee?"

Richard Fee was the team goalie.

"He's committed to Boston College."

"But he's only a freshman," Corinne said.

"I know, right? I mean, are they going to start drafting them out of the womb?"

"It's ridiculous," Corinne agreed. "How do they know what kind of student he's going to be? He just got into high school."

Becky and Corinne continued, but Adam was already tuning them out. They didn't seem to care, so Adam dutifully took this as his cue to leave the ladies and maybe stand by himself for a bit. He gave Becky a quick cheek peck and started on his way. Becky and Corinne had known each other since childhood. They had both been born in Cedarfield. Becky had never left the town.

Corinne had not been so lucky.

Adam moved toward a spot halfway between the moms and the dads in the corner, hoping to carve out a little space for himself. He glanced over at the group of fathers. Tripp Evans met his eye and nodded as though he understood. Tripp probably didn't want the crowd either, but he was the guy who drew it. Local celebrity, Adam thought. Deal with it.

When the horn blew, ending the first quarter, Adam looked back toward his wife. She was chatting away with Becky, both women animated. He just stared for a moment, lost and scared. He knew Corinne so well. He knew everything about her. And paradoxically, because he knew her so well, he knew that what the stranger had told him had the echo of truth.

What will we do to protect our family?

The horn sounded, and the players took the field. Every parent now checked to see whether his or her kid was still in the game. Thomas was. Becky continued to talk. Corinne quieted now, nodding along, but she kept her focus on Thomas. Corinne was good with focus. Adam had originally loved that quality in his wife. Corinne knew what she wanted from life, and she could laser in on the goals that would help achieve it. When they met, Adam had fuzzy future plans at best—something about working with the underserved and downtrodden—but he had no specifics about where he wanted to live or what kind of life he wanted to lead or how to form that life or that nuclear family. It was all vast and vague to him—and here, in stark contrast, was this spectacular, beautiful, intelligent woman who knew exactly what they both should do.

There was a freedom in that surrender.

It was then, thinking about the decisions (or lack thereof) he had made to get him to this point in life, when Thomas got the ball behind the goal, faked a pass down the middle, drove to the right, cranked back his stick, and shot a beauty low and in the corner.

Goal.

The fathers and mothers cheered. Thomas's team-

mates came over and congratulated him, slapping him
good-naturedly on the helmet. His son stayed calm, following that old adage "Act like you've been there." But
even at this distance, even through his son's face mask,
even behind the mouth guard, Adam knew that Thomas,
his oldest child, was smiling, that he was happy, that it
was Adam's job as a father, first and foremost, to keep
that boy and his brother smiling and happy and safe.

What would he do to keep his boys happy and safe?

Anything.

But it wasn't all about what you'd do or sacrifice, was
it? Life was also about luck, about randomness, about
chaos. So he could and would do whatever was possible
to protect his children. But he somehow knew—knew
with absolute certainty—that it wouldn't be enough, that
luck, randomness, and chaos had other plans, that the
happiness and safety were going to dissolve in the still
springtime air.

CHAPTER 7

THOMAS ended up scoring his second goal—the game winner!—with fewer than twenty seconds on the clock.

This was the hypocrisy in Adam's cynicism about the overly intense sports world: Despite everything, when Thomas scored that final goal, Adam leapt in the air, pumped his fist, and shouted, "Yes!" Like it or not, he felt a rush of pure, undiluted joy. His better angels would say that it had nothing to do with Adam himself, that the joy emanated from the knowledge that his son was feeling even greater joy, and that it was natural and healthy for a parent to feel that way for his own child. Adam reminded himself that he was not one of those parents who lived through his kids or looked at lacrosse as a ticket to a better college. He enjoyed the sport for one simple reason: His sons loved playing.

But parents all tell themselves a lot of things. The Croatian hunchback, right?

When the game ended, Corinne took Ryan home in her car. She was going to get dinner ready. Adam waited for Thomas in the Cedarfield High School parking lot. It would, of course, have been much easier to simply take him home right after the game, but there were rules about the kids taking the team bus for insurance purposes. So Adam, along with a bunch of other parents, followed the bus back to Cedarfield and waited for their sons to disembark. He got out of his car and made his way toward the school's back entrance.

"Hey, Adam."

Cal Gottesman walked toward him. Adam said hey back. The two fathers shook hands.

"Great win," Cal said.

"Yes indeed."

"Thomas played a hell of a game."

"So did Eric."

Cal's glasses never seemed to fit right. They kept slipping down his nose, forcing him to push them back up with his index finger, only to have them immediately start their nasal descent again. "You, uh, you seemed distracted."

"Pardon?"

"At the game," Cal said. He had one of those voices where everything sounded like a whine. "You seemed, I don't know, bothered."

"Did I?"

"Yes." He pushed the glasses up his nose. "I also couldn't help but notice your look of, shall we say, disgust."

"I'm not sure what—"

"When I was correcting the referees."

Correcting, Adam thought. But he didn't want to get into that. "I didn't even notice."

"You should have. The ref was going to call a crosscheck on Thomas when he got the ball at X."

Adam made a face. "I'm not following."

"I ride the refs," Cal said in a conspiratorial tone,

"with purpose. You should appreciate that. It benefited your son tonight."

"Right," Adam said. Then—because who the hell was this guy to approach him like this?—he added, "And why do we sign that sportsmanship waiver at the beginning of the season?"

"Which one?"

"The one where we promise not to verbally abuse any players, coaches, or referees," Adam said. "That one."

"You're being naïve," Cal said. "Do you know who Moskowitz is?"

"Does he live on Spenser Place? Trades bonds?"

"No, no," Cal replied with an impatient snap. "Professor Tobias Moskowitz at the University of Chicago."

"Uh, no."

"Fifty-seven percent."

"What?"

"Studies show that fifty-seven percent of the time the home team wins a sporting event—what we call a home-field advantage."

"So?"

"So the home-field advantage is real. It exists. It exists across all sports, during all time periods, in all geographies. Professor Moskowitz noted that it is remarkably consistent."

Adam said, "So?" again.

"Now, you've probably heard many of the normal reasons given to explain this advantage. Travel fatigue—the away team has to go on a bus or a plane or what have you. Or maybe you've heard that it's familiarity with the playing field. Or that some teams are used to cold weather or warm weather—"

"We live in neighboring towns," Adam said.

"Right, exactly, which just strengthens my point."

Boy, was Adam not in the mood. Where the heck was Thomas?

"So," Cal continued, "what do you think Moskowitz found?"

"Excuse me?"

"What do you think explains home-field advantage, Adam?"

"I don't know," Adam said. "Crowd support maybe."

Cal Gottesman clearly liked that answer. "Yes. And no."

Adam tried not to sigh.

"Professor Moskowitz and others like him have run studies on home-field advantage. They aren't saying things like travel fatigue aren't a factor, but there is pretty much no data supporting those theories—just some anecdotal evidence. No, the fact is, only one reason for the home-field advantage is supported by hard, cold data." He held up his index finger in case Adam didn't know what *one* meant. Then, just in case he was being too subtle, he said, "Just one."

"And that is?"

Cal lowered the finger into a fist. "Referee bias. That's it. The home team gets more of the calls."

"So you're saying the refs are throwing the game?"

"No, no. See, that's the key to the study. It isn't as though the referees are purposely favoring the home team. The bias is completely unintentional. It's not conscious. It's all related to social conformity." Cal's scientist hat was strapped down tightly now. "In short, we all want to be liked. The refs, like all humans, are all social creatures and assimilate the emotions of the crowd. Every once in a while, a referee will subconsciously make a call that will make the crowd happier. Ever watch a basketball game? All coaches work the refs because they understand human nature better than anyone. Do you see?"

Adam nodded slowly. "I do."

"So that's it, Adam." Cal spread his hands. "That's the whole home-field advantage in a nutshell—the human desire to conform and be liked."

"And so you yell at the referees—"

"At away games," he interrupted. "I mean, we need to keep our advantage at home. But at away games, sure, scientifically speaking, you need it for balance. Staying quiet could actually hurt you."

Adam looked away.

"What?"

"Nothing."

"No, I want to hear it. You're an attorney, right? You work in an adversarial business."

"I do."

"And you do what you can to influence the judge or opposing counsel."

"I do."

"So?"

"Nothing. I got your point."

"But you don't agree with it."

"I don't really want to get into it."

"But the data is pretty clear."

"Right."

"So what's your issue?"

Adam hesitated and then figured, why not? "It's just a game, Cal. Home-field advantage is part of it. It's why we play half of the games home, half away. So it balances out. In my view—and hey, it's only mine—you're justifying bad behavior. Let it just play out, bad calls and all.

It's a better example to the boys than screaming at referees. And if we lose an extra game or two a year, which I doubt, it's a small price to pay for decorum and dignity, don't you think?"

Cal Gottesman started working up his counter when Thomas came out of the locker room. Adam held up a hand and said, "No big deal, Cal, just my take. Excuse me, okay?"

Adam hurried back to the car and watched his son cross the field. There is a definite walk when you feel good about a win. Thomas stood more upright, a bounce in his step. There was a hint of a smile on his face. Thomas didn't want to let that joy out, Adam knew, until he was in the car. He waved to a few friends, ever the politician. Ryan was on the quiet side, but Thomas could be mayor of this town.

Thomas threw his lacrosse bag into the backseat. The stink from the much-sweated-in pads began their assault. Adam slid open the windows. That did some good, but after a game in the warm weather, it was never enough.

Thomas waited for them to get about a block away before allowing his face to light up. "Did you see that first goal?"

Adam grinned. "Sick."

"Yeah. Only my second goal using my left."

"It was a nice move. The game winner was sweet too."

They went on like this for quite some time. Some might think it was being boastful. It was actually the opposite. With his teammates and coaches, Thomas was modest and generous. He always gave credit to someone else—the guy who made the pass, the kid who made the steal—and grew shy and embarrassed whenever he was made the center of attention on an athletic field.

But alone with his family, Thomas felt comfortable cutting loose. He loved to go into details about the game, not just about his goals but about the entirety of play, what the other kids said, who had played well, who hadn't. Home was a secure haven for that—a familial cone of honesty, if you will. Corny as it sounded, that was what family should be. He didn't have to worry about sounding like a braggart or a phony or any of that. He just spoke freely.

"He's home!" Corinne shouted as Thomas walked through the door. He shrugged his lax bag off his shoulder and left it in the mudroom. Thomas let his mother hug him.

"Great game, honey."

"Thanks."

Ryan offered his brother a fist bump of congratulations.

"What's for dinner?" Thomas asked.

"I got one of those marinated skirt steaks on the grill."

"Oh yeah."

The steaks were Thomas's favorite. Not wanting to break the mood, Adam dutifully gave his wife a kiss. They all washed up. Ryan set the table, which meant that Thomas would have to clear it. There was water for everyone. Corinne had poured two glasses of wine for the adults. She laid out the food on the kitchen island. Everyone grabbed plates and served themselves.

It was a strikingly ordinary, albeit cherished, family dinner, and yet it felt to Adam as though there were a ticking bomb under their table. It was only a matter of time now. The dinner would end and the boys would do their homework or watch TV or mess around on the computer or play a video game. Would he wait until Thomas and Ryan went to bed? Probably. Except that over the past year or two, he or Corinne would fall asleep before Thomas. So he'd have to get Thomas in his room with the door closed before he could confront his wife with what he had learned.

Tick, tick, tick . . .

For most of the meal, Thomas held court. Ryan listened raptly. Corinne told a story about how one of the teachers got drunk in Atlantic City and threw up in the casino. The boys loved it.

"Did you win any money?" Thomas asked.

"I never gamble," Corinne said, ever the mom, "and you shouldn't either."

Both boys rolled their eyes.

"I'm serious. It's a terrible vice."

Now both boys shook their heads.

"What?"

"You're so lame sometimes," Thomas said.

"I am not."

"Always with the life-lesson stuff," Ryan added with a laugh. "Cut it out."

Corinne looked to Adam for help. "Do you hear your sons?"

Adam just shrugged. The subject changed. Adam didn't remember to what. He was having trouble focusing. It was as though he were watching a movie montage of his own life—the happy family he and Corinne had created, having dinner, enjoying one another's company. He could almost see the camera slowly circling the table, getting everyone's face, getting everyone's back. It was so everyday, so hackneyed, so perfect.

Tick, tick, tick . . .

A half hour later, the kitchen was cleaned. The boys headed upstairs. As soon as they were out of sight, Corinne's smile dropped off her face. She turned to Adam.

"What's wrong?"

Amazing when he thought about it. He had lived with Corinne for eighteen years. He had seen her in every kind of mood, had experienced her every emotion. He knew when to approach, when to stay away, when she needed a hug, when she needed a kind word. He knew her well enough to finish her sentences and even her thoughts. He knew everything about her.

There had been, he thought, no surprises. He even knew her well enough to know that what the stranger had alleged was indeed possible.

Yet he hadn't seen this. He hadn't realized that Corinne could read him too, that she had known, despite his best effort to hide it, that something serious had upset him, that it wasn't just a normal thing, that it was something big and maybe life-altering.

Corinne stood there and waited for the blow. So he delivered it.

"Did you fake your pregnancy?"

CHAPTER 8

THE stranger sat at a corner table at the Red Lobster in Beachwood, Ohio, just outside of Cleveland.

He nursed his Red Lobster "specialty cocktail," a mango mai tai. His garlic shrimp scampi had started to congeal into something resembling tile caulk. The waiter had tried to take it from him twice, but the stranger had shooed him away. Ingrid sat across the table. She sighed and checked her watch.

"This has to be the longest lunch ever."

The stranger nodded. "Almost two hours."

They were watching a table with four women who were on their third "specialty cocktail" round and it wasn't yet two thirty. Two of them had done Crabfest, the variety dish served on a plate the approximate circumference of a manhole cover. The third woman had ordered the shrimp linguini Alfredo. The cream sauce kept getting caught up in the corners of her pink-lipsticked mouth.

The fourth woman, whose name they knew was Heidi Dann, was the reason they were there. Heidi had ordered the wood-grilled salmon. She was forty-nine, big and bouncy with strawlike hair. She wore a tiger-print top with a somewhat plunging neckline. Heidi had a boister-ous yet melodic laugh. The stranger had been listening to it for the past two hours. There was something mesmer-izing in the sound.

"I've grown to like her," the stranger said.

"Me too." Ingrid pulled her blond hair back with both hands, forming an imaginary ponytail and then letting it free. She did that a lot. She had the kind of long, too-straight hair that constantly fell in front of her face. "There's a certain zest for life there, you know?"

He knew exactly what Ingrid meant.

"In the end," Ingrid said, "we are doing her a favor."

That was the justification. The stranger agreed with it. If the foundation is rotten, you need to demolish the en-tire house. You can't just fix it with a coat of paint or a few planks of wood. He knew that. He understood it. He lived it.

He believed it.

But that didn't mean that he relished being the one to work the explosives. That was also how he looked at it. He was the one who blew up the house with the rotting foundation—but he never stuck around to see how or if it was rebuilt.

He didn't even stick around to make sure that no one had been left inside the house when it went up.

The waitress came over and gave the ladies the check. Everyone dug into their purses with care and produced cash. The woman who had the linguini did the math, di-viding the bill up with precision. The two Crabfest eaters pulled out bills one at a time. Then they each opened their change purse as though it were a rusted chastity belt.

Heidi just threw in some twenties.

Something about the way she did it—with care and ease—touched him. He guessed that the Danns were okay with money, but who knew in today's world? Heidi and her husband, Marty, had been married twenty years. They had three kids. Their oldest daughter, Kimberly, was a freshman at NYU in Manhattan. The two boys, Charlie and John, were still in high school. Heidi worked various makeup counters at the Macy's in University Heights. Marty Dann was a vice president in sales and marketing for TTI Floor Care in Glenwillow. TTI was all about vacuum cleaners. They owned Hoover, Oreck, Royal, and the division where Marty had worked for the past eleven years, Dirt Devil. He traveled a lot for his job, mostly to Bentonville, Arkansas, because that was where Walmart's corporate offices were.

Ingrid was studying the stranger's face. "I can handle this on my own, if you'd like."

He shook his head. This was his job. Ingrid was here because he would need to approach a woman and that sometimes looked odd. A man-and-woman couple approaching someone? No worries. A man approaching another man in, say, a bar or American Legion Hall? Again no worries. But if a twenty-seven-year-old man approached a forty-nine-year-old woman near, say, a Red Lobster?

That could get tricky.

Ingrid had already paid the bill, so they moved quickly. Heidi had arrived on her own in a gray Nissan Sentra. He and Ingrid had parked their rent-a-car two spots away. They waited by the car, key in hand, ready to pretend that they were about to get in it and drive off.

They didn't want to draw attention to themselves.

Five minutes later, the four women exited the restaurant. They hoped Heidi would end up alone now, but they had no way of knowing for certain. One of her friends could walk her to the car, in which case they would have to follow Heidi back to her house and either try to confront her there (never a good idea to confront a victim on their own property—it made them more defensive) or wait until she headed out again.

The women all bid one another adieu with hugs. Heidi, he could see, was a good hugger. She hugged as though she meant it. When she hugged, her eyes closed and the person she hugged closed hers too. It was that kind of hug.

The three other women headed off in the opposite direction. Perfect.

Heidi started toward her car. She wore Capri pants. Her high heels made her stagger a little after the drinks, but she handled it with practiced aplomb. She was smiling. Ingrid nodded a get-ready at the stranger. They both did all they could to look harmless.

"Heidi Dann?"

He tried to keep his expression friendly or, at worst, neutral. Heidi turned and met his eye. The smile dropped off her face as though someone had attached an anchor to it.

She knew.

He wasn't surprised. Many somehow did, though denial also worked big-time when the stranger called. But he sensed strength and intelligence in her. Heidi already knew that what he was about to say would change everything.

"Yes?"

"There's a website called FindYourSugarBaby.com," he said.

The stranger had learned that you had to leap directly into it. You didn't ask the victim if they had time to talk or if they wanted to sit down or go someplace quiet. You just launched.

"What?"

"It purports to be a modern online dating service. But it's not. Men—supposedly wealthy men with disposable income—sign up to meet, well, sugar babies. Have you heard of it?"

Heidi looked at him another second. Then she turned her gaze toward Ingrid. Ingrid tried to smile reassuringly.

"Who are you two?"

"That's not important," he said.

Some people fight it. Other people see that it's an irrelevant waste of time in the big picture. Heidi was in the latter group. "No, I've never heard of it. It sounds like one of those sites married people use to cheat."

The stranger made a yes-no gesture with his head and said, "Not really. This site caters to more of a business transaction, if you know what I mean."

"I don't know what you mean at all," Heidi said.

"You should read the material when you have a chance. The site talks about how every relationship is really a transaction and how important it is to define your roles, to know what is expected of you and what is expected of your lover."

Heidi's face was losing color. "Lover?"

"So here is how it works," the stranger continued. "A man signs on, for example. He looks through a list of women, usually much younger. He finds one he likes. If she accepts, they start negotiating."

"Negotiating?"

"He's looking for what we call a sugar baby. The website defines that as a woman he'd maybe take out to dinner or escort to a business conference, that kind of thing."

"But that's not what really happens," Heidi said.

"No," the stranger said. "That's not what happens."

Heidi let loose a long breath. She put her hands on her hips. "Go on."

"So they negotiate."

"The rich guy and his sugar baby."

"Right. The site tells the girl all sorts of nonsense. How everything is defined. How dating like this means no game playing. How the men are rich and sophisticated and will treat her well and buy her gifts and take her to exotic overseas locales."

Heidi shook her head. "Do the girls really fall for that?"

"Some, maybe. But I doubt too many. Most understand the score."

It was as though Heidi had expected him to visit, expected this news. She was calm now, though he could still sense the devastation. "So they negotiate?" she prompted.

"Right. Eventually, they reach an understanding. It's all spelled out in an online contract. In one case, for example, the young woman agrees to be with the man five times per month. They spell out possible days of the week. He offers eight hundred dollars."

"Each time?"

"Per month."

"Cheap."

"Well, that's how it starts. But she counters with two thousand dollars. They go back and forth."

"Do they reach an agreement?" Heidi asked.

Her eyes were wet now.

The stranger nodded. "In this case, they settle for twelve hundred dollars per month."

"That's fourteen thousand four hundred dollars per year," Heidi said with a sad smile. "I'm good at math."

"That's correct."

"And the girl," Heidi said. "What does she tell the guy she is? Wait, don't tell me. She says she's a college student and needs help with her tuition."

"In this case, yes."

"Ugh," Heidi said.

"And in this case," the stranger continued, "the girl is telling the truth."

"She's a student?" Heidi shook her head. "Terrific."

"But the girl, in this case, doesn't stop there," the stranger said. "The girl sets up different days of the week with different sugar daddies."

"Oh, that's gross."

"So with one guy, she's always Tuesdays. Another guy is Thursdays. Someone else gets weekends."

"Must add up. The money, I mean."

"It does."

"Not to mention the venereal diseases," Heidi said.

"That I can't comment on."

"Meaning?"

"Meaning we don't know if she uses condoms or what. We don't have her medical records. We don't even know exactly what she does with all these men."

"I doubt she's playing cribbage."

"I doubt it too."

"Why are you telling me this?"

The stranger looked at Ingrid. For the first time, Ingrid spoke. "Because you deserve to know."

"That's it?"

"That's all we can tell you, yes," the stranger said.

"Twenty years." Heidi shook her head and bit back her tears. "That bastard."

"Pardon?"

"Marty. That bastard."

"Oh, we're not talking about Marty," the stranger said.

Now, for the first time, Heidi looked completely baffled. "What? Then who?"

"We're talking about your daughter, Kimberly."

CHAPTER 9

CORINNE took the blow, stumbled back, stayed standing.

"What the hell are you talking about?"

"Can we skip this part?" Adam asked.

"What?"

"The part where you pretend you have no idea what I'm talking about. Let's skip the denials, okay? I know you faked the pregnancy."

She tried to gather herself, pick up the pieces one at a time. "If you know, why are you asking?"

"How about the boys?"

That puzzled her. "What about them?"

"Are they mine?"

Corinne's eyes went wide. "Are you out of your mind?"

"You faked a pregnancy. Who knows what else you're capable of?"

Corinne just stood there.

"Well?"

"Jesus, Adam, look at them."

He said nothing.

"Of course they're yours."

"There are tests, you know. DNA. You can buy them at Walgreens, for crying out loud."

"Then buy them," she snapped. "Those boys are yours. You know that."

They stood on either side of the kitchen island. Even now, even in the midst of his anger and confusion, he could not help but see how beautiful she was. He couldn't believe that with all the guys who wanted her, she had somehow chosen him. Corinne was the girl men wanted to marry. That was how guys foolishly looked at women when they were younger. They broke them down into two camps. One camp made guys think of lust-filled nights and legs in the air. Camp Two made them think of moonlight walks and canopies and wedding vows. Corinne was squarely in Camp Two.

Adam's own mother had been eccentric to the point of bipolarity. That had been what foolishly attracted his father. "Her crackle," Dad had explained. But the crackle turned more into mania as time passed. The crackle was fun and spontaneous, but the unpredictability wore his father down, aged him. There were great ups, but they were eventually decimated by the growing number of great downs. Adam did not make that mistake. Life is a series of reactions. His reaction to the mistake of his father was to marry a woman he considered steady, consistent, controlled, as though people were just that simple.

"Talk to me," Adam said.

"What makes you think I faked the pregnancy?"

"The Visa charge to Novelty Funsy," he said. "You told me it was for school decorations. It wasn't. It's a billing name for Fake-A-Pregnancy.com."

She looked confused now. "I don't understand. What made you go through a charge from two years ago?"

"It's not important."

"It is to me. You didn't casually decide to start checking old bills."

"Did you do it, Corinne?"

Her gaze was down on the granite top of the island. Corinne had taken forever to find the exact shade of granite, finally finding something called Ontario Brown. She spotted some dried debris and started working it free with her fingernail.

"Corinne?"

"Do you remember when I had two school periods off during lunch?"

The change of subject threw him for a moment. "What about it?"

The debris came loose. Corinne stopped. "It was the only time in my teaching career I had that big of a time window. I got permission to go off school grounds for lunch."

"I remember."

"I used to go to that café in Bookends. They made a great panini sandwich. I'd get one and a glass of homemade iced tea or a coffee. I'd sit at this corner table and read a book." A small smile came to her face. "It was bliss."

Adam nodded. "Great story, Corinne."

"Don't be sarcastic."

"No, no, seriously, it's gripping and so relevant. I mean, I'm asking you to tell me about faking a pregnancy, but really this story is much better. What kind of panini was your favorite, anyway? I like the turkey and swiss myself."

She closed her eyes. "You've always used sarcasm as a defense mechanism."

"Oh, right, and you've always been great with timing. Like now, Corinne. Now is the time to psychoanalyze me."

There was a pleading in her voice now. "I'm trying to tell you something, okay?"

He shrugged. "So tell me."

She took a few seconds to gather herself before she began speaking again. When she did, her voice had a far-off quality to it. "I'd go to Bookends pretty much every day, and after a while, you become—I don't know—a regular. The same people would be there all the time. It was like a community. Or like *Cheers*. There was Jerry, who was unemployed. And Eddie was an outpatient at Bergen Pines. Debbie would bring her laptop and write—"

"Corinne . . ."

She held up her hand. "And then there was Suzanne, who was, like, eight months pregnant."

Silence.

Corinne turned behind her. "Where's that bottle of wine?"

"I don't see where you're going with this."

"I just need some more wine."

"I put it in the cabinet above the sink."

She headed over to it, opened the door, and snatched out the bottle. Corinne grabbed her glass and started to pour. "Suzanne Hope was maybe twenty-five years old. It was her first baby. You know how young mothers-to-be are—all glowing and over-the-top happy, like they're the first people to ever get pregnant. Suzanne was really nice. We all talked to her about the pregnancy and the baby. You know. She'd tell us about her prenatal vitamins. She ran names by us. She didn't want to know if it was a boy or girl. She wanted to be surprised. Everyone liked her."

He bit back the sarcastic rejoinder. Instead, he replaced it with an obvious observation. "I thought you were there for quiet and reading."

"I was. I mean, that's how it started. But somewhere along the way, I started to cherish this social circle. I know it sounds pathetic, but I looked forward to seeing these people. And it was like they only existed in that time and space, you know? It's like when you used to play pickup basketball. You loved those guys on the court, but you didn't know a thing about them off it. One guy owned that restaurant we went to and you didn't even know, remember?"

"I remember, Corinne. But I don't see the point."

"I'm just trying to explain. I made friends. People came in and out without warning. Like Jerry. One day, Jerry disappeared. We assumed he got a job, but it's not like he came in and told us. He just stopped coming. Suzanne too. We figured that she had the baby. She was way overdue. And then sadly, when the new semester started, double lunch ended for me, and so I guess I faded away too. That's how it worked. It was cyclical. The cast rotated."

He had no idea where she was going with this, but there was no reason to rush her either. In a way, he wanted things to slow down now. He wanted to consider all options. He glanced back over at the kitchen table where Thomas and Ryan had just eaten and laughed and thought that they were secure.

Corinne took a deep sip of her wine. To move it along, Adam asked, "Did you ever see any of them again?"

Corinne almost smiled. "That's the point of the story."

"What is?"

"I saw Suzanne again. Maybe three months later."

"At Bookends?"

She shook her head. "No. It was a Starbucks in Ramsey."

"Did she have a boy or girl?"

A sad smile toyed with Corinne's lips. "Neither."

He didn't know what to make of that or how to follow it up, so he simply said, "Oh."

Corinne met his eye. "She was pregnant."

"Suzanne was?"

"Yes."

"When you saw her at Starbucks?"

"Yes. Except it was only three months after I last saw her. And she still looked eight months pregnant."

Adam nodded, finally seeing where she was going. "Which is, of course, impossible."

"Of course."

"She was faking."

"Yes. See, I had to go to Ramsey to check out this new textbook. It was lunchtime again. Suzanne must have figured that there'd be no chance one of us from Bookends would be there. That Starbucks is, what, a fifteen-minute drive from Bookends?"

"At least."

"So I was up at the counter ordering a latte and I heard that voice and there she was, sitting in the corner, telling a rapt group of patrons about her prenatal vitamin regimen."

"I don't get it."

Corinne tilted her head. "Really?"

"You do?"

"Sure. I got it right away. Suzanne was holding court in the corner, and then I started walking toward her.

When she spotted me, that glow just vanished. I mean, you can imagine. How do you explain being eight months pregnant for, like, what, half a year? I just stood there and waited. I think she hoped that I'd leave. But I didn't. I was supposed to go to school, but later, I told them I got a flat tire. Kristin covered my classes for me."

"You and Suzanne eventually talked?"

"Yes."

"And?"

"She said that she really lives in Nyack, New York."

That was about thirty minutes from both Bookends and that Starbucks, Adam figured.

"She told me a story about having a stillborn. I don't think it's true, but it could be. But in many ways, Suzanne's story is simpler. Some women love being pregnant. Not because of the hormonal rush or because they have a baby growing inside of them. Their reasons are much more base. It is the one time in their life they feel special. People hold doors for them. People ask them about their day. They ask them when they're due and how they're feeling. In short, they get attention. It's a little like being famous. Suzanne was nothing special to look at. She didn't strike me as being particularly smart or interesting. Being pregnant made her feel like a celebrity. It was like a drug."

Adam shook his head. He remembered the wording on the Fake-A-Pregnancy website: *Nothing throws you in the spotlight like being pregnant!*

"So she faked being pregnant in order to maintain the high?"

"Yes. She'd slap on the fake belly. She'd go to the coffee shop. Instant attention."

"But there was only so long that she could get away with that," he said. "You can't be eight months pregnant for more than, well, a month or two."

"Right. So she moved lunch spots. Who knows how long she'd been at it—or if she's still doing it. She said her husband didn't care about her. He came home and went right to the TV or stayed at the bar with the guys. Again, I don't know if that's a lie. It doesn't matter. Oh, and Suzanne did it other places too. Like instead of going to the supermarket in her hometown, she'd go to ones farther away and smile at people and they'd always smile back. If she went to the movies and wanted a good seat, she'd use it. Same with airplane rides."

"Wow," Adam said. "That's pretty sick."

"But you don't get it?"

"I get it. She should see a shrink."

"I don't know. It seems pretty harmless."

"Strapping on a fake belly to gain attention?"

Corinne shrugged. "I admit it's extreme, but some people get attention because they're beautiful. Some because they inherited money or have a fancy job."

"And some get it by lying about being pregnant," Adam said.

Silence.

"So I assume your friend Suzanne told you about the Fake-A-Pregnancy website?"

She turned away.

"Corinne?"

"That's all I'm willing to say right now."

"You're kidding, right?"

"No."

"Wait, are you telling me you crave attention like this Suzanne? I mean, this isn't normal behavior. You know that, right? This has to be a mental disorder of some kind."

"I need to think about it."

"Think about what?"

"It's late. I'm tired."

"Are you out of your mind?"

"Stop."

"What?"

Corinne turned back to him. "You feel it too, don't you, Adam?"

"What are you talking about?"

"We're in a minefield," she said. "Like someone just dropped us right in the middle of it, and if we move too fast in any direction, we're going to step on an explosive and blow this whole thing up."

She looked at him. He looked at her.

"I didn't drop us in the minefield," he said through gritted teeth. "You did."

"I'm going up to bed. We can talk about this in the morning."

Adam blocked her path. "You're not going anywhere."

"What are you going to do, Adam? Beat it out of me?"

"You owe me an explanation."

She shook her head. "You don't understand."

"Don't understand what?"

She looked up into his eyes. "How did you find out, Adam?"

"It doesn't matter."

"You have no idea how much it matters," she said in a soft voice. "Who told you to look at the charge on the Visa bill?"

"A stranger," he said.

She took a step back. "Who?"

"I don't know. Some guy. I'd never seen him before. He came up to me at the American Legion and told me what you'd done."

She shook her head as though trying to clear it. "I don't understand. What guy?"

"I just told you. A stranger."

"We need to think about this," she said.

"No, you need to tell me what's going on."

"Not tonight." She put her hands on his shoulders. He backed away as though her touch scalded him. "It isn't what you think, Adam. There's more to this."

"Mom?"

Adam spun toward the voice. Ryan stood at the top of the steps.

"Can one of you help me with my math?" he asked.

Corinne didn't hesitate. The smile was back in place. "I'll be right up, honey." She turned to Adam. "Tomorrow," she whispered to him. There was a pleading in her voice. "The stakes are so high. Please. Just give me until tomorrow."

CHAPTER 10

WHAT could he do?

Corinne simply shut down. Later, alone in their bedroom, he tried anger, pleading, demanding, threats. He used words of love, ridicule, shame, pride. She wouldn't respond. It was so frustrating.

At midnight, Corinne carefully took off the anniversary diamond studs and placed them on her night table. She turned off the lights, wished him a good night, and closed her eyes. He was at a loss. He came close—maybe too close—to doing something physical. He debated ripping off her covers, but what would that do? He wanted to—dare he even admit it to himself?—put his hands on her, to shake her and make her talk or at least see reason. But when Adam was twelve, he had seen his father put his hands on his mother. Mom had egged him on— that was how she was, sadly. She would call him names or insult his manhood until eventually he cracked. One night, he saw his father wrap his hands around his mother's neck and start to choke her.

Oddly enough, it wasn't so much the fear, horror, and danger of seeing his father use force against his mother that bothered him. It was how pitiful and weak this act of dominance made his father look, how, even though she was on the receiving end, his mother had manipulated his father into becoming something so pathetic that he had to resort to doing something so out of character, so not him.

Adam could never lay a hand on a woman. Not just because it was wrong. But because of what it would do to him.

Unsure what to do, he slipped into bed next to Corinne. He pounded his pillow into the right shape, laid his head on it, and closed his eyes. He gave it ten minutes. Uh-uh, no way. He headed downstairs, pillow in hand, and tried to sleep on the couch.

He set his alarm for 5:00 A.M. so he'd be sure to get back upstairs into his bedroom before the boys woke up. There was no need. If sleep paid any visit, it was too brief to register. Corinne was deep in sleep when he went back up. He knew by her breathing that this wasn't an act—she was out cold. Funny, that. He couldn't sleep. She could. He remembered reading somewhere that cops could often tell guilt or innocence by suspects who slept. An innocent man left alone in an interrogation room, the theory went, stayed awake because of confusion and nerves about being falsely accused. A guilty man fell asleep. Adam had never bought the theory, one of those things that sounds cute but doesn't really hold up. Yet here he was, the innocent guy staying awake while his wife—the guilty?—slept like a newborn.

Adam was tempted to shake her awake, catch her on that cusp between dream and consciousness, maybe get the groggy truth out of her, but he had come to the conclusion that it wouldn't work. She had a point about being careful. But more than that, she was going to work in her own time frame. He couldn't push it too much. And maybe that was best.

The question was, what was he going to do now?

He knew the truth, didn't he? Did he really have to wait for her to confirm that she'd faked a pregnancy and a miscarriage? If she hadn't, he would have heard the denials by now. She was stalling—perhaps to come up with a reasonable rationale or perhaps to give him time to calm down and consider his alternatives.

Because what could he do here?

Was he ready to walk out the door? Was he ready to divorce her?

He didn't know the answer. Adam stood over the bed and stared down at her. How did he feel about her? He told himself, right now, without thinking about it, answer this: If it was true, did he still love her and want to be with her for the rest of his life?

His feelings were jumbled, but his gut reaction: Yes.

Take a step back. How big a deal was this deception? It was huge. No question about it. Huge.

But was it something that should destroy their lives—or was it something that they could live with? All families ignore the elephants in the room. Could he one day ignore this one?

He didn't know. Which was why he would have to be careful. He would have to wait. He would have to listen to her reasoning, even if that seemed almost obscene to him.

"It isn't what you think, Adam. There's more to this."

That was what Corinne said, but he couldn't imagine what. He slipped under the covers and closed his eyes for a moment.

When he opened them again, it was three hours later.

Exhaustion had sneaked up on on him and dragged him down. He checked the bed next to him. Empty. He swung his legs out of bed, his feet landing on the floor with a dull thud. From downstairs he heard Thomas's voice. Thomas the talker. Ryan the listener.

And Corinne?

He glanced out the bedroom window. Her minivan was still in the driveway. He crept quietly down the stairs. He probably couldn't articulate exactly why—probably something to do with sneaking up on Corinne before she had a chance to leave for work. The boys were at the table. Corinne had made Adam his favorite—she was big on making favorites all of a sudden, wasn't she?—a bacon, egg, and cheese sandwich on a sesame bagel. Ryan was eating a bowl of Reese's Puffs—health food—reading the back of the box as though it were religious scripture.

"Hey, guys."

Two grunts. Whatever their personalities might be like later in the day, neither boy was big on pre-school conversation with his parents.

"Where's your mother?"

Two shrugs.

He stepped fully into the kitchen and looked out the window and into the backyard. Corinne was out there. Her back was turned. A phone was pressed up to her ear.

Adam felt his face redden.

When he pulled open the back door, Corinne spun toward him and put up a "wait a sec" finger. He didn't. He stormed toward her. She hung up the phone and slipped it into her pocket.

"Who was that?"

"The school."

"Bullshit. Let me see the phone."

"Adam . . ."

He put out his hand. "Give it to me."

"Don't make a scene in front of the boys."

"Cut the crap, Corinne. I want to know what's going on."

"There's no time. I have to be at school in ten minutes. Do you mind driving the boys?"

"Are you for real?"

She stepped close to him. "I can't tell you what you want to know yet."

He almost punched her. He almost reared back his fist and . . . "What's your strategy here, Corinne?"

"What's yours?"

"Huh?"

"What's your worst-case scenario?" she asked. "Think about it. And if it's true, are you going to leave us?"

"Us?"

"You know what I mean."

It took a second for him to get the words out. "I can't live with someone I can't trust," he said.

She tilted her head. "And you don't trust me?"

He said nothing.

"We all have our secrets, don't we? Even you, Adam."

"I've never kept anything like this from you. But clearly, I have my answer."

"No, you don't." She moved close to him and looked up into his eyes. "You will soon. I promise."

He bit back and said, "When?"

"Let's meet for dinner tonight. Janice's Bistro at seven. Back table. We can talk there."

CHAPTER 11

HUMMEL figurines sat on the top shelf. There was a little girl with a donkey, three children playing follow-the-leader, a little boy with a beer stein, and finally a boy pushing a girl on a swing.

"Eunice loves them," the old man told Adam. "Me, I can't stand the damn things. They creep me out. I keep thinking someone should make a horror film with them, you know? Like instead of that scary clown or leprechaun. Can you imagine if those things came to life?"

The kitchen was old wood paneling. A *Viva Las Vegas* magnet was on the fridge. There was a snow globe with three pink flamingos on the ledge above the sink. The mounting read MIAMI, FLA in a florid-script font—"Fla" in case you weren't sure which Miami, Adam guessed. *The Wizard of Oz* collectible plates and an owl clock with moving eyes took up the wall on the right. The wall on the left had numerous yet fading police-related certificates and plaques, a retrospective of the long and distinguished career of retired Lieutenant Colonel Michael Rinsky.

Rinsky noticed Adam reading the certificates and muttered, "Eunice insisted we hang them up."

"She's proud of you," Adam said.

"Yeah, whatever."

Adam turned back toward him. "So tell me about the mayor's visit."

"Mayor Rick Gusherowski. Busted him twice when he was in high school, once for drunk driving."

"Was he charged?"

"Nah, just called his old man to pick him up. This was, what, thirty years ago? We did that more back in those days. Considered drunk driving a minor offense. Stupid."

Adam nodded to let him know that he was listening.

"They're real strict with the drunk-driving stuff now. Saves lives. But anyway, Rick comes to my door. Mr. Mayor now. Got the suit, with the American flag in the lapel. Don't join the military; don't help out the little guy; don't take in your tired, your poor, your huddled masses—but if you wear a little flag, you're a patriot."

Adam tried not to smile.

"So Rick comes in with his chest out and this big grin. 'The developers are offering you a lot of money,' he says to me. Goes on and on about how generous they're being."

"What do you say?"

"Nothing yet. I just kinda stare at him. Let him bloviate."

He signaled to the kitchen table for them to sit. Adam didn't want to sit in Eunice's chair—it felt wrong somehow—so he asked, "Which chair?"

"Any's fine."

Adam took one. Then Rinsky sat. The vinyl tablecloth was old and a little sticky and felt just right. There were still five chairs here, though the three boys he and Eunice had raised in this very house were grown and gone.

"Then he starts in on me with the good-of-the-community stuff. 'You're standing in the way of progress,' he tells me. 'People will lose their jobs because of you. Crime will increase.' You know the deal."

"I do, yes," Adam said.

Adam had heard it before many times, and he wasn't unsympathetic. Over the years, this downtown neighborhood had gone to seed. Some developer, getting a ton of tax breaks, had come in and bought up every building on the block on the cheap. He wanted to knock down all the dilapidated homes, apartments, storefronts, and build shiny new condos and Gap stores and tony restaurants. It wasn't a bad idea, really. You could make fun of the gentrification, but towns needed new blood too.

"So he keeps talking, about the shiny new Kasselton, how it will make the neighborhood safe and bring people back and all that. Then he comes up with his big pot sweetener. The developer has new senior-living housing in the heights. And then he has the gall to lean across and give me the sad eyes and say, 'You need to think about Eunice.'"

"Wow," Adam said.

"I know, right? Then he says I should take this deal because the next one will be worse and they can throw me out. Can they really do that?"

"They can," Adam said.

"We bought this house in 1970 off my GI Bill. Eunice ... she's fine, but sometimes her mind isn't on the track it's supposed to be. So she gets real scared in strange places. She starts to cry and shake even, but then she gets home, right? She sees this kitchen, she sees her creepy figurines or that rusty old refrigerator, and she's okay again. Do you understand?"

"I do."

"Can you help us?"

Adam leaned back. "Oh yes, I think I can."

Rinsky studied him for a few moments, his eyes penetrating. Adam shifted in the chair. He could tell what a great cop he must have been. "You got a funny look on your face, Mr. Price."

"Call me Adam. What kind of funny look?"

"I'm an old cop, remember?"

"Of course."

"I pride myself on reading faces."

"And what are you seeing on mine?" Adam asked.

"That you're cooking up a badass, killer idea."

"I may be," Adam said. "I think I can end this quickly if you have the stomach for it."

The old man smiled. "Do I look like I'm afraid of a fight?"

CHAPTER 12

WHEN Adam got home at six P.M., Corinne's car wasn't in the driveway.

He didn't know whether that surprised him. Corinne was usually home before him, but she probably wisely figured that there might be a scene if they met up at home before their Janice's Bistro dinner, so it would be best to avoid him. He hung up his coat and placed his briefcase in the corner. The boys' backpacks and sweatshirts were strewn across the floor, as though they were debris from a plane crash.

"Hello?" he shouted. "Thomas? Ryan?"

No answer. There was a time in this world when that meant something, maybe was even a cause for concern, but with the video games and the headphones and the teenage boys' constant need to "shower"—was that a euphemism?—any concern was short-lived. He started up the stairs. Sure enough, the shower was running. Probably Thomas. The door to Ryan's room was closed. Adam gave it a brief knuckle rap but opened without waiting for a response. If the headphones were loud enough, Ryan might never reply; if he just opened it, he felt as though he was completely invading his son's privacy. The knock-and-open somehow felt like a parentally fair way to handle the dilemma.

As expected, Ryan was lying in bed with his headphones on, fiddling with his iPhone. He slipped them off and sat up. "Hey."

"Hey."

"What's for dinner?" Ryan asked.

"Good, thanks. Work was busy, sure, but overall, yeah, I'd say I had an okay day. How about you?"

Ryan just stared at his father. Ryan often just stared at his father.

"Have you seen your mother?" Adam asked.

"No."

"She and I are going to Janice's tonight. You want me to order you two a pizza from Pizzaiola?"

There are few questions more rhetorical than asking your child whether they want you to order them pizza for dinner. Ryan didn't even bother with the yes, heading straight to the "Can we get buffalo chicken topping?"

"Your brother likes pepperoni," Adam said, "so I'll go half-and-half."

Ryan frowned.

"What?"

"Just one pie?"

"It's only the two of you."

Ryan did not seem placated.

"If that's not enough, there are Chipwiches in the freezer for dessert," Adam said. "That okay?"

Grudgingly: "I guess."

Adam headed back down the hall and into his bedroom. He sat on the bed and called the pizzeria, adding an order of mozzarella sticks. Feeding teenage boys was like filling a bathtub with a grapefruit spoon. Corinne

was always complaining—happily, for the most part—
that she had to food shop every other day at the least.

"Hey, Dad."

Thomas wore a towel around his waist. Water dripped
from his hair. He smiled and said, "What's for dinner?"

"I just ordered you guys pizza."

"Pepperoni?"

"Half pepperoni, half buffalo chicken." Adam held up
his hand before Thomas could say more. "And an order
of mozzarella sticks."

Thomas gave his father a thumbs-up. "Nice."

"You don't have to eat it all. Just leave the leftovers in
the fridge."

Thomas made a confused face. "What is this leftovers
of which you speak?"

Adam shook his head and chuckled. "Did you leave
me any hot water?"

"Some."

"Great."

Adam normally wouldn't shower and change, but he
had time and felt oddly nervous. He showered quickly,
managing to stay seconds ahead of the hot water, and
shaved away the Homer Simpson five-o'clock shadow. He
reached into the back of his cabinet and pulled out an
aftershave he knew Corinne liked. He hadn't worn it in a
while. Why he hadn't worn it recently, he couldn't say. Why
he had chosen to wear it tonight, he couldn't say either.

He put on a blue shirt because Corinne used to say that
blue worked with his eyes. He felt stupid about that and
almost changed, but then he figured, what the hell? When
he started out the bedroom door, he turned around and
took a long look at this room that had been theirs for so
long. The king-size bed was neatly made. There were too

many pillows on it—when had people started putting so many pillows on a bed?—but he and Corinne had spent a lot of years here. A simple and insipid thought, but there you go. It was just a room, just a bed.

Yet a voice in Adam's head couldn't help but wonder: Depending on how this dinner went, he and Corinne might never spend another night in here together.

That was melodramatic, of course. Pure hyperbole. But if hyperbole couldn't feel free to roam in his head, where could it roam?

The doorbell rang. No movement from the boys. There never was. They had been trained somehow to never answer the house phone (it wasn't for them, after all) and to never answer the doorbell (it was usually a delivery guy). As soon as Adam paid and closed the door, the boys clumped down the stairs like runaway Clydesdales. The house shook but held its ground.

"Paper plates okay?" Thomas asked.

Thomas and Ryan would eat on paper plates exclusively because it meant easier cleanup, but tonight, with the parents away, it was pretty much a given that if he forced real plates on them, they'd be in the sink when he and Corinne came home. Corinne would then complain to Adam. Adam would then have to scream for the boys to come down and put their plates in the dishwasher. The boys would claim that they were just about to do it— yeah, right—but not to worry because they'd be down and do it when their show was over in five (read: fifteen) minutes. Five (read: fifteen) minutes would pass, and then Corinne would complain to Adam again about how irresponsible the boys were, and he'd shout up to them with a little more anger in his voice.

The cycles of domesticity.

"Paper plates are fine," Adam said.

The two boys attacked the pizza as if they were rehearsing the finale of *The Day of the Locust*. Between bites, Ryan looked at his father curiously.

"What?" Adam said.

Ryan managed to swallow. "I thought you were just going to Janice's for dinner."

"We are."

"So what's with the getup?"

"It isn't a getup."

"And what's the smell?" Thomas added.

"Are you wearing cologne?"

"Eeew. It's ruining the taste of the pizza."

"Knock it off," Adam said.

"Want to trade a slice of pepperoni for a slice of buffalo chicken?"

"No."

"Come on, just one slice."

"Throw in a mozzarella stick."

"No way. Half a mozzarella stick."

Adam started for the door as the negotiations wore down. "We won't be late. Get your homework done, and please stick the pizza box in the recycling, okay?"

He drove past the new hot yoga place on Franklin Avenue—by *hot* he meant temperature of the class, not popularity or looks—and found parking across the street from Janice's. Five minutes early. He looked for Corinne's car. No sign of it, but she could be parked in the back lot.

David, Janice's son and quasi maître d', greeted him at the door and brought him to the back table. No Corinne. Well, okay, he was here first. No big deal. Janice came out of the kitchen two minutes later. Adam rose and kissed her on the cheek.

"Where's your wine?" Janice asked. Her bistro was BYO. Adam and Corinne always brought a bottle.

"Forgot."

"Maybe Corinne will bring some?"

"I doubt it."

"I can send David to Carlo Russo's."

Carlo Russo's was the wine store down the street.

"That's okay."

"It's no hassle. It's quiet right now. David?" Janice turned back to Adam. "What are you having tonight?"

"Probably the veal Milanese."

"David, get Adam and Corinne a bottle of the Paraduxx Z blend."

David brought back the wine. Corinne still wasn't there. David opened the bottle and poured two glasses. Corinne still wasn't there. At seven fifteen, Adam started to get that sinking feeling in his gut. He texted Corinne. No answer. At seven thirty, Janice came over to him and asked if everything was okay. He assured her that it was, that Corinne was probably just caught up in some parent-teacher conference.

Adam stared at his phone, willing it to buzz. At 7:45 P.M., it did.

It was a text from Corinne:

MAYBE WE NEED SOME TIME APART. YOU TAKE CARE OF THE KIDS. DON'T TRY TO CONTACT ME. IT WILL BE OKAY.

Then:

JUST GIVE ME A FEW DAYS. PLEASE.

CHAPTER 13

ADAM sent several desperate texts to try to get Corinne to reply. They included: "this isn't the way to handle this," "please call me," "where are you," "how many days," "how can you do this to us"—stuff like that. He tried nice, mean, calm, angry.

But there was no reaction.

Was Corinne okay?

He gave Janice some lame excuse about Corinne still being stuck and having to cancel. Janice insisted that he take two veal Milanese home with him. He was going to fight it, but there seemed little point.

As he pulled onto his street, he still held out hope that Corinne had changed her mind and gone home. It was one thing to be mad at him. It was another thing to take it out on the boys. But her car wasn't in the drive, and the first thing Ryan said to him when he opened the door was "Where's Mom?"

"She has some work thing," Adam said in a voice equally vague and dismissive.

"I need my home uniform."

"So?"

"So I threw it in the wash. Do you know if Mom did the laundry?"

"No," Adam said. "Why don't you check the basket?"

"I did."

"How about your drawers?"

"I checked there too."

You always see your or your spouse's flaws in your child. Ryan had Corinne's anxiety over small matters. Big matters—house payments, illness, destruction, accidents—didn't bother Corinne. She rose to the occasion. Maybe because she overcompensated by worrying the minor stuff into a ground stump, or maybe, in life, like a great athlete, Corinne was clutch when it mattered.

Of course, to be fair, this was no small matter to Ryan.

"Then maybe it's in the washer or dryer," Adam said.

"Already looked."

"Then I don't know what to tell you, kid."

"When will Mom be home?"

"I don't know."

"Like at ten?"

"What part of 'I don't know' is confusing you exactly?"

There was more snap in his tone than expected. Ryan was also, like his mother, supersensitive.

"I didn't mean—"

"I'll text Mom."

"That's a good idea. Oh, let me know what she says, okay?"

Ryan nodded and texted.

Corinne didn't reply to him right away. Nor in an hour. Or even two. Adam made up some excuse about her teachers' conference being extended. The boys bought it because the boys never looked too closely at stuff like that. He promised Ryan that he'd find the uniform before his game.

Adam was, of course, blocking to some extent. Was Corinne safe? Had something terrible happened to her? Should he go to the police?

The last part felt foolish. The police would hear about their big fight, see Corinne's text about letting her be, and shake their heads. And really, when you step back, is it so bizarre that his wife would want a little distance after what Adam had just learned?

Sleep came in small chunks. Adam constantly checked his phone for texts from Corinne. Nothing. At 3:00 A.M., he sneaked into Ryan's room and checked his son's phone. Nothing. This made no sense. Trying to avoid Adam, okay, he could get that. She might be angry or scared or confused or feeling cornered. It would make sense that she might want to get away from him for a few days.

But her boys?

Would Corinne really just up and leave her boys in the lurch like this? Did she expect him to just make excuses?

. . . YOU TAKE CARE OF THE KIDS. DON'T TRY TO CONTACT ME. . . .

What was that all about? Why shouldn't he try to contact her? And what about . . . ?

He sat up as the sun came through the windows. Hello.

Corinne could abandon him. She could even want to—he didn't know—force him to take care of the boys.

But what about her students?

She took her teaching responsibilities, like most things that mattered, very seriously. She was also a bit of a control freak and hated the idea of some ill-prepared substitute taking over her class for even a day. Funny now that he thought about it. Over the past four years, Corinne had missed only one day of school.

The day after her "miscarriage."

It had been a Thursday. He had come home late from work to find her crying in bed. When the bad cramping started, she had driven herself to the doctor. It was too late, but in truth, she said, the doctor wouldn't have been able to do anything anyway. These things happen, the doctor had told her.

"Why didn't you call me?" Adam had asked.

"I didn't want you to worry or rush home. There was nothing you could do."

And he had bought it.

Corinne had wanted to go to work the next day, but Adam put his foot down. She had gone through something traumatic. You don't just get up and go to work the next day. He had picked up the phone and handed it to her.

"Call the school. Tell them you won't be in."

She had reluctantly made the call, informing the school that she would be back by Monday. Adam had thought at the time that this was simply Corinne's way. Get back to life. Get back to work. No reason to dwell. He had been amazed at the speed of her recovery.

Man, how naïve could one man be?

But then again, was that his fault? Who the hell would be looking for dishonesty in such a traumatic moment? Why would he question her word on something so serious? Even now, in hindsight, he had no idea why Corinne would have done something so . . . heinous? Crazy? Desperate? Manipulative?

What?

But that didn't matter right now. The point was, Corinne would be at school. She might choose to take time off from him and maybe even her boys, but there was no reason why she wouldn't be at school today.

The boys were old enough to get ready for school on their own. Adam managed to avoid them, ducking their questions about Mom's whereabouts with quick shout-outs from his bedroom and the pretense of a long morning shower.

When the boys were gone, he drove over to the high school. The bell for homeroom would have just sounded. That would be perfect. Adam could enter and confront her as she walked between homeroom and first period. Her homeroom class was room 233. He would wait for her by the door.

The high school had been built in the seventies and reeked of it. What had been considered sleek and modern had weathered like an old sci-fi movie set, like *Logan's Run* or something. The building was gray with fading aqua trim. It was the edificial equivalent of Cheez Whiz or a hockey player's mullet.

There were no free spaces in the school's parking lot. Adam ended up parking illegally—live on the edge—and hurrying toward the school. The side door was locked. Adam had never done this before—visited Corinne during a school day—but he knew that all schools had taken up stringent security protocols in the wake of shootings and other violence. He circled toward the front door. It was also locked. Adam pressed the intercom button.

A camera whirred down on him, and the weary female voice that could only belong to someone working in a school's main office asked him who he was.

He put on his most disarming smile. "It's Adam Price. Corinne's husband."

The door buzzed. Adam pushed through the doors. A

sign read CHECK IN AT THE MAIN DESK. He wasn't sure what to do here. If he signed in, they would want to know why and probably buzz down to the classroom. He didn't want that. He wanted to surprise Corinne or, at the very least, not need to explain to the staff why he was here. The office was on the right. Adam was about to turn left and just hurry down the opposite way when he saw the armed security guard. He aimed his most disarming smile at the guard. The guard offered one back. No choice now. He'd have to go to the main office. He veered through the door and weaved past a few local moms. There was a huge laundry basket in the middle of the floor where parents dropped off lunches for their kids who forgot to bring them in the morning.

The clock on the wall grunted and ticked. It read 8:17 A.M. Three minutes until the bell rang. Okay, good. The sign-up sheet was on the tall counter. He picked up the pen as casually as possible—Mr. Without A Care—and quickly signed in with intentionally messy handwriting. He grabbed a visitor pass. The two women behind the desk were busy. They didn't bother to even glance his way.

No reason to wait, was there?

He hurried back down the hall, flashing his visitor pass at the guard. Like most high schools, there had been additions over the years, and that helped make traversing your way inside these arteries somewhat tricky. Still, when the bell sounded, Adam was perfectly situated to observe the door to room 233.

The students streamed out and collided and clogged the corridors like some medical documentary on heart disease. He waited until the flow of students petered out and then halted. Then, a few seconds later, a young man Adam guessed was probably under thirty came out and turned left.

A substitute.

Adam just stood there, pressing himself against the wall to let the student stream rush past him and not get caught in its current. He wasn't sure what to think or do. Was he even surprised by this development? He didn't know. He tried to put it together, tried to think about the links here—the fake pregnancy, the stranger, the confrontation—that had led to his wife's choosing to run off for a few days.

It made no sense.

So what next?

Nothing, he supposed. At least, not right this very moment. Go to work. Do your job. Think it through. He was missing something. He knew that. Corinne had as much as admitted that, hadn't she?

"It isn't what you think, Adam. There's more to this."

When the flow of students turned into a trickle, he started back toward the front exit. He was lost in thought and about to make a turn when he felt fingers like a steel talon grip his arm. He turned and saw his wife's friend, Kristin Hoy.

"What the hell is going on?" she whispered.

"What?"

Her muscles clearly were not just for show. She pulled him into an empty chemistry classroom and closed the door. There were workstations and beakers and sinks with high faucets. A giant chart of the periodic table of elements, both a staple of every science classroom and a cliché, dominated the far wall.

"Where is she?" Kristin asked.

Adam wasn't sure how to play it, so he went with honesty. "I don't know."

"How can you not know?"

"We were supposed to meet for dinner last night. She never showed."

"She just didn't . . . ?" Kristin shook her head in confusion. "Did you call the police?"

"What? No."

"Why not?"

"I don't know. She sent a text. She said she needed some time away."

"From what?"

Adam just looked at her.

Kristin said, "You?"

"Seems so."

"Oh. Sorry." Kristin stepped back, chastened. "So why are you here?"

"Because I want to make sure she's okay. I figured she'd be at work. She never calls in sick."

"Never," Kristin agreed.

"Except, it seems, today."

Kristin considered that. "I guess you guys have been fighting a lot."

Adam didn't really want to get into it, but what choice did he have? "Something has recently come up," he said in his most noncommittal legal voice.

"It isn't any of my business, right?"

"Right."

"But it is kinda my business because Corinne made it part of my business."

"What do you mean?"

Kristin sighed and put her hand to her mouth. Outside the school, her outfits were all about accentuating her toned body. She wore sleeveless blouses and either shorts or small skirts, even when the weather didn't exactly call for it. In here, her blouse was more conservative, though you could still see the muscles near the clavicle and neck.

"I got a text too," she said.

"What did it say?"

"Adam?"

"What?"

"I don't want to get in the middle of this. You get that, right? You two have been having issues. I get that."

"We haven't been having issues."

"But you just said—"

"We have *an* issue, one, and, well, it just came up."

"When?"

"When did the issue come up?"

"Yes."

"The day before yesterday."

"Oh," Kristin said.

"What do you mean, 'Oh'?"

"It's just that ... I mean, Corinne has been acting strangely for the past month or so."

Adam tried to keep a straight face. "Strange how?"

"Just, I don't know, different. Distracted. She missed a class or two and asked me to cover for her. She missed a few workouts and said ..."

Kristin stopped.

"Said what?" Adam prodded.

"Said if anybody asked where she was, to just say that she was there with me."

Silence.

"Did she mean me, Kristin?"

"She never said that, no. Look, I better get back. I have class—"

Adam stepped in her path. "What did her text say?"

"What?"

"You said she sent you a text yesterday. What did it say?"

"Look, she's my friend. You get that, right?"

"I'm not asking you to betray confidences."

"Yeah, Adam, you kinda are."

"I just want to make sure she's okay."

"Why wouldn't she be?"

"Because this isn't like her."

"Maybe it's just what she said to you. She needs time."

"Is that what she texted you?"

"Something like that, yes."

"When?"

"Yesterday afternoon."

"Wait, when? After school?"

"No," Kristin said too slowly. "During."

"During school?"

"Yes."

"What time?"

"I don't know. Around two o'clock."

"Wasn't she at school?"

"No."

"She missed school yesterday too?"

"No," Kristin said. "I saw Corinne in the morning. She was acting a little shaky. I guess that's because you guys were fighting."

Adam said nothing.

"She was supposed to oversee study hall during lunch break, but she asked me to cover for her. I did. I saw her run out to her car."

"Where was she going?"

"I don't know. She didn't say."

Silence.

"Did she come back to school?"

Kristin shook her head. "No, Adam, she never came back."

CHAPTER 14

THE stranger had given Heidi the link to FindYour SugarBaby.com as well as her daughter's user ID and password. With a heavy heart, Heidi signed in as Kimberly and found out all she needed to confirm that everything the stranger had told her was true.

The stranger had not just told her out of the kindness (or emptiness) of his heart. He made money demands, of course. Ten grand was the amount. If she didn't pay it in three days, the news of Kimberly's "hobby" would go viral.

Heidi signed out and sat on the couch. She debated pouring herself a glass of wine and decided against it. Then Heidi had a good, long cry. When she finished, she headed to the bathroom, washed her face, and sat back on the couch.

Okay, she thought, what do I do about this?

Heidi's first decision was almost the simplest: Don't tell Marty. She didn't like to keep secrets from her husband, but then again, she didn't hate it either. It was part of life, wasn't it? Marty would absolutely lose it if he found out what his little girl was up to while she was supposedly studying at NYU. Marty was prone to over-reaction, and Heidi could see him hopping in his car, driving to Manhattan, and dragging his daughter back by the hair.

Marty didn't need to know the truth. Come to think of it, neither did Heidi.

Damn those two strangers.

When Kimberly was in high school, she had gotten drunk at a party at a classmate's house. Intoxication led, as it often does, to going a little too far with a boy. Not all the way. But too far. Another mother in town, a busybody who meant well, had overheard her daughter talking about the incident. She had called Heidi and said, "I hate to tell you this, but if our roles were reversed, I would want to know."

So she told Heidi about the incident. Heidi had told Marty, who had completely overreacted. The relationship between father and daughter had never really been the same. What, Heidi wondered, would have been the outcome if that busybody had never called? In the end, what good had it done? It embarrassed her daughter. It strained the relationship between father and daughter. It had, Heidi believed, been a huge part of Kimberly's decision to go to college so far away. And maybe that stupid phone call from that stupid busybody had even led Kimberly and ultimately Heidi to this terrible website and the horrific nature of her daughter's relationship with three different men.

Heidi didn't want to believe it, but the evidence was right there in the "secret" communications between her young daughter and these older men. Dress it up all she wanted, but there was no way around the fact that her daughter was involved in straight-up prostitution.

She wanted to cry again. She wanted to do nothing

and forget those two calm strangers had ever said anything to her. But she had no choice now, did she? The secret had been thrust in her face. She couldn't put that horse back in the barn, to mix her metaphors. It was a parental paradox probably as old as time: She didn't want to know, but she did want to know.

When she called her daughter's cell phone, Kimberly had answered with breathless enthusiasm. "Hi, Mom."

"Hey, sweetheart."

"Everything okay? Your voice sounds funny."

At first Kimberly had denied it. That was to be expected. Then she tried to make it sound innocent. That, too, was to be expected. Then Kimberly tried defiance, accusing her mother of hacking into her account and invading her privacy. Again expected.

Heidi kept her voice steady, even as her heart cracked in her chest and filled it with pain. She explained to Kimberly about the stranger. She recounted what they had told her and what she had seen on her own. Patiently. Calmly. At least, on the outside.

It took some time, but they both knew where this conversation was headed. Cornered, the shock slowly wearing off, Kimberly started to open up. Money was tight, she explained.

"You can't believe how expensive everything is here."

A classmate had told Kimberly about the site. You didn't really have to do anything with the guys, she'd been told. They just wanted young girls for the company. Heidi almost laughed out loud at that one. Men, as Heidi knew all too well and Kimberly quickly learned, never really just wanted company. That was merely the loss leader to get you in the store.

Heidi and Kimberly talked for two hours. At the end

of the conversation, Kimberly asked her mother what she should do.

"Break it off with them. Today. Now."

Kimberly promised she would do just that. The next question was how to proceed. Heidi said she would take some time off and come up and spend some time in New York. Kimberly balked.

"The semester will be over in two weeks. Let's just wait till then."

Heidi didn't like that idea. In the end, they agreed to discuss it further in the morning. Before they hung up, Kimberly said, "Mom?"

"Yes?"

"Please don't tell Dad."

Already decided, but she didn't tell Kimberly that. When Marty came home, she said nothing. Marty cooked up burgers on the grill in the yard. Heidi poured them both drinks. He talked about his day. She talked about hers. The secret was there, of course. It sat at the kitchen table in Kimberly's old chair, never speaking but never budging, either.

In the morning, after Marty left for work, there was a knock on the door.

"Who is it?"

"Mrs. Dann? I'm Detective John Kuntz with the New York Police Department. May I speak with you for—"

Heidi threw open the door, nearly collapsing in the process. "Oh my God, my daughter . . . ?"

"Oh, she's fine, ma'am," Kuntz said quickly, stepping forward to help support her. "Wow, jeez, I'm sorry. I guess I should have told you that right away. I'm just imagining— your daughter is in school in New York and an NYPD officer shows up at your door." Kuntz shook his head. "I have kids too. I get it. But don't worry, Kimberly is fine. I mean, healthwise. There are other factors ..."

"Factors?"

Kuntz smiled. There was a little too much space between each tooth. He sported a terrible comb-over, the kind of thing that made you want to grab a pair of scissors, pull the few hairs taut, and snip them off. She placed him in his midforties, paunchy with stooped shoulders and the sunken eyes of someone who didn't eat well or get enough sleep.

"May I come in for a moment?"

Kuntz held up his badge. It looked, to Heidi's amateur eye, to be legitimate.

"What's this about?"

"I think you probably have some idea." Kuntz nodded toward the door. "May I?"

Heidi stepped back. "I don't."

"Don't what?"

"Have any idea what this is about."

Kuntz stepped inside and looked around as though he were there to buy the place. He smoothed down a few of the comb-over hairs that had started to make a static-electrical escape. "Well, you called your daughter last night. Is that correct?"

Heidi wasn't sure how to answer. Didn't matter. Kuntz plowed ahead without waiting for one anyway.

"We are aware that your daughter has been involved in activity that could be illegal."

"What do you mean?"

He sat on the couch. She sat on the chair across from him.

"Can I ask a favor, Mrs. Dann?"

"What's that?"

"It's a small one, but I think it would really simplify this conversation for all concerned. Let's stop with the pretense, okay? It just wastes time. Your daughter, Kimberly, was involved in online prostitution."

Heidi just sat there.

"Mrs. Dann?"

"I think you better leave."

"I'm trying to help."

"It sounds like you're making accusations. I better talk to an attorney."

Kuntz pushed down the stray strands again. "You got it wrong."

"How so?"

"We don't care about what your daughter may or may not have done. It's petty and I will grant you this: With the online stuff, there is a fine line between business relationship and prostitution. Then again, maybe there has always been. We aren't interested in hassling you or your daughter."

"Then what do you want?" Heidi asked.

"Your cooperation. That's all. If you and Kimberly cooperate, we see no reason why we can't just forget about her role in all this."

"Her role in what?"

"Let's take it a step at a time, shall we?" Kuntz reached into his pocket and pulled out a small pad. Then he took out one of those small pencils golfers use to keep score. He licked the pencil's tip and turned his attention back toward Heidi. "First off, how did you find out about your daughter's involvement with that sugar babies website?"

"What difference does that make?"

Kuntz shrugged. "Just a routine question."

Heidi said nothing. The small tingling at the base of her neck had started to grow.

"Mrs. Dann?"

"I think I better talk to an attorney."

"Oh," Kuntz said. He made a face as though he were a teacher suddenly disappointed by a favorite pupil. "Then your daughter lied to us. That won't look good here, I gotta be honest."

Heidi knew that he wanted her to bite. The silence between them grew so big, Heidi could hardly breathe. She couldn't take it, so she asked: "Why do you think my daughter lied?"

"Simple. Kimberly told us you found out about the website in a completely legal way. She said that two people—a man and a woman—stopped you outside a restaurant and informed you of what was going on. But see, if that were true, I don't get why you wouldn't want to tell us that. There is nothing illegal in that activity."

Heidi's head started spinning. "I don't understand any of this. What are you doing here exactly?"

"That's a fair question, I guess." Kuntz sighed and adjusted himself on the couch. "Do you know what the Cyber Crime Unit is?"

"I imagine it has something to do with crimes on the Internet."

"Exactly. I'm with the CCU—that stands for Cyber Crime Unit—which is a fairly new division of the NYPD. We bust criminals who use the Internet in nefarious ways—hackers, scammers, that kind of thing—and we suspect that the person or persons who approached you at the restaurant are part of an elusive cyber criminal syndicate we've been after for a long time."

Heidi swallowed. "I see."

"And we would like your help in finding and identifying whoever might have been involved in these crimes. Does that make sense? So let's get back to it, okay? Yes or no, did two people approach you in the parking lot of a restaurant?"

The tingling was still there, but she said, "Yes."

"Great." Kuntz smiled with the spaced teeth again. He wrote something down and looked back up at her. "What restaurant?"

She hesitated.

"Mrs. Dann?"

"I don't understand something," Heidi said slowly.

"What's that, ma'am?"

"I just talked to my daughter yesterday afternoon."

"Yes."

"So when did you talk to her?"

"Last night."

"And how did you get here so fast?"

"This matter is of great importance to us. I flew in this morning."

"But how did you even know about it?"

"Pardon?"

"My daughter didn't say anything about calling the police. So how would you know . . . ?" She stopped. Her mind traveled down a few possible paths. All of them were pretty dark.

"Mrs. Dann?"

"I think you better leave."

Kuntz nodded. He started working the few strands of hair again, sweeping them from one ear to the other. Then he said, "I'm sorry, but I can't do that."

Heidi stood and moved toward the door. "I'm not going to talk to you."

"Yes, you are."

Still sitting and with something approaching a sigh, Kuntz took out his gun, aimed with precision at Heidi's kneecap, and pulled the trigger. The sound of the weapon was quieter than she would have thought, but the impact was more immense. She collapsed to the floor like a broken folding chair. He moved fast, covering her mouth to smother her scream. He lowered his lips to her ear.

"If you scream, I'll finish you off slowly and then I'll start on your daughter," Kuntz whispered. "Do you understand?"

The pain came in waves, nearly making her pass out. Kuntz took the muzzle and pressed it against the other knee. "Do you understand, Mrs. Dann?"

She nodded.

"Terrific. Now let's try this again. What was the name of the restaurant?"

CHAPTER 15

ADAM sat in his office, going over everything for the thousandth time in his head, when a simple question came to him: If Corinne had indeed decided to run away from life, where would she go?

Truth? He had no idea.

He and Corinne were such a couple, such a unit, that the idea of her running away someplace without him or their family was completely anathema to him. There were friends Corinne might call, he guessed. Some women she knew in college. There were a few family members too. But he couldn't see her confiding in or staying with any of them under this sort of circumstance. She just wasn't that open with anyone other than . . . well, other than Adam.

So maybe Corinne was alone.

That seemed most likely. She would be staying in a hotel. But either way—and this was the key here—whatever she was doing would require means, aka the use of a credit card or cash. That meant somewhere there were credit card charges or ATM withdrawals.

So look them up, dummy.

He and Corinne had two accounts, both held jointly. They used a debit card for one and a Visa charge card for the other. Corinne wasn't good with the finances. Adam handled all that as part of their domestic division of labor. He also knew all the user names and passwords.

In short, he could see her every charge or withdrawal.

For the next twenty minutes, Adam went through her charge cards and bank accounts. He started by searching from the most recent backward—any activity from today and yesterday. But there was nothing. He started traveling back a few days, just to see if there were any patterns. Corinne wasn't big on using cash. Credit cards were both easier and offered points on every purchase. She liked that.

Everything—her entire financial life or, well, spending life—was there and unsurprising. She had gone to the A&P supermarket, Starbucks, the Lax Shop. She had lunch at Baumgart's and picked up takeout at Ho-Ho-Kus Sushi. There were the automatic gym payments taken off the card and something she had ordered online from Banana Republic. Normal-life stuff. There was also pretty much at least one charge every single day.

But not today. And not yesterday.

No charges at all.

So what should he make of that?

For one thing, Corinne might be naïve in the ways of bill paying, but she wasn't dumb. If she wanted to stay hidden, Corinne might have realized that he could check the credit card statements online and track her down that way.

Right. So what would she do instead? She'd use cash.

He checked the ATM withdrawals. The last one she made had been two weeks ago for $200.

Was that enough to run away on?

Doubtful. He thought about it.

If she were driving for any length of time, she would need to buy gas. So how much cash did she have on her now? It wasn't as though she planned to run. She couldn't have known that he would confront her about the fake pregnancy or that the stranger would visit. . . .

Or had she?

He stopped. Could Corinne have put money away, knowing that something like this would happen? He tried to think back. Had she been surprised when he confronted her? Or had she been more like . . . resigned?

Had she somehow suspected that one day her deception would come to light?

He didn't know. When he sat back and tried to think it through, he realized that he didn't know a damn thing for anything close to certain. In her text, Corinne had asked him—no, the text equivalent of begged him, what with her "JUST GIVE ME A FEW DAYS. PLEASE."—to let her be. Maybe that was best. Maybe he should just let her blow off steam or do whatever it was she was doing and be patient and wait. That was what she had specifically asked for in that text, right?

But then again, for all he knew, Corinne had driven away from the school and met some horrible fate. Maybe she knew the stranger. Maybe she drove to the stranger and confronted him and he got angry and kidnapped her, or worse. Except the stranger didn't seem the type. And those texts had come in, telling him that she needed time and to give her a few days. But then again—this was how his head was reeling back and forth right now—anyone could have sent those texts.

A killer even.

Maybe someone had killed Corinne and taken her phone and . . .

Whoa, slow down a sec. Let's not get ahead of ourselves.

He could actually feel his heart pounding against his chest. Now that this worry had entered his head—check that, it had been in his head, but now he had all but voiced it—the fear stayed there, unmoving, like some unwelcome relative who wouldn't leave. He looked at her text again:

MAYBE WE NEED SOME TIME APART. YOU TAKE CARE OF THE KIDS. DON'T TRY TO CONTACT ME. IT WILL BE OKAY.

And then:

JUST GIVE ME A FEW DAYS. PLEASE.

Something about the texts was off, but he couldn't figure out what. Suppose Corinne was in real danger. He again wondered whether he should go to the police. Kristin Hoy had asked him about that right away, hadn't she? She asked him whether he had called the police if his wife was missing. Only she wasn't missing. She had sent that text. Unless she didn't send that text.

His head started spinning.

Okay, let's say he went to the police. Then what? He would have to go to the town cops. And what would he say exactly? They'd take one look at the text and say to give it time, wouldn't they? And in town, as much as he hated to admit it mattered, the cops would talk. He knew most of them. Len Gilman was the top cop in Cedarfield. He'd take his complaint, most likely. He had a son Ryan's age. They were in the same homeroom. Gossip and rumors about Corinne would spread like, well, gossip and rumors. Did he care? Easy to say no, but he knew that Corinne would. This was her town. She had battled to make it her own again and make a life.

"Hey, bro."

Andy Gribbel entered the office with a big smile on his bearded face. He wore sunglasses inside today, not because he wanted to look cool so much as to cover the red from either a late night or something more herbal.

"Hey," Adam said. "How did the gig go the other night?"

"The band totally kicked ass," Gribbel said. "Kicked ass and took names."

Adam leaned back, welcoming the interruption. "What did you open with?"

"'Dust in the Wind.' Kansas."

"Hmm," Adam said.

"What?"

"Opening with a slow ballad?"

"Right, but it totally worked. Dark bar, low lights, atmospheric, and then we directly segued, no break, into 'Paradise by the Dashboard Light.' Blew the roof off the place."

"Meat Loaf," Adam said with a nod. "Nice."

"Right?"

"Wait, since when do you have a female vocalist?"

"We don't."

"But 'Paradise' is a male-female duet."

"I know."

"A rather aggressive one," Adam continued, "with all the 'Will you love me forever's and him pleading for her to let him sleep on it."

"I know."

"And you guys do it without a female vocalist?"

"I do both parts," Gribbel said.

Adam sat up, tried to picture this. "You do the male-female duet yourself?"

"Always."

"That must be a hell of a rendition."

"You should hear me do 'Don't Go Breaking My Heart.' One second I'm Elton. The next, Kiki Dee. Brings tears to your eyes, really. Speaking of which . . ."

"What?"

"You and Corinne need a night out. I mean, *you* do anyway. If those bags under your eyes get any heavier, you'll have to pay surcharge when you check in for your flight."

Adam frowned. "Reaching."

"Come on, it wasn't that bad."

"We all set up for Mike and Eunice Rinsky tomorrow?"

"That's why I wanted to see you."

"Problem?"

"Nope, but Mayor Gush-something-ski wants to talk to you about the Rinsky eviction. He's got some town hall at seven and asked if you could stop by after. I texted you the address."

Adam checked his phone. "Yeah, okay, I guess we should hear him out."

"I'll let his people know. Have a good night, my man."

Adam checked his watch. He was surprised to see that it was six o'clock already. "Good night."

"Let me know if we're on for tomorrow."

"Will do."

Gribbel took off then, leaving Adam alone. Adam stopped and listened for a second. The sounds were distant, the office in its slow nightly death throes. Okay, so back up a step. Play it through. Go back to what he knew for certain.

One, he knew that Corinne had gone to school yesterday. Two, around lunchtime, Kristin had seen Corinne pull out of the school parking lot. Three . . . okay, no three, but . . .

Tollbooths.

If Corinne had gone any distance at all, there would be a record of it via the tollbooths. The school was near tolls on the Garden State Parkway, so that would show up in her E-ZPass records. Would Corinne remember to pocket her E-ZPass for the tolls? Probably not. E-ZPass was the kind of thing you stuck on your windshield and forgot about. There were times when it worked the opposite way, when Adam had rented a car and driven through the E-ZPass lanes, forgetting that he didn't have his E-Z Pass.

Worth a try anyhow.

He found the E-ZPass website via a Google search, but it required both an account number and a password. He didn't have them—had never, in fact, gone on the website—but they'd be on the bills at home. Okay, good. Time to go home anyway.

He grabbed his jacket and hurried to the car. When he merged onto Interstate 80, his mobile rang. It was Thomas.

"Where's Mom?"

He debated how to play it, but now was not the time for detailed honesty. "She's away."

"Where?"

"I'll tell you about it later."

"Will you be home for dinner?"

"I'm on my way now. Do me a favor. Take burgers out

of the freezer for you and your brother. I'll grill them when I get home."

"I don't really like those burgers."

"Too bad. I'll see you in half an hour."

He flipped through the music stations as he drove, searching for some nonexistent perfect song that would be, as Stevie Nicks might sing, "hauntingly familiar" yet not played so often as to beat it into submission. When he did find such a song—a rarity—it was always the last verse, and so the flipping would start anew.

When he pulled onto his street, Adam was surprised to see the Evanses' Dodge Durango in the driveway. Tripp Evans was getting out of the vehicle as Adam pulled in beside him. The two men greeted each other with handshakes and slaps on the back. Both were wearing business suits with loosened ties, and suddenly, the lacrosse draft at the American Legion Hall, just three days earlier, seemed very far away.

"Hey, Adam."

"Hey, Tripp."

"Sorry to just stop by like this."

"No worries. What can I do for you?"

Tripp was a big man with big hands. He was the kind of guy who never looked comfortable in a business suit. The shoulders were too tight or one sleeve was too long, something, so that he was always adjusting himself and you could see all he really wanted to do was rip the damn thing off. Lots of guys looked like that to Adam. Somewhere along the way, the suit had been strapped to them like the proverbial straitjacket, and now they simply couldn't get it off.

"I was hoping to talk to Corinne for a sec," Tripp said.

Adam stood there, hoping nothing showed on his face.

"I texted her a few times," Tripp continued, "but, uh, she hasn't replied. So I just figured I'd stop by."

"Can I ask what it's about?"

"No big deal, really," he said in a voice that for a guy as forthright as Tripp felt awfully forced. "It's just some lacrosse business."

Might be just Adam's imagination. Might be just the craziness of the past couple of days. But it felt as though some sort of tension was gathering in the air between them.

"What kind of lacrosse business?" Adam asked.

"The board met last night. Corinne never showed. Which was odd, I guess. I wanted to fill her in on some stuff, that's all." He looked toward the house as though he expected her to appear at the door. "It can wait."

"She's not here," Adam said.

"Okay, fine. Just tell her I stopped by." Tripp turned and met Adam's eye. That tension in the air seemed to thicken. "Everything okay?"

"Yeah," Adam said. "I'm fine."

"Let's grab a beer soon."

"I'd like that."

Tripp opened his car door. "Adam?"

"Yeah?"

"I'll be honest here," Tripp said. "You look a little rattled."

"Tripp?"

"What?"

"I'll be honest here. You do too."

Tripp tried to smile it off. "It's really no big deal."

"Yeah, you said that before. No offense, but I don't believe you."

"It's lacrosse business. That's the truth. I'm still hoping it's nothing, but I can't tell you more right now."

"Why not?"

"Board confidentiality."

"Are you serious?"

But he was. Adam could see that Tripp wouldn't budge on the subject, but then again, if Tripp was telling the truth, what the hell could the lacrosse board have to do with anything truly relevant in this?

Tripp Evans slipped back into his car. "Just tell Corinne to give me a call when she can. Have a good night, Adam."

CHAPTER 16

ADAM expected Mayor Gusherowski to look like a fat-cat politico fresh off the graft train—soft build, ruddy complexion, practiced smile, maybe a pinkie ring—and in this particular case, Adam was not disappointed. Adam wondered whether Gusherowski had always looked like a poster boy for corrupt politicians or if, over his years of "service," it had just become part of his DNA.

Three of the past four mayors of Kasselton had been indicted by the US Attorney's office. Rick Gusherowski had served in two of those administrations and been on the town council for the third. Adam wouldn't judge the man strictly on his looks or even legacy, but when it came to New Jersey small-town corruption, where there was smoke, there was usually a blazing, supernova-like bonfire.

The sparsely attended town hall meeting was breaking up when Adam arrived. The median age of the audience appeared to be in the mideighties, but that could be because this particular town hall meeting was being held at the brand-spanking-new PineCliff Luxury Village, which was unquestionably a euphemism for nursing and/or retirement home.

Mayor Gusherowski approached Adam with a Guy

Smiley smile—the perfect blend of game show host and Muppet. "Wonderful to meet you, Adam!" He gave Adam the perfunctory too-enthusiastic handshake, adding that little pull toward him that politicians believed made the recipient feel somehow inferior or obligated. "Can I call you Adam?"

"Sure, Mr. Mayor."

"Oh, we'll have none of that. Call me Gush."

Gush? Oh, Adam didn't think so.

The mayor spread his arms. "What do you think of the place? Beautiful, am I right?"

It looked to Adam like a conference room at a Court-yard Marriott, which was to say neat, generic, and impersonal. Adam gave a noncommittal head nod.

"Walk with me, Adam. I want to give you a little tour." He started down a corridor with forest green walls. "Great, isn't it? Everything here is state-of-the-art."

"What does that mean?" Adam asked.

"Huh?"

"State-of-the-art. How is it state-of-the-art?"

The mayor rubbed his chin, signaling deep thought. "Well, for one thing, they have flat-screen televisions."

"So does almost every house in America."

"There's Internet service."

"Again, like almost every house, not to mention café, library, and McDonald's, in America."

Gush—Adam was warming to the name—volleyed the question away by reigniting the smile. "Let me show you our deluxe unit."

He used a key to unlock the door and opened it with the flourish of—maybe Adam's mind was on game shows now—a model on *The Price Is Right.* "Well?"

Adam stepped inside.

"What do you think?" Gush asked.

"It looks like a Courtyard Marriott."

Gush's smile flickered. "These are brand-new and state—" He stopped himself. "Modern."

"It doesn't matter," Adam said. "Frankly, it doesn't matter if it looks like a Ritz-Carlton. My client doesn't want to move."

Gush nodded with great sympathy. "I get that. I really do. We all want to hold on to our memories, am I right? But sometimes memories hold us back. They force us to live in the past instead of the present."

Adam just stared at him.

"And sometimes, as a member of a community, we have to think about more than just ourselves. Have you been to the Rinsky house?"

"I have."

"It's a dump," Gush said. "Oh, I don't mean it like that. I grew up in that neighborhood. I say this as a man who worked his way up from those very streets."

Adam waited for the bootstraps analogy. He was somewhat disappointed when it didn't come.

"We have a chance of making real progress, Adam. We have a chance to chase away the urban blight of crime and bring sunshine to a part of our city that could use it. I'm talking new housing. A real community center. Restaurants. Quality shopping. Real jobs."

"I've seen the plans," Adam said.

"Progressive, am I right?"

"I don't care about that."

"Oh?"

"I represent the Rinskys. I care about them. I don't care about the profit margins of Old Navy or the Home Depot."

"That's not fair, Adam. We both know the community would be better served with this project coming to fruition."

"We both don't know that," Adam said. "But either way, I don't represent the community. I represent the Rinskys."

"And let's be honest. Look around you. They'd be happier living here."

"Doubtful, but maybe," Adam said. "But see, in the United States, the government doesn't decide what makes a man happy. The government doesn't decide that a couple who worked hard and bought their own home and raised their family would now be happier living somewhere else."

The smile slowly returned to Gush's face. "May I be blunt for a moment, Adam?"

"What, you haven't been so far?"

"How much?"

Adam steepled his fingers and did his best movie villain voice. "One billion dollars."

"I'm serious. Now, I could play games and do it the way the developer asked me to—bargain with you, go up in ten-thousand-dollar increments. But let's cut to the chase, shall we? I've been authorized to increase the offer by another fifty thousand dollars."

"And I've been authorized to tell you no."

"You're being unreasonable."

Adam didn't bother responding.

"You know that a judge already gave us the okay on our eminent domain case, right?"

"I do."

"And that Mr. Rinsky's previous attorney already lost the appeal. That's why he's gone now."

"I know that too."

Gush smiled. "Well, you leave me no choice."

"Sure I do," Adam said. "You don't just work for the developer, do you, Gush? You're a man of the people. So build your strip mall around his house. Change the plans. It can be done."

"No," Gush said, the smile gone now. "It can't."

"So you'll throw them out?"

"The law is on my side. And after the way you guys have behaved?" Gush leaned in close enough for Adam to smell the Tic Tac and whispered, "With pleasure."

Adam stepped back, nodding. "Yeah, I figured that."

"So you'll listen to reason?"

"If I ever hear it." Adam gave a little wave and turned to go. "Have a good night, Gush. We'll talk again soon."

CHAPTER 17

THE stranger hated to do this one.

But Michaela Siegel, who was now weaving her way into view, deserved to know the truth before she made a terrible mistake. The stranger thought about Adam Price. He thought about Heidi Dann. They may have been devastated by his visit, but this time, in the case of Michaela Siegel, it would be much, much worse.

Or maybe not.

Maybe Michaela would feel relief. Maybe, after the initial devastation, the truth would set her free. Maybe the truth would bring back balance to her life and put her back on the road she should and would have taken.

You never knew how someone would react until the pin in the grenade was pulled out, right?

It was late, nearly two in the morning. Michaela Siegel hugged her noisy friends good-bye. They were all somewhat inebriated from that night's festivities. The stranger had already tried twice earlier to get Michaela alone. It hadn't worked. He hoped that now she might head for the elevator by herself, and he could start the process.

Michaela Siegel. Age twenty-six. She was in her third year of residency in internal medicine at Mount Sinai

Hospital after graduating from Columbia University College of Physicians and Surgeons. She had started as an intern at Johns Hopkins Hospital, but after what happened, she and the hospital administrator felt that it would be best for all if she switched locations.

As she semistumbled toward the elevator, the stranger stepped into view. "Congratulations, Michaela."

She turned with a crooked smile. She was, he already knew, a rather sexy woman, which in a sense made this violation all the worse. The stranger felt a flush in his cheeks, remembering what he had seen, but he pushed on.

"Hmm," she said.

"Hmm?"

"Are you serving me with a subpoena or something?"

"No."

"And you're not hitting on me, are you? I'm engaged."

"No."

"I didn't think so," Michaela Siegel said. There was the slight slur of drink in her voice. "I don't really talk to strangers."

"I get that," he said, and because he feared losing her, he dropped the bombshell. "Do you know a man named David Thornton?"

Her face slammed shut like a car door. The stranger had anticipated that. "Did he send you?" she asked.

The slur was gone from her voice.

"No."

"Are you some kind of weird perv or something?"

"No."

"But you've seen—"

"Yes," he said. "Just for two seconds. I didn't watch it all or stare or anything. It was just . . . I had to make sure."

He could see now that she was facing the same dilemma so many he approached faced—flee this lunatic or hear him out? Most of the time, curiosity won them over, but he never knew how it would go.

Michaela Siegel shook her head and voiced that dilemma. "Why am I still talking to you?"

"They say I have an honest face."

It was true. That was why it was almost always he who took on this task. Eduardo and Merton had strengths, but if they approached you like this, your first instinct would be to run fast.

"That's what I used to think about David. That he had an honest face." She tilted her head. "Who are you?"

"That's not important."

"Why are you here? This is all in my past."

"No," he said.

"No?"

"It's not in your past. I wish it was."

Her voice was a scared whisper. "What the hell are you talking about?"

"You and David broke up."

"Well, duh," she snapped. "I'm getting married to Marcus this weekend."

She showed him the engagement ring on her finger.

"No," the stranger said. "I mean . . . I'm not saying this right. Do you mind if I go through it step-by-step?"

"I don't care how honest your face is," Michaela said. "I don't want to rehash this."

"I know."

"It's behind me."

"It's not. Not yet, anyway. That's why I'm here."

Michaela just stared at him.

"Were you and David broken up when...?" He didn't know how to put it, so he just sort of moved his hands back and forth.

"You can say it." Michaela straightened her back. "It's called revenge porn. I'm told it's quite the craze."

"That's not what I'm asking," the stranger said. "I'm asking about the state of your relationship *before* he put that video online."

"Everyone saw it, you know."

"I know."

"My friends. My patients. My teachers. Everyone at the hospital. My parents ..."

"I know," the stranger said softly. "Were you and David Thornton broken up?"

"We'd had a big fight."

"That's not what I asked."

"I don't get—"

"Were you two broken up before that video went public?"

"What difference does it make now?"

"Please," the stranger said.

Michaela shrugged. "I don't know."

"You still loved him. That's why it hurt so much."

"No," she said. "It hurt so much because it was a terrible betrayal. It hurt so much because the man I was dating went on a revenge porn site and put up a sex tape of us doing ..." She stopped. "Can you imagine? We had a fight, and that was how he reacted."

"He denied putting it up, right?"

"Of course he did. He didn't have the courage—"

"He was telling you the truth."

There were people around them. One guy stepped in

an elevator. Two women hurried outside. A concierge was behind the desk. They were all there, and right now, none of them were there.

Her voice was distant, hollow. "What are you talking about?"

"David Thornton didn't put that tape online."

"Are you a friend of his or something?"

"I've never seen or spoken to him."

Michaela swallowed. "Are you the one who posted the video?"

"No, of course not."

"Then how can you—?"

"The IP address."

"What?"

The stranger took a step closer to her. "The site claims to keep the user's IP address anonymous. That way, no one can know or prosecute the person who put it up."

"But you know?"

"Yes."

"How?"

"People think a site is anonymous because the site says so. That's a lie by definition. Behind every secret site on the Internet, there is a human being monitoring every keystroke. Nothing is really secret or anonymous."

Silence.

They were there now. The stranger waited. It wouldn't be long. He could see the quake by her mouth.

"So whose IP address was it?"

"I think you know already."

Her face twisted up in pain. She closed her eyes. "Was it Marcus?"

The stranger didn't answer yes or no. There was no need.

"They were close friends, weren't they?" the stranger said.

"Bastard."

"Roommates, even. I don't know the exact details. But you and David fought. Marcus saw an opportunity and seized it." The stranger reached into his pocket and pulled out an envelope. "I have the proof right here."

Michaela held up her palm. "I don't need to see it."

The stranger nodded, put the envelope away.

"Why are you telling me?" she asked.

"It's what we do."

"The wedding is four days away." She looked up at him. "So now what do I do?"

"That's not up to me," the stranger said.

"Right, of course." There was bitterness in her voice. "You just rip open lives. Closing them back up again—that's not up to you."

The stranger said nothing.

"I guess you figured, what, I'll go back to David now? Tell him I know the truth and ask his forgiveness? And then what? He'll take me in his arms and we'll live happily ever after? Is that how you see this working out? You being the hero of our love?"

In truth, the thought had occurred to the stranger, though not the hero part. But that idea of righting a wrong, that idea of restoring balance, that idea of putting her back on the life path she'd been taking—yes, he had hoped for that sort of resolution.

"But here's the problem, Mr. Secret Revealer." Michaela stepped closer to him. "Even when I was dating David, I had a crush on Marcus. That's the irony, right? Marcus didn't have to do this. We would have ended up together. Maybe, I don't know, but maybe Marcus feels bad about what he did. Guilty. Maybe he's trying to make up for it, and that's why he's so good to me."

"That's not a reason to be good to someone."

"Oh, so now you're offering life advice?" she snapped. "Do you know what choices you've left me with? I can blow up my life or I can live a lie."

"You're still young and attractive—"

"And I'm in love. With Marcus."

"Even now? Even though you know he's capable of doing something like this?"

"People are capable of doing all sorts of things in the name of love."

Her voice was soft now. The fight had gone out of it. She turned away and pressed the call button on the elevator. "Are you going to tell anyone else about this?" she asked.

"No."

"Good night."

"So you're still going to marry him?"

The elevator doors opened. Michaela stepped inside and turned to face him. "You didn't reveal a secret," she said. "You just created another one."

CHAPTER 18

ADAM pulled over when he hit the Cedarfield town line. He took out his phone and texted Corinne again:

I'M WORRIED. THE BOYS ARE WORRIED.
PLEASE COME HOME.

He hit SEND and put the car back into drive. Adam started to wonder, not for the first time, how he ended up spending his life in the town of Cedarfield. It was a simple thought, and yet the obvious implications weighed on him. Had something this important been a conscious choice? He didn't think so. He and Corinne could, he knew, have chosen to live anywhere, but then again, what was wrong with Cedarfield? It was, in many ways, the winner's spoils in the war we call the American dream. Cedarfield had picturesque homes with expansive yards. There was a lovely town center with a variety of restaurants and shops and even a movie theater. There were updated sports facilities, a modern library, and a duck pond. No less a nearly biblical authority than *Money* magazine had ranked Cedarfield the twenty-seventh "Best Place to Live in America" last year. According to the New Jersey Department of Education, Cedarfield was classified in the socioeconomic District Factor Group of J, the highest of eight categories. Yes, the government ranks towns in this way for real. Why they do this ranking is anybody's guess.

In fairness, Cedarfield was a great place to raise your kids, even though you were raising them to be you. Some thought of it as the cycle of life, but for Adam, it felt more like a shampoo-rinse-repeat existence, with so many of their neighbors and friends—good, solid people whom Adam liked a lot—growing up in Cedarfield, leaving for four-year stints to college, returning, marrying, raising their own children in Cedarfield, who would grow up here and leave for four-year stints to college, in the hopes of returning, marrying, and raising their own children here.

Nothing wrong with that, was there?

After all, Corinne, who had spent the first ten years of her life in Cedarfield, had not, it seemed, been fortunate enough to follow this well-trodden trajectory. When she was in fourth grade, this town and its values already deeply ingrained in her DNA, Corinne's father was killed in a car accident. He had been only thirty-seven, too young presumably to have worried about stuff like his own mortality or estate planning. His insurance coverage was a pittance, and soon after, Corinne's mother had to sell the house and downsize with Corinne and her older sister, Rose, to a brick garden apartment in the somewhat less upscale city of Hackensack.

For a few months, Corinne's mother had made the ten-mile trek between Hackensack and Cedarfield so that Corinne could still see her old friends. But then school started and predictably her friends got busy with town sports and dance classes Corinne could no longer afford, and while the physical distance stayed the same, the societal chasm grew too far to bridge. The childhood relationships quickly frayed on their way to completely falling apart.

Corinne's sister, Rose, acted out conventionally, doing poorly in school, rebelling against her mother, experimenting with a potpourri of recreational drugs and dead-end boys. Corinne, on the other hand, channeled the deep hurt and resentment into what most might consider positive outlets. She grew focused in school and in life, determined to do her best in all endeavors. Corinne kept her head down, studied hard, ignored the normal teenage temptations, and silently vowed to return victorious to the place where she'd been a seemingly happy girl with a father. Corinne spent the next two decades like a child with her face pressed against the upper suburban glass, until, at long last, the window opened or—just as likely—shattered.

Corinne and Adam had bought a house that looked suspiciously like the one in which Corinne had been raised. If it had bothered him at the time, Adam didn't recall it, but maybe by then, he shared her quest. When you marry, you marry your spouse's hopes and dreams too. Hers were to triumphantly return to a place that had cast her aside. There was a thrill, he now guessed, in helping Corinne fulfill that twenty-year odyssey.

The lights were still on at the aptly named Hard-core Gym (motto: You're Not Hard-core Unless You Lift Hard-core). Adam took a quick gander at the parking lot and spotted Kristin Hoy's car. He hit the speed dial for Thomas's cell phone—again, no point in calling the home phone; neither boy would ever answer it—and waited. Thomas answered on the third ring and gave his customary distracted and barely audible "Hullo?"

"All okay at home?"

"Yeah."

"What are you doing?"

"Nothing."

"And by nothing, you mean?"

"Playing *Call of Duty*. I just started."

Right.

"Homework done?" Adam asked out of habit. It was an oft-repeated parent-child verbal hamster-wheel of a question, never going anywhere, though somehow still mandatory.

"Pretty much."

He didn't bother telling him to "pretty much" finish it first. Pointless. Let the kid do it on his own. Let go a little.

"Where's your brother?"

"I don't know."

"But he's home, right?"

"I guess."

Brothers. "Just make sure he's okay. I'll be home soon."

"Okay. Dad?"

"Yeah?"

"Where's Mom?"

"She's away," he said again.

"Where?"

"It's some teachers' thing. We can talk about it when I get home, okay?"

The pause was long. "Yeah, okay."

He parked next to Kristin's Audi convertible and headed inside. The bloated musclehead behind the desk looked

Adam up and down and clearly found him wanting. He had the Cro-Magnon brow. His lips were frozen in a sneer of disdain. He wore some kind of sleeveless unitard. Adam feared the man might call him Brah.

"Help ya?"

"I'm looking for Kristin Hoy."

"Member?"

"What?"

"You a member?"

"No, I'm a friend. My wife's a member. Corinne Price."

He nodded as if that explained everything. Then he asked, "She okay?"

The question surprised Adam. "Why wouldn't she be?"

He might have shrugged, but the bowling balls flanking his head barely budged. "Big week to miss. Competition next Friday."

Corinne, he knew, didn't compete. She was nicely built and all, but there was no way she'd don one of those skimpy suits and start posing. She had, however, attended nationals with Kristin last year.

Musclehead pointed—he actually flexed when he did so—toward a corner in the back of the gym. "Room B."

Adam pushed through the glass door. Some gyms were quiet. Some featured loud music. And some, like this one, echoed with primordial grunts and the clank of heavy metal weights. All the walls were mirrored, and here, and only here, primping and posing for self-pleasure was not only acceptable but expected. The place reeked of sweat, disinfectant, and what he imagined from the commercials Axe cologne smelled like.

He found room B, knocked lightly, and pushed it open. It looked like a yoga studio with blond wood

floors, a balance beam, and, yep, tons of mirrors. A super-
toned woman tottered out onto the floor in a bikini and
ridiculously high heels.

"Stop," Kristin shouted.

The woman did so. Kristin strutted over in a skimpy
pink bikini and the same ridiculously high heels. There
was no totter, no awkwardness, no hesitation. She stalked
across the floor as though it owed her something.

"Your smile is weak. You look as though you've never
been in high heels before."

"I don't normally wear them," the woman said.

"Well, you're going to have to practice. They will judge
you on everything—how you enter, how you exit, how
you walk, your poise, your smile, your confidence, your
demeanor, your facial expression. You get one chance to
make that first impression. You can lose the competition
with your very first step. Okay, all of you sit." Five other
super-toned women sat on the floor. Kristin stood in front
of them, pacing back and forth. Her muscles coiled and
uncoiled with each step.

"You should all still be leaning out," Kristin said. "Thirty-
six hours before competition, most of you will carbo-load.
This will prevent your muscles from flattening out and get
them to have that natural puff look we're going for. Right
now, you should still be eating ninety percent protein. You
all have the specific diet plan, am I right?"

Nods.

"Follow it like a religious scripture. You should all be
drinking one and a half gallons of water per day. That's
a minimum. We'll start scaling that down as we get closer.
Only sips the day before Nationals and no water at all on
competition day. I have water pills if any of you are still
retaining water weight. Any questions?"

One hand went up.

"Yes?"

"Will we rehearse the evening gown competition?"

"We will. Remember, ladies. Most people think this is a bodybuilding competition. It is not. The WBFF is about fitness. You will have your poses and pose-off, just as we've been doing. But the judges now are looking for Miss America, Victoria's Secret, Fashion Week, and yes, *MuscleMag* all wrapped into one elegant package. Harriet will help you coordinate your evening gowns. Oh, and now let's go over travel necessities. Please bring with you the following: butt glue for your bikini, tape for the top of your suit, E6000 glue, breast pad petals, blister bandages, shoe glue—we always have last-minute strap disasters—tanner, gloves for your tanner, tan-block cream for those palms and feet bottoms, teeth whitener strips, red-eye drops—"

It was then that she spotted Adam in the mirror. Her face changed all at once. Gone was the taskmaster preparing for the WBFF nationals. Back was the friend and fellow teacher. It was amazing how easily we all slip in and out of roles, Adam thought.

"Work on your starting poses," Kristin said, her eyes on Adam now. "When you first walk out, you do one front, then one back, then you walk away. That's it. Okay, Harriet will lead you out. I'll be right back."

Kristin headed toward him without pause, again crossing the room in the high heels that made her nearly as tall as he was. "Anything new?" she asked him.

"Not really."

Kristin led him into the corner. "So what's up?"

It shouldn't be awkward talking to a woman standing in ridiculously high heels and sporting a skimpy bikini.

But it was. When Adam was eighteen, he spent two weeks in Spain's Costa del Sol. Many of the women went topless, and Adam had fancied himself too mature to ogle. He didn't ogle, but he did feel a little awkward. That feeling was coming back to him now.

"I guess you're preparing for a show," Adam said.

"Not just any show, but Nationals. If I can be selfish for a moment? Corinne left at a bad time. She's my travel partner. I know in the scheme of things, this doesn't seem like much, but this is my first show since turning pro and . . . okay, that's a dumb thing to care about. But that's a small part of how I'm feeling. The bigger part, though, is I'm really worried. This isn't like her."

"I know," Adam said. "It's why I want to ask you something."

"Go ahead."

He didn't know how to do it, so he just dove in. "It's about her pregnancy two years ago."

Pay dirt.

His words hit Kristin Hoy like a surprise wave at the beach. Now it was Kristin's turn to teeter on the ridiculously high heels. "What about it?"

"You look surprised," he said.

"What?"

"When I mentioned her pregnancy. You looked like you'd seen a ghost or something."

Her eyes darted everywhere but on him. "I guess I was surprised. I mean, she disappears, and for some reason, you start asking about something that happened two years ago. I don't see the connection."

"But you remember her pregnancy?"

"Of course. Why?"

"How did she tell you?"

"About being pregnant?"

"Yes."

"Oh, I don't remember." But she did. He could tell. Kristin was lying to him. "What's the difference how she told me?"

"I need you to think. Do you remember anything odd about it?"

"No."

"Nothing unusual about the pregnancy at all?"

Kristin put her hands on her hips. Her skin glistened from a fine sheen of perspiration or maybe something left over from a bronzer. "What are you trying to get at?"

"How about when she miscarried?" Adam tried. "How was she acting then?"

Oddly enough, those two questions seemed to center her somehow. Kristin took her time now, breathing slowly as though meditating, the prominent clavicle rising and falling. "Funny."

"Yes?"

"I thought her reaction was low-key."

"Meaning?"

"Well, I was thinking about it. She was so good about getting over it. So after you left school today, I started thinking—I mean, at first—that maybe Corinne had been too good after the miscarriage."

"I'm not following."

"A person needs to grieve, Adam. A person needs to express and feel. If you don't express and feel, toxins develop in your bloodstream."

Adam tried not to frown at the new age babble.

"It seemed to me like maybe Corinne had bottled up her pain," she continued. "And when you do that, you create not only toxins but internal pressure. Eventually, something has to give. So after you left, I started wondering. Maybe Corinne had submerged the pain of losing the baby. Maybe she pushed it down and tried to keep it down, but now, two years later, whatever walls she had built suddenly gave way."

Adam just looked at her. "At first."

"What?"

"You said you started thinking this 'at first.' So somewhere along the line you changed your mind."

She didn't reply.

"Why?"

"She's my friend, Adam."

"I know that."

"You're the husband she's trying to get away from, right? I mean, if you're telling the truth and nothing bad happened to her."

"Are you serious?"

"I am." Kristin swallowed hard. "You walk down the streets where we all live. You see the nice neighborhoods and the manicured lawns and the nice patio furniture in the backyard. But none of us knows what really goes on behind those facades, do we?"

He stood there.

"For all I know, Adam, you abuse her."

"Oh, come on—"

Kristin held up her hand. "I'm not saying you do. I'm just giving you an example. We just don't know." There were tears in her eyes, and now he wondered about her husband, Hank, and why, with this physique, she sometimes wore those long sleeves and cover-ups. He had thought that maybe she had wanted to be modest. But that might not be it.

She had a point, though. They might live in a seemingly friendly community or a close-knit neighborhood, but every home is its own island with its own secrets.

"You know something about this," Adam said to her.

"I don't. And I really have to get back to the girls now."

Kristin turned away from him. Adam almost reached out and grabbed her arm. Instead, he said, "I don't think Corinne was really pregnant."

Kristin stopped.

"You knew, didn't you?"

With her back still turned, she shook her head. "Corinne never said anything to me."

"But you knew."

"I knew nothing," Kristin said in a low voice. "You need to go now."

CHAPTER 19

RYAN was at the back door waiting for him.

"Where's Mom?"

"She's away," Adam said.

"What do you mean, away?"

"She's traveling."

"Where?"

"It's a teacher's thing. She'll be home soon."

Ryan's voice was a panicked whine. "I need my uniform, remember?"

"Did you check your drawer?"

"Yes!" The panicked whine had upgraded itself to a shout. "You asked me that yesterday! I checked the drawer and the laundry basket!"

"How about the washer and dryer?"

"I checked both of those too! I checked everywhere!"

"Okay," Adam said, "calm down."

"But I need my uniform! If you don't have your uniform, Coach Jauss makes you run extra laps and miss a game."

"No problem. Let's look for it."

"You never find anything! We need Mom! Why isn't she answering my texts?"

"She's out of range."

"You don't get it! You don't—"

"No, Ryan, you don't get it!"

Adam heard his voice boom through the house. Ryan stopped. Adam didn't.

"You think your mother and I exist only to serve you? Is that what you think? Well, here's something you should learn right now, pal. Your mom and I are human beings too. Big surprise, right? We have lives too. We get sad, just like you. We worry about our lives, just like you. We aren't here just to serve you or do your bidding. Now do you get it?"

Tears filled his son's eyes. Adam heard footsteps. He turned toward them. Thomas was at the top of the steps, staring down at his father in disbelief.

"I'm sorry, Ryan. I didn't mean—"

Ryan sprinted up the stairs.

"Ryan!"

Ryan ran past his brother. Adam heard the bedroom door slam shut. Thomas stayed at the top of the stairs and looked at him.

"I lost my temper," Adam said. "It happens."

Thomas didn't say anything for a long moment. Then he said, "Dad?"

"What?"

"Where's Mom?"

He closed his eyes. "I told you. She's away at a teachers' thing."

"She was just away at a teachers' thing."

"There's another."

"Where?"

"Atlantic City."

Thomas shook his head. "No."

"What do you mean, no?"

"I know where she is," Thomas said. "And it's no-where near Atlantic City."

CHAPTER 20

COME in here, please," Adam said.

Thomas hesitated before heading down the stairs into the kitchen. Ryan was still in his room with the door closed. That was probably best. Give everyone a chance to cool down. But right now, Adam desperately needed to follow up on what Thomas had just told him.

"Do you know where your mother is?" he asked.

"Sort of."

"What do you mean, sort of? Did she call you?"

"No."

"Did she text or e-mail you?"

"No," Thomas said. "Nothing like that."

"But you know she isn't anywhere near Atlantic City." He nodded.

"How do you know that?"

His son lowered his head. There were times when he would see Thomas move a certain way or make a gesture and realize that it was an echo of himself. He had no doubt that Thomas was his son. The similarities were too great. Did he have doubts about Ryan? He never had before, but in some secret, dark corner in the heart, all men have that misgiving. They never voice it. It rarely reaches their consciousness. But it's there, sleeping in that dark corner, and now the stranger had poked the fear and dragged it into the light.

Did that explain Adam's stupid outburst?

He had lost his temper with Ryan, and yes, under the circumstances, it was more than understandable, the way the boy was carrying on about his uniform.

But was there more to it than that?

"Thomas?"

"Mom will get mad."

"No, she won't."

"I promised her I'd never do it," Thomas said. "But, I mean, she always texts me back. I don't get what's going on. So I did something I shouldn't have done."

"It's okay," Adam said, trying to keep the desperation from his voice. "Just tell me what happened."

He let out a deep breath and gathered himself. "Okay, you remember before you went out, I asked you where Mom was?"

"Yes."

"And, I don't know, you sounded . . . it was just weird, that's all. First, you not saying where Mom is, then Mom's not answering my texts . . ." He looked up. "Dad?"

"What?"

"When you said all that stuff about Mom being at a teachers' conference, were you telling the truth?"

Adam thought about it, but not long. "No."

"Do you know where Mom is?"

"No. We had a fight, I guess."

His son nodded in too sagely a way. "So Mom, what, ran out on you?"

"I don't know, Thomas. That's what I'm trying to figure out."

Thomas nodded some more. "So maybe Mom wouldn't want me to tell you where she is."

Adam sat back and rubbed his chin. "That's a possibility," he admitted.

Thomas put his hands on the table. He wore a silicone wristband, the kind people use to promote causes, though this one read CEDARFIELD LACROSSE. He started using his free hand to snap the band against his wrist.

"But here's the problem," Adam said. "I don't know what happened here, okay? If your mom contacted you and told you not to tell me where she is, well, I would listen to her on that. But I don't think she did. I don't think she'd put you or Ryan in that position."

"Mom didn't," Thomas said, still staring at the band on his arm.

"Okay."

"But she did make me promise never to sign into this."

"Sign into what?"

"This app."

"Thomas?"

The boy looked up.

"I have no idea what you're talking about."

"See, we made a deal. Mom and me."

"What kind of deal?"

"She would only use the app in emergencies, not to spy on me. But I was never allowed to use it."

"What do you mean, emergencies?"

"Like if I'd gone missing or she really couldn't reach me."

Adam felt himself spinning again. He stopped and tried to center himself. "Maybe you should explain about this app."

"It's called a phone locator, and it's supposed to help you find your phone, you know, in case you lose it or someone steals it."

"Okay."

"So it shows you where your phone is on this map. All phones come with an app like this, I think, but this is an upgrade. So see, if something happened to us, or Mom couldn't find me or Ryan, she could look us up on the app and know exactly where we were."

"From the phone?"

"Right."

Adam reached out his hand. "Let me see."

Thomas hesitated. "But that's the thing. I wasn't supposed to use it."

"But you did, right?"

He lowered his head and nodded.

"You signed in and you saw where your mother is?"

Another nod.

Adam put his hand on his son's shoulder. "I'm not mad," he said. "But could you let me see the app?"

Thomas took out his phone. His fingers danced across the screen. When he was done, he handed the phone to his father. Adam looked at it. There was a map showing Cedarfield. Three blinking dots were coming from the same place. One dot was blue, another green, another red.

"So these dots . . . ," Adam began.

"That's us."

"Us?"

"Right. You, me, and Ryan."

The pulse in Adam's head started to thrum. When he spoke, his voice sounded far away. "Me?"

"Sure."

"There's a dot representing me?"

"Yeah. You're the green one."

His mouth went dry. "So, in other words, if your mom wanted, she could track . . ." He stopped. There was no need to finish the thought. "How long has this app been on our phones?"

"I don't know. Three, four years maybe."

Adam just sat there as the realization rolled over him. Three or four years. For three or four years, Corinne had that ability to sign into some app and see exactly where her children and, more important, her husband were at any given moment.

"Dad?"

He had prided himself on his naïveté when it came to this technological mastery that had enslaved the masses, that forced us to ignore one another and obey its insatiable demand for attention. Adam's phone had, to his knowledge, no unnecessary apps. No games, no Twitter, no Facebook, no shopping, no scores, no weather reports, none of that. He had the apps the phone came with—e-mail, texts, phone, stuff like that. He had Ryan put on a GPS that mapped out the best driving routes, taking into account the traffic.

But that was it.

"So why can't I see Mom on this thing?" Adam asked.

"You need to zoom out."

"How?"

Thomas took back the phone, placed two fingers on the screen, pinched them. He handed the phone back to his father. Adam could now see the entire state of New Jersey and to the west, Pennsylvania. An orange dot was on the left part of the screen. Adam tapped on it and the phone zoomed in again.

Pittsburgh?

Adam had made the drive to Pittsburgh once to bail a client out of jail. The ride had taken him more than six hours.

"Why isn't the dot blinking?" Adam asked.

"Because it's not active."

"What do you mean?"

Thomas bit back the sigh he always sounded when he had to explain technology to his father. "When I checked the app a few hours ago, she was still moving. But then, about an hour ago, well, that's where Mom was."

"So she stopped here?"

"I don't think so. See, if you click here ..." He reached over and touched the screen. An image of a mobile phone with the word CORINNE'S came up. "It puts the battery power left up here on the right. See? So when I checked it then, her phone only had about four percent left. It's out now, so the dot stopped blinking."

"So is she still where this dot is?"

"I don't know. It only shows where she was before the battery died."

"And you can't see where she is anymore?"

Thomas shook his head. "Not until Mom charges her phone. There's also no point in texting or calling right now."

"Because her phone is dead."

"Right."

Adam nodded. "But if we keep watching this, we can see when she's powered back up?"

"Right."

Pittsburgh. Why on earth would Corinne have gone to Pittsburgh? To his knowledge, she didn't know anybody there. To his knowledge, she had never been there. He didn't remember her ever talking about the city or having any friends or relatives who'd moved there.

He zoomed in on the orange dot. The address read South Braddock Avenue. He clicked the button for a satellite photo. She'd been in or near a strip mall of some sort. There was a supermarket, a dollar store, a Foot Locker, a GameStop. Maybe she had stopped there to grab something to eat or get supplies or something.

Or maybe she was meeting the stranger.

"Thomas?"

"Yeah?"

"Is this app on my phone?"

"It has to be. If someone can see you, then you can see them."

"Can you show me where it is?"

Adam handed him the phone. His son narrowed his eyes and started with the fingers again. Finally, he said, "I found it."

"How come I never saw it before?"

"It was grouped on the last page with a bunch of other apps you probably never use."

"So if I sign in right now," Adam said, "I can keep an eye on Mom's phone?"

"Like I said, the battery's dead right now."

"But if she charges it?"

"Yeah, you'll be able to tell. You just need the password."

"What is it?"

Thomas hesitated.

"Thomas?"

"LoveMyFamily," he said. "All one word. And you need to capitalize the *L*, *M*, and *F*."

CHAPTER 21

OH yeah, hotshot, in your face.

Bob Baime—or, as Adam preferred, Gaston—hit yet another turnaround jumper. Yep, Big Bob was in the zone tonight. He was on fire. *En fuego.*

This was pickup basketball at Beth Lutheran Church. A rotating group of guys, mostly town fathers, played two nights a week. The players varied in ability. Some guys were great—one guy had even been an all-American at Duke and a first-round draft pick of the Boston Celtics before crapping out with a knee injury—and some guys sucked eggs so badly they could barely walk.

But today, Bob Baime, Big Bob Baime, was the man, the go-to guy, the automatic basket machine. Under the boards, he was a one-man rebounding wrecking crew. He used his two-hundred-seventy-pound frame and moved people out of the way. He knocked over the all-American, Mr. Basketball Superstar. The all-American shot him a look, but Big Bob Baime stared right back at him.

The all-American shook his head and started running downcourt.

Yeah, asshole, keep moving, so you don't get your ass kicked.

Ladies and gentlemen, Big Bob Baime was back. That all-American with his stupid knee brace usually got the best of him. But not today. Uh-uh, no way. Bob had held his ground. Man, his old man would have been proud. His old man, who'd spent most of Bob's childhood calling him Betty instead of Bobby, calling him worthless and weak, and worse, a pussy, a faggot, and even a girl. His father, the tough son of a bitch, had been the athletic director at Cedarfield High School for thirty years. Look up *old-school* in the dictionary, you'll see a picture of Robert Baime Senior. It had been hard growing up with a guy like that, but in the end, no doubt, the hard love had been worth it.

Too bad. Too bad his old man couldn't see how his only son had become such a big man in this town. Bob no longer lived on the crummy side of town where the teachers and blue-collar guys tried to survive. No, he bought the big manor with the mansard roof in the ritzy "country club" section of town. He and Melanie drove his-and-hers Mercedes. People respected them. Bob had been invited to join the exclusive Cedarfield Golf Club, a place his dad once went as a guest. Bob had three kids, great athletes all of them, even if Pete was having a tough time in lacrosse right now, maybe losing his chance at a scholarship now that Thomas Price was taking his position. But still, it had all been good.

And now it would again.

Too bad his father hadn't seen this part either. Too bad he hadn't seen his son lose his job, because then he would have seen exactly what kind of man Bob was—a survivor; a winner; a man who, when faced with adversity, perseveres. He was about to close the page on this awful chapter in his life and become Big Bob the big breadwinner again. Even Melanie would see. Melanie, his wife, the former cheerleading captain. She used to look at him with something close to worship, but since the downturn, she'd been in full nag mode, riding him for being so generous in the past, being a show-off with the money, leaving them with no savings when he lost his job. Yep, the vultures had been circling. The bank was ready to foreclose on the house. The repo man had been talking smack about the two Mercedes S coupes.

Well, who was going to have the last laugh now?

Jimmy Hoch's dad, a top headhunter in New York, had lined him up for an interview today, and to put it simply, Bob Baime nailed it. Crushed it like an empty soda can. The guy doing the interview had been eating out of Big Bob's hand. Sure, the call hadn't come in yet—Bob kept eyeing the phone on the sideline—but it wouldn't be long now. He was going to land that job, maybe even insist on a better buy-in, and then, well, he'd officially be back. Wait till he told Melanie about the interview. She would finally put out again, maybe throw on that little pink thing he loved so much.

Back on the court, Bob got the ball, drove hard to the hoop, and scored the winning basket.

Oh yeah, Bob was back and better than ever. Man, he wished that he had felt this way the other night when that prig Adam Price was riding him over picking Jimmy Hoch for the lacrosse team. For crying out loud, all three of those kids sucked. They'd all end up being glorified towel boys. Who cared that a tenth of a point assigned by some bored evaluators who only paid attention to the good players separated them? He wasn't about to blow this big job interview. Not that it should matter. It wasn't like him and Jimmy Hoch's dad had any kind of quid pro quo, but hey, life was about mutual back-scratching. Sports were a life lesson, right? Kids might as well learn that now too.

Bob's team was about to take the floor for a new game when his phone rang.

He grabbed the phone fast, his hand actually shaking as he checked out the incoming number.

GOLDMAN.

So this was it.

"Bob, you ready?"

"Start the game without me, fellas. I have to take this."

Bob headed out into the corridor for privacy. He cleared his throat and smiled, because if you smiled for real, that confident tone would even travel through the phone.

"Hello?"

"Mr. Baime?"

"Speaking."

"This is Jerry Katz with Goldman."

"Yes, hey, Jerry. Nice to hear from you."

"I'm afraid that it isn't good news, Mr. Baime."

Bob felt his heart plummet. Jerry Katz said some more stuff about how competitive the market was and how much he enjoyed talking with him, but the words started to blur into a barely audible haze. Jerry, the scrawny idiot, was still jabbering away. Darkness seeped into Bob's chest, and as it did, a memory came over him. He thought again about the other night, about Adam openly challenging him on selecting Jimmy Hoch. It had, Bob realized now, surprised him in more ways than one. First, what business was it of his, a guy who wasn't even going to coach the travel team, which players Bob selected? Adam and Corinne's kid was on the team. So what difference could Jimmy Hoch make to him?

But more important, especially now that he thought about it: How did Adam recover so quickly from the devastating news that he had received just minutes earlier at the American Legion bar?

Jerry still talked. Bob still smiled. Smiled and smiled. Smiled like an idiot, and when he finally said, "Well, I appreciate you calling me and letting me know," Bob bet that he sounded like a truly confident idiot.

He hung up.

"Bob, you ready?"

"Come on, man, we need you."

And they did. Maybe, Bob thought, that was what the other night had been with Adam. In the same way Bob would go back on the court and find an outlet for his rage, maybe Adam had attacked him for picking Jimmy because he, too, needed the outlet.

What, Bob wondered, would be Adam's reaction if he knew the full truth about his wife? Not the betrayal stuff he thought he knew now. But the full truth.

Well, Bob thought as he jogged back toward the court, he'd find out soon enough, wouldn't he?

CHAPTER 22

IT was two in the morning when Adam remembered something—or, to be more precise, someone.

Suzanne Hope from Nyack, New York.

She had been the one to steer Corinne to the Fake-A-Pregnancy website. That was where this all started, right? Corinne meets Suzanne. Suzanne fakes a pregnancy. Corinne, for some reason, decides to do the same. Maybe. And then the stranger shows up.

He brought up the search engine on his smartphone and typed in *Suzanne Hope Nyack, New York*. He figured that this would probably not work, that this woman had probably given a fake name or fake town to go along with her fake pregnancy, but almost immediately he found hits.

The White Pages listed a Suzanne Hope of Nyack, New York, as being between the ages of thirty and thirty-five. There was both a telephone number and a street address given. Adam was about to write them down when he remembered something Ryan had taught him a few weeks back—pressing two buttons on the phone simultaneously so it takes a screenshot. He tried it, checked the image in the photo app, and saw that it was legible.

He turned off the phone and tried again to drift off to sleep.

THE cramped living room in Old Man Rinsky's house smelled of Pine-Sol and cat piss. The room was packed, but that only meant that there were maybe ten people there. Still, that was all Adam would need. He spotted the bald guy who normally covered sports for *The Star-Ledger*. There was the woman reporter he liked from the Bergen *Record*. According to Adam's paralegal extraordinaire, Andy Gribbel, the *Asbury Park Press* and the *New Jersey Herald* were also there. The major networks weren't interested yet, but News 12 New Jersey had sent out a camera crew.

It would be enough.

Adam leaned close to Rinsky. "You're sure you're okay with this?"

"You kidding?" The old man arched an eyebrow. "I'm just going to try not to enjoy it."

Three of the reporters were jammed into the plastic-covered sofa. Another leaned on the upright piano against the wall. A birdhouse-shaped cuckoo clock hung on the far wall. There were more Hummel figurines on the end table. The once shag carpet had been trampled into something resembling artificial turf.

Adam checked his phone one last time. Still nothing on the phone tracker about Corinne. She either hadn't charged up her phone or . . . no point in thinking about that now. The reporters were looking at him both expectantly and skeptically, half "let's see what you got," half "this is a waste of time." Adam stepped forward. Mr. Rinsky stayed where he was.

"In 1970," Adam began without preamble, "Michael J. Rinsky returned home after serving his country in the most hostile battlegrounds of Vietnam. He came back here, to his beloved hometown, and married his high school sweetheart, Eunice Schaeffer. Then, using the money he earned from his GI Bill, Mike Rinsky bought a home."

Adam paused. Then he added, "This home."

The reporters scribbled.

"Mike and Eunice had three boys and raised them in this very house. Mike got a job with the local police, starting as a rookie patrolman, and moved up the ranks until he was chief. He and Eunice have been important members of this community for many years. They volunteered at the local shelter, the town library, the Biddy Basketball program, the July Fourth parade. In the past nearly fifty years, Mike and Eunice touched so many lives in this town. They worked hard. When Mike left the stresses of work, he came home to relax in this very house. He rebuilt the boiler in the basement on his own. His children grew older, graduated, and moved out. Mike kept working and eventually, after thirty years, he paid off the mortgage. Now he owns this house—the house we are all in right now—outright."

Adam glanced behind him. As if on cue—well, it was on cue—the old man hunched his shoulders, made his face droop, and held an old framed photograph of Eunice in front of him.

"And then," Adam continued, "Eunice Rinsky got sick. We won't invade her privacy by going into the details. But Eunice loves this house. It comforts her. New places frighten her now, and she finds solace in the place where she and her beloved husband raised Mike Junior,

Danny, and Bill. And now, after a lifetime of work and sacrifice, the government wants to take this home—her home—away from her."

The scribbling stopped. Adam wanted to let the moment weigh on them, so he reached behind him, took hold of the water bottle, and wetted his throat. When he started up again, his voice seethed and started cracking with barely controlled rage.

"The government wants to throw Mike and Eunice out of the only home they've ever known so some wealthy conglomerate can knock it down and build a Banana Republic." Not strictly true, Adam thought, but close enough. "This man"—Adam gestured behind him at Old Man Rinsky, who was playing his part with gusto, managing to look even more fragile somehow—"this American hero and patriot, just wants to keep the home he worked so hard to own. That's all. And they want to take it away from him. I ask you, does that sound like the United States of America? Does our government seize hardworking people's property and give it to the rich? Do we throw war heroes and elderly women into the streets? Do we just take away their home after they've worked a lifetime to pay it off? Do we just bulldoze their dreams to create yet another strip mall?"

They were all looking at Old Man Rinsky now. Even Adam was starting to well up for real. Sure, he had left some parts out—how they had offered to pay the Rinskys more than the house was worth, for example—but this wasn't about being balanced. Attorneys take sides. The other side, if and when they responded, would give their spin. You were supposed to be biased. That was how the system worked.

Someone snapped a photograph of Old Man Rinsky.

Then someone else. Hands were raised for questions. A reporter shouted out, asking Old Man Rinksy how he felt. He played it smart, looking lost and fragile, not so much angry as bewildered. He shrugged, held up the picture of his wife, and simply said, "Eunice wants to spend her last days here."

Game, set, match, Adam thought.

Let the other side spin the facts all they want. The sound bite belonged to them. The better story—and that was really what the media always wanted, not the truest story but the best—belonged to them. What would make a more compelling narrative—a big conglomerate throwing a war hero and his ill wife out of their home, or a stubborn old man who is preventing rejuvenation by not taking money and moving into better digs?

It wouldn't be close.

A half hour later, with the reporters gone, Gribbel smiled and tapped Adam on the shoulder. "It's Mayor Gush for you."

Adam took the phone. "Hello, Mr. Mayor."

"You think this is going to work?"

"The *Today* show just called. They want us to come in tomorrow morning for an exclusive interview. I said not yet."

It was a bluff, but a pretty good one.

"You know how fast a news cycle is nowadays?" Gush countered. "We can ride it out."

"Oh, I don't think so," Adam said.

"Why not?"

"Because for now, we have decided to make our case impersonal and corporate. But our next move will be to take it a step further."

"Meaning?"

"Meaning that we will reveal that the mayor, who is working so hard to throw an old couple out of their home, may have a personal grudge against an honest cop who once arrested him, even though he let him go."

Silence. Then: "I was a teenager."

"Yeah, I'm sure that will play well in the press."

"You don't know who you're messing with, pal."

"I think I have a pretty good idea," Adam said. "Gush?"

"What?"

"Build your new village around the house. It's doable. Oh, and have a nice day."

EVERYONE had cleared out of the Rinskys' house.

Adam heard the clacking of a keyboard in the breakfast nook off the kitchen. When he entered the room, he was taken aback by the sheer amount of technology that surrounded him. There were two big-screen computers and a laser printer sitting on the Formica desk. One wall was entirely corked. Photographs, clippings from newspapers, and articles printed off the Internet were hung on it with pushpins.

Rinsky had reading glasses low on his nose. The reflection of the screen made the blue in his eyes deepen.

"What's all this?" Adam asked.

"Just keeping busy." He leaned back and took off the glasses. "It's a hobby."

"Surfing the Web?"

"Not exactly." He pointed behind him. "See this photograph?"

It was a picture of a girl with her eyes closed who Adam guessed was probably between eighteen and twenty. "Is she dead?"

"Since 1984," Rinsky said. "Her body was found in Madison, Wisconsin."

"A student?"

"Doubt it," he said. "You'd think a student would be easy to identify. No one ever has."

"She's a Jane Doe?"

"Right. So you see, me and some fellas online, we crowdsource the problem. Share information."

"You're solving cold cases?"

"Well, we try." He gave Adam his "aw shucks" smile. "Like I said, it's a hobby. Keeps an old cop busy."

"Hey, I have a quick question for you."

Rinsky gestured for Adam to go ahead.

"I have a witness I need to reach. I'm a firm believer in doing it in person."

"Always better," Rinsky agreed.

"Right, but I'm not sure if she's home or not, and I don't want to warn her or ask her to meet me."

"You want to surprise her?"

"Right."

"What's her name?"

"Suzanne Hope," Adam said.

"You have her phone number?"

"Yeah, Andy found it for me online."

"Okay. How far away does she live?"

"Probably a twenty-minute drive."

"Give me the number." Rinksy stuck out his hand and wiggled his fingers. "I'll show you a clever little cop technique you can use, but I'd appreciate it if you kept it to yourself."

Adam handed him the phone. Rinsky lowered his reading glasses back down his nose, picked up the kind of black telephone Adam hadn't seen since his childhood, and dialed the number. "Don't worry," he said. "I got a block on my caller ID." Two rings later, a woman's voice answered. "Hello?"

"Suzanne Hope?"

"Who's asking?"

"I work for the Acme Chimney Cleaning Service—"

"Not interested, take me off your list."

Click.

Rinsky shrugged and smiled. "She's home."

CHAPTER 23

THE drive took exactly twenty minutes.

Adam pulled up to one of those sad garden apartment complexes of monotonous brick that catered to young couples saving up to buy a first home and divorced dads who were broke and/or wanted to stay near the kids. He found apartment 9B and knocked on the door.

"Who is it?"

It was a woman's voice. She hadn't opened the door.

"Suzanne Hope?"

"What do you want?"

He actually hadn't planned for this. For some strange reason, he had figured that she'd open the door and invite him in and then he could explain his reason for coming here, even though he still wasn't sure what that reason was. Suzanne Hope was a potential thin thread, a tenuous connection to what had led Corinne to run off. Maybe he could gently pull on the thread and, to mix metaphors, learn something.

"My name is Adam Price," he said to the closed door. "My wife is Corinne."

Silence.

"Do you remember her? Corinne Price?"

"She's not here," the voice he assumed was Suzanne Hope's said.

"I didn't think she was," he replied, though now that he thought about it, perhaps he had held out the smallest unspoken hope that finding Corinne would be that easy.

"What do you want?"

"Can we talk a second?"

"What about?"

"About Corinne."

"This isn't my business."

Shouting through a door felt distant, of course, but Suzanne Hope was clearly not yet comfortable opening it. He didn't want to push it and lose her completely. "What's not your business?" he asked.

"You and Corinne. Whatever troubles you're having."

"What makes you think we're having troubles?"

"Why else would you be here?"

Why indeed. Score one for Suzanne Hope. "Do you know where Corinne is?"

Down the concrete path and to the right, a postal worker eyed Adam with suspicion. Not surprising. He had thought about the divorced dads who show up here, but of course there were divorced moms too. Adam tried to nod at the postal worker to show him that he meant no harm, but that didn't seem to help.

"Why would I know?" the voice asked.

"She's missing," Adam said. "I'm trying to find her."

Several seconds passed. Adam took a step back and kept his hands at his sides, trying to look as unthreatening as possible. Eventually, the door opened a crack. The chain was still in place, but now he could see a sliver of Suzanne Hope's face. He still wanted to come inside and sit down, talk to her face-to-face, engage, disarm, distract, whatever it would take. But if a chain made Suzanne Hope feel safe, then so be it.

"When was the last time you saw Corinne?" he asked her.

"A long time ago."

"How long?"

Adam saw her eyes look up to the right. He didn't necessarily buy the idea that you could tell lies by the way the eyes move, but he did know that when someone's eyes look up and to the right, it usually indicated that the person was visually *remembering* things, as opposed to the left, which meant visually *constructing* things. Of course, like most generalizations, you couldn't really count on it, and visually constructing did not mean lying. If you asked someone to think of a purple cow, that would lead to visual construction, which isn't a lie or deception.

Either way, he didn't think she was lying.

"Maybe two, three years ago."

"Where?"

"It was a Starbucks."

"So you haven't seen her since . . ."

"Since the time she figured out I was lying about being pregnant," she finished for him. "That's right."

Adam hadn't expected that answer. "No phone calls?"

"No phone calls, no e-mails, no letters, nothing. I'm sorry I can't help you."

The postal worker kept moving, kept delivering the mail, kept eyeing Adam. Adam put his hands to his eyes to shade the sun. "Corinne followed your lead, you know."

"What do you mean?" she asked.

"You know what I mean."

Through the crack in the door, he could see Suzanne Hope nod. "She did ask me a lot of questions."

"What kind of questions?"

"Where did I buy the prosthetic belly, how did I get the sonogram pictures, stuff like that."

"So you directed her to Fake-A-Pregnancy.com."

Suzanne Hope put her left hand against the frame of the door. "I didn't 'direct' her anywhere." Her voice had a little snap in it now.

"That's not what I meant."

"Corinne asked, and I told her about it. That's all. But yeah, she was almost too curious. Like we were kindred spirits."

"I'm not following."

"I thought she'd judge me. I mean, most people would, right? Who could blame them? Weird lady pretending she's pregnant. But it was like we were kindred spirits. She got me right away."

Wonderful, Adam thought, but he kept the sarcasm to himself. "If I may be so bold," he said slowly, "how much did you lie to my wife?"

"What do you mean?"

"For one thing"—he pointed to the hand on the door-frame—"there's no wedding band on your finger."

"Wow, aren't you a real-life Sherlock?"

"Were you even married?"

"Yes."

He could hear the regret in her voice, and for a moment, he thought she would slip that hand back inside and slam the door shut.

"I'm sorry," Adam said. "I didn't mean—"

"It was his fault, you know."

"What was?"

"That we couldn't have kids. So you'd think Harold would have been more sympathetic, right? He was the one with the low sperm count. Shooting blanks. Bad swimmers. I never blamed him. It was his fault, but it wasn't his fault, if you know what I mean."

"I do," he said. "So you've never really been pregnant?"

"Never," she said, and he could hear the devastation in her voice.

"You told Corinne you had a stillborn."

"I thought maybe she'd understand better if I said that. Or, well, not understand. Just the opposite, really. That she would sympathize anyway. But I wanted to be pregnant so badly, and maybe that was my fault. Harold saw that. It made him withdraw. Maybe. Or maybe he never really loved me. I don't know anymore. But I always wanted kids. Even as a little girl, I wanted a big family. My sister Sarah, who swore she'd never have any, well, she has three. And I remember how happy she was when she was pregnant. How she glowed. I guess I just wanted to see what it was like. Sarah said being pregnant made her feel like somebody important, everyone always asking when the baby was due and wishing her luck and all that. So one day, I did it."

"Pretended you were pregnant?"

Suzanne nodded in the doorframe. "As a gag, really. Just to see what it would be like. And Sarah was right. People held doors for me. They wanted to carry my groceries or give me their parking spot. They asked me how I was doing and really seemed to care about the answer. People get hooked on drugs, right? They get hooked on highs, and I read it's all because of some dopamine release. Well, that's what this did. It was a dopamine release for me."

"Do you still do it?" he asked, though he didn't know why he cared. Suzanne Hope had pointed his wife toward the website. He had already figured that out. There was nothing really new to learn here.

"No," she said. "Like all addicts, I stopped when I hit rock bottom."

"Do you mind my asking you when that was?"

"Four months ago. When Harold found out and discarded me like an old tissue."

"I'm sorry," he said.

"Don't be. It's for the best. I'm in therapy now, and while I own this illness—it's me, not anyone else— Harold didn't love me. That's what I realize now. Maybe he never did, I don't know. Or maybe it's because he started resenting me. A man can't have a child and it hits home with his manhood. So maybe that's it. But either way, I looked for validation elsewhere. Our relationship had become toxic."

"I'm sorry," Adam said.

"It doesn't matter. You didn't come to hear about that. Suffice it to say I'm happy I didn't pay the money. Maybe that guy telling Harold my secret was the best thing to happen to me."

A chill started somewhere in Adam's chest and spread to his fingers. His voice seemed to be coming from somewhere else, somewhere far away. "What guy?"

"What?"

"You said a guy told your husband your secret," he said. "What guy?"

"Oh my God." Suzanne Hope finally opened the door and looked at him in anguish. "He told you too."

CHAPTER 24

ADAM sat on the couch across from Suzanne Hope. Her apartment had white walls and white furniture and yet somehow it still seemed dark and depressing. There were windows, but little natural light seeped in. There were no visible stains or dirt and yet the apartment felt grimy. The artwork, if that was what one would call it, would be considered too generic for a Motel 6.

"Is that how you found out about the fake pregnancy?" Suzanne Hope asked. "Did that guy visit you too?"

He sat there, still feeling that chill. Suzanne Hope had her hair piled high in what might have started as a bun. A tortoiseshell hair clip kept what was left in place. A ton of bracelets adorned her right wrist, Gypsy-style, and whenever she moved, they jingled. Her eyes were big and wide and blinked a lot, the kind of eyes that had probably made her appear eager and animated in her youth, though now they looked as though she were awaiting a blow.

Adam leaned forward. "You said you didn't pay the money."

"That's right."

"Tell me what happened."

Suzanne Hope stood. "Would you like some wine?"

"No."

"I probably shouldn't have any either."

"What happened, Suzanne?"

She looked longingly toward the kitchen. Adam remembered another rule of interrogation, if not life: Alcohol lowers inhibitions. It makes people talk, and while scientists debate this, Adam was convinced that it was also a truth serum. Either way, if he accepted her hospitality, she would probably be more apt to talk.

"Maybe a small glass," he said.

"White or red?"

"Either."

She headed toward the kitchen with a bounce in her step that felt out of place in this depressing apartment. As she reached into the refrigerator, Suzanne said, "I work part-time as a cashier at Kohl's. I like it. I get an employee discount, and the people there are nice."

She took out two glasses and started to pour.

"So one day I go outside for my lunch break. They have these picnic tables in the back. I go out there and this guy in a baseball cap is waiting for me."

Baseball cap. He swallowed. "What did he look like?"

"Young, white, skinny. Kind of a geek. I know this sounds odd, especially with what happened next, but he had a nice way about him. Like he was my friend. He had this smile that made me relax a little."

She poured the wine.

"So what happened?" Adam asked.

"Out of nowhere he just says, does your husband know? I stop and say, excuse me, something like that. And he says, does your husband know you faked your pregnancy?"

Suzanne picked up one of the glasses and took a deep

sip. Adam stood and walked toward her. She handed him the glass and then made a motion to clink glasses. He did so.

"Go on," Adam said.

"He asked me if my husband knew about my lie. I asked him who he was. He didn't say. He just said something about the stranger who reveals truth, something like that. He says he has proof I've been lying about being pregnant. At first I figured that he had seen me at Bookends or Starbucks, you know, like Corinne. But I hadn't seen him before and something in the way he spoke . . . it just didn't add up to that."

Suzanne Hope took another sip. He took one too. The wine tasted like fish ass.

"So the guy says that he wants five thousand dollars. He says if I pay it, he'll go away and I'll never see him again. Though—and this was really odd—he said that I couldn't lie again."

"What did he mean?"

"That's what he said. He said, here's the deal. You pay me five thousand dollars and stop faking the pregnancy, and I'll go away for good. But if I kept up the deception— that was the word he used, *deception*—he would tell my husband the truth. He also promised it was a onetime payment."

"What did you say?"

"First, I asked him how I knew I could trust him. If I gave him the money, how did I know he wouldn't ask for more?"

"How did he respond to that?"

"He gave me that smile again and said that's not what we do, that's not how we operate. And you know, this is weird. I believed him. Maybe it was the smile, maybe not. I don't know. But I think he was being straight with me."

"But you didn't pay, did you?"

"How did you know? Oh, wait, I already told you. Funny. At first, I started thinking, how am I going to get that kind of money? And then, when I stopped and thought about it, I thought, wait, what did I do wrong here? I lied to a bunch of strangers. It's not like I lied to Harold, right?"

Adam took another sip, taste be damned. "Right."

"Maybe, I don't know, maybe I was calling the guy's bluff. Maybe I didn't care. Or heck, maybe I wanted him to tell Harold. The truth will set you free, right? Maybe that's what I wanted in the end. Harold would see this as a cry for help. He'd show me more attention."

"But that wasn't what happened," Adam said.

"Not even close," she said. "I don't know when or how the guy told Harold. But he did. He gave Harold some Web link so he could see all the stuff I ordered from that pregnancy-faking website. Harold went ballistic. I thought it would open his eyes to my pain, but really, it did the opposite. It played into all his insecurities. All that stuff about not being a real man—it all came roaring to a head. It's complicated, you know. A man is supposed to spread his seed and if the seed isn't any good, well, it goes right to his core. Stupid."

She took another sip and looked him straight in the eye.

"I'm surprised," Suzanne said.

"Surprised about what?"

"That Corinne made the same choice. I would have figured that she'd pay the money."

"What makes you say that?"

Suzanne shrugged. "Because she loved you. Because she had so much to lose."

CHAPTER 25

COULD it be that simple?

Could it all be a blackmail scam that went south? The stranger had gone to Suzanne Hope and asked for money in exchange for silence. She refused to pay. The stranger then told her husband about her faking the pregnancy.

Was that what happened with Corinne and Adam?

On the one hand, it made perfect sense. The Hopes had been blackmailed. Why couldn't it have happened to Corinne and him? You ask for money, you don't get it, you tell. That's how blackmail works. But as Adam started on his way back home, as he let the reality of what he just heard roll around in his head, something about it all didn't feel right. He couldn't put his finger on it. For some reason, something about the obvious blackmail theory didn't quite pass the smell test.

Corinne was driven and smart. She was a worrier and a planner. If the stranger had threatened her with blackmail and if she had made the decision not to pay up, Corinne, ever the perfect student, would have been prepared. Yet when Adam confronted her after the stranger's visit, Corinne had been at a loss. She had no ready answer. She weakly tried to stall. There was no doubt in his mind that Corinne had been surprised.

Why? If she'd been blackmailed, wouldn't she have at least suspected that the stranger would tell Adam?

She had also reacted by, what, running away? Did that make sense? She had run so quickly and haphazardly, barely contacting him and the school and, most surprising of all, just leaving the boys in the lurch.

That wasn't Corinne.

Something else was going on here.

He did a mental rewind to the night at the American Legion Hall. He thought about the stranger. He thought about the young blond woman with him. He thought about how calm and concerned the stranger seemed. The stranger took no joy in telling Adam what Corinne had done—nothing about him indicated psycho or even socio—but then again, he hadn't seemed businesslike, either.

For the hundredth time that day, Adam checked the phone-locator app, hoping that Corinne had charged her phone back up since her visit to Pittsburgh. He wondered again whether she had chosen to stay there or was just traveling through. He bet traveling through. He also bet that she had realized somewhere along the way that one of the boys would put together that they could find her on the phone locator, so she had simply turned off the power or maybe found a way to turn off the app.

Okay, so if Corinne were traveling from Cedarfield through Pittsburgh, where would she be going?

He didn't have a clue. But something was really, *really* wrong. Duh, thank you, Captain Obvious. Still, Corinne had told him to stay away. Shouldn't he listen to that? Should he sit back and see how it all played out? Or was the threat too real to be idle?

Should he get help? Should he contact the police or just let it be?

Adam couldn't say which side of the fence he would have fallen on—both options were fraught with problems—but suddenly, as he made the turn onto his street, that didn't seem like an issue anymore. As he pulled up to his house, Adam noticed three men standing on the curb in front of his lawn. One was his neighbor, Cal Gottesman, who was pushing those glasses up his nose. The other two were Tripp Evans and Bob "Gaston" Baime.

What the . . . ?

For a moment, just a split second, Adam expected the worst: Something horrible had happened to Corinne. But no, these guys wouldn't be the ones to tell him. Len Gilman, the town cop who also had two kids in the lax program, would be the one.

As if someone had heard his thoughts, a squad car with the words CEDARFIELD POLICE DEPARTMENT emblazoned across the sides turned onto the road and slid into the spot where the three men were standing. Len Gilman was in the driver's seat.

Adam felt his heart drop.

He quickly put the car in park and swung the car door open. Gilman was doing the same. When Adam stood, his knees almost gave way. On teetering legs, he sprinted toward where the four men had congregated, on the curb right in front of Adam's house.

All four men looked at him solemnly.

"We need to talk," Len Gilman said.

CHAPTER 26

BEACHWOOD, Ohio, Police Chief Johanna Griffin had never been to a homicide scene.

She had seen her share of dead bodies, of course. Plenty of people called the police when they found that a loved one had died of natural causes. Same with a drug overdose or a suicide, so, yeah, Johanna had been around death and then some. There'd also been a fair number of gory car crashes over the years. Two months ago, a semi cut across the divider line, and when it slammed into a Ford Fiesta, the car's driver had been decapitated and his wife's skull had been crushed like a Styrofoam cup.

Bloody and gross and even dead didn't bother Johanna. But boy, this did.

Why? First off: murder. It was just hard to get around the word. *Murder.* Just say it out loud and feel the chill. Nothing compared, really. It was one thing to lose your life to illness or accident. But to have your life snatched away from you intentionally, to have a fellow human being actually decide to snuff out your very existence— that just offended on so many levels. It was an obscenity. It was something beyond a crime. It was playing God in the most ungodly way possible.

But even that, Johanna might have been able to live with.

Johanna tried to keep her breath steady, but she could feel it coming in hurried gulps. She stared down at the corpse. Heidi Dann stared back up out of unblinking eyes. There was a bullet hole in Heidi's forehead. A second bullet—or maybe the first bullet, come to think of it—had blown away her kneecap. Heidi had bled out on the Oriental carpet she'd bought for a song from a guy named Ravi, who sold them out of a truck in front of the Whole Foods. Johanna had halfheartedly chased Ravi off more than once, but Ravi, who gave his customers great value and a ready smile, always came back.

The rookie working with her, a kid named Norbert Pendergast, was trying not to look too excited. He sidled up to Johanna and said, "The county guys are on their way. They're going to take this away from us, aren't they?"

They would, Johanna knew. Local cops in this area spent most of their days dealing with traffic violations and bicycle licenses and maybe a domestic dispute. Major crimes, like murder, were handled by the county police. So yep, in a few minutes, the big boys would come in, swinging their little dicks to make sure everyone knew they were in charge now. They would cast her aside, and not to sound overly melodramatic, but this was her town. Johanna had grown up here. She knew the lay of the land. And she knew the people. She knew, for example, that Heidi loved to dance and played a great game of bridge and had a naughty, contagious laugh. She knew that Heidi enjoyed experimenting with weird-color nail polish, that her favorite TV shows of all time were *The Mary Tyler Moore* and *Breaking Bad* (yep, that was Heidi), and that she had bought the Oriental rug on which she had bled out from Ravi in front of the Whole Foods for $400.

"Norbert?"

"Yeah?"

"Where's Marty?" Johanna asked.

"Who?"

"The husband."

Norbert pointed behind him. "He's in the kitchen."

Johanna hoisted up her pants—no matter how hard she tried, the pants waist on the police uniform never quite fit—and started toward the kitchen. Marty's pale face tilted up when she entered as though pulled on a string. His eyes were shattered marbles.

"Johanna?"

The voice was hollow and ghostlike.

"I'm so sorry, Marty."

"I don't understand. . . ."

"Let's take it a step at a time." Johanna pulled out the kitchen chair across from him—yes, that had been Heidi's chair—and sat down. "I need to ask you some questions, Marty. That okay with you?"

The county swinging dicks would spend a long time looking at Marty as the perp. He hadn't done it. Johanna knew that, but there'd be no point in trying to explain, because the truth was, she knew because, well, she knew. The county dicks would laugh that off and talk about the percentage of murders like this being committed by the husband. Fine with her. And who knew? Maybe they were right (they weren't), but either way, the county dicks could go in that direction. She'd try others.

Marty nodded numbly. "Yeah, okay."

"So you just got home, right?"

"Yeah. I was at a convention in Columbus."

No reason to ask for confirmation. The county dicks could chase that down. "So what happened?"

"I parked in the driveway." His voice was flat and very far away somehow, beyond detached. "I opened the door with my key. I called out to Heidi—I knew she was home because her car was there. I walked into the den and . . ." Marty's face twisted into something barely human and then collapsed into something all too human.

Normally, Johanna would give a grieving spouse time to recover, but the county dicks would be here soon. "Marty?"

He tried to regain his composure.

"Is anything missing?"

"What?"

"Like in a robbery."

"I don't think so. I don't see anything missing. But I didn't really look."

A robbery, she knew, was unlikely. The contents of the house didn't have a lot of value, for one thing. For another, Heidi's engagement ring, which Johanna knew had been her grandmother's and was the most expensive thing she owned, was still on her finger. A thief would have taken that for certain.

"Marty?"

"Yeah?"

"Who's the first person to pop into your head?"

"What do you mean?"

"Who might have done this?"

Marty stopped and thought about it. Then his face twisted up again. "You know my Heidi, Johanna."

Know. Still using the present tense.

"She doesn't have an enemy in the world."

Johanna took out her notepad. She opened it to an empty page and stared at it and hoped that no one would see her eyes well up. "Think, Marty."

"I am." He let out a moan. "Oh my God, I have to tell Kimberly and the boys. How am I going to tell them?"

"I can help with that, if you'd like."

Marty leapt on that like onto a lifeboat. "Would you?" He was a nice guy, Johanna thought, but no way had he ever been good enough for someone like Heidi. Heidi was special. Heidi was the kind of person who always made everyone around her feel special. Simply put, Heidi was magic.

"The kids adore you, you know. So did Heidi. She'd want you to be the one."

Johanna kept her eyes on the blank page. "Has anything happened lately?"

"What? You mean, anything like this?"

"I mean, anything like anything. Have you gotten any frightening calls? Did Heidi get in an argument with someone at Macy's? Did someone cut her off in traffic on 271? Did she give someone the finger when they cut the line at Jack's? Anything."

He slowly shook his head.

"Come on, Marty. Think."

"Nothing," he said. He looked up at her, his face lined with anguish. "I got nothing."

"What's going on here?"

The authoritative voice came from behind her, and Johanna knew that her time was up. She stood and faced two county dicks. She introduced herself. They eyed her as though she might steal silverware, and then they told her that they would take over now.

And so they would. Johanna would let them. They

had experience at this, and Heidi deserved the best. Johanna headed out, content to let the homicide detectives do their thing.

But she'd be damned if that meant she wasn't going to do her thing too.

CHAPTER 27

ARE your kids home?" Len Gilman asked.

Adam shook his head. The five of them were still standing on the curb. Len Gilman didn't look like a cop, though he had the gruff part down to an art form. He reminded Adam of one of those aging motorcycle gang members who still wears leather and hangs out in dive bars. Gilman's graying handlebar mustache had yellow nicotine stains. He favored short-sleeved shirts, even when in uniform, and had enough hair on his arms to be mistaken for a bear.

For a moment, no one moved, just five town dads hanging by the curb on a Thursday night.

This made no sense, Adam thought, and maybe that was a good thing.

If Len Gilman had come here in his capacity as a police officer to deliver the worst kind of news, why would he bring Tripp, Gaston, and Cal with him?

"Maybe we could go inside," Len said, "and talk."

"What's this about?"

"It's better if we do this in private."

Adam was tempted to say that they were in private, on the curb in front of his lawn where no one else could hear them, but Len was already starting up the walk and Adam didn't want to do anything that might delay the conversation any more. The other three men waited for Adam. Gaston had his head down, studying the grass. Cal was jittery, but that was pretty much his default state. Tripp was noncommittal.

Adam moved in behind Len, the other three trailing on the path. When they got to the door, Len stepped aside and let Adam use the key. Jersey the dog rushed toward them, nails clacking on the hardwood, but, perhaps sensing something wasn't quite right, her greeting was muted and perfunctory. Jersey quickly sized up the situation and slinked back to the kitchen.

The house fell into silence, the kind of silence that seemed deliberate, as though even the walls and furniture were conspiring to keep everything still. Adam didn't bother with niceties. He didn't ask anyone if they wanted to take a seat or have a drink. Len Gilman headed into the living room, as though he either owned the place or was a cop comfortable in his own skin.

"What's going on?" Adam asked.

Len did the talking for the group. "Where is Corinne?"

Two things hit Adam at once. First: relief. If she'd been hurt or worse, Len would know where she was. So whatever was going on here, even if it was something bad, it wasn't the worst-case scenario. Second: fear. Because, yes, Corinne seemed safe for the moment, but whatever this visit entailed, by both this show of force and the tone of Len's voice, it was indeed going to be something bad.

"She's not home," Adam said.

"Yes, we can see that. Would you mind telling us where she is?"

"Would you mind telling me why you want to know?"

Len Gilman kept his gaze on Adam. The other men stood and shifted their feet. "Why don't we sit down?"

Adam was about to protest that this was his house and that he'd tell everyone when or where to sit, but that seemed pointless and a waste of energy. Len collapsed with a sigh in the big chair usually reserved for Adam. Adam noted that it was probably a power move, but again no reason to fret over the irrelevant. The other three men sat on the couch like the speak-no-hear-no-see-no monkeys. Adam stayed standing.

"What the hell is going on?" Adam asked again.

Len Gilman stroked his handlebar mustache as though it were a small pet. "I just want to make something clear right off the bat. I'm here in my role as a friend and a neighbor. I'm not here as the chief of police."

"Oh, that's encouraging."

Len ignored the sarcasm and continued. "So as a friend and neighbor, I'm telling you that we are looking for Corinne."

"And as a friend and neighbor, not to mention a concerned husband, I'm asking you why."

Len Gilman nodded, buying time, trying to figure how to play this. "I know Tripp stopped by here yesterday."

"Right."

"He mentioned that we had a lacrosse board meeting."

Len Gilman then stopped talking, doing that cop thing where you wait and hope your subject says something. Adam knew the technique all too well from his days in the prosecutor's office. He also knew that those who played it back, who tried to outwait the cop, were usually hiding something. Adam wasn't. He also wanted to move this along, so he said, "Right," again.

"Corinne didn't come to the meeting. She didn't show."

"Só what? Does she need an absence note from a parent?"

"Don't be a wiseass, Adam."

Len was right. He needed to clamp down on the sarcasm.

"Are you a member of the board, Len?" Adam asked.

"I'm a member at large."

"What's that mean?"

Len smiled and spread his hands. "Damned if I know. Tripp is the president. Bob here is the VP. And Cal is the secretary."

"I know and, man, am I impressed." Again he scolded himself for the tone. This wasn't the time. "But I still don't know why you're all looking for Corinne."

"And we don't know why we can't find her," Len countered, spreading his meaty paws. "It's a mystery, isn't it? We've texted her. We've e-mailed her. We've called her mobile and your house. Heck, I even stopped by the school. Did you know that?"

Adam bit back his reply.

"Corinne wasn't there. She was absent—and there was no absence note from a parent. So I talked to Tom." Tom Gorman was the principal. He, too, lived in town and had three kids. Towns like this got ridiculously incestuous. "He says Corinne normally has the best attendance record of any teacher in the district, but suddenly she's a no-show. He was concerned."

"Len?"

"Yes?"

"Can you cut the crap and tell me why you're all so anxious to find my wife?"

Len looked over at the three monkeys on the couch. Bob's face was set in stone. Cal was busy cleaning his glasses. That left it up to Tripp Evans. Tripp cleared his throat and said, "There seems to be some discrepancies with the lacrosse financials."

Boom.

Or maybe the opposite of boom. The house grew even quieter. Adam was sure that he could actually hear his own heart beating in his chest. He found the seat behind him and lowered himself onto it.

"What are you talking about?"

But of course, he already knew, didn't he?

Bob now found his voice. "What do you think we're talking about?" he half snapped. "There's money missing from the account."

Cal nodded, just to do something.

"And you think . . . ?" Adam didn't finish the thought. First off, it was obvious what they thought. Two, it would not do to even voice such a ridiculous accusation.

But was it ridiculous?

"Let's not get ahead of ourselves," Len said, playing Mr. Reasonable. "Right now, we just want to talk to Corinne. As I told you before, I'm here as a friend and neighbor and maybe a board member. That's why we are all here. We're Corinne's friends. And yours. We want to keep this between us."

Lots of nods.

"Meaning what?"

"Meaning," Len said, leaning forward in a conspiratorial way, "that if the books get straightened out, that will be the end of it. It stays in this room. No questions will be asked. If the discrepancies go away, if the ledger is made whole again, well, we don't really care about the hows or whys. We all move on."

Adam stayed quiet. Organizations are all the same.

Cover-ups and lies. The greater good and all that. Through his confusion and fear, part of Adam couldn't help but feel disgust. But that was beside the point. He needed to be very careful here. Despite Len Gilman's twice-repeated "friend/neighbor/board member" spiel, he was a cop. He wasn't here as a nicety. He was here to gather information. Adam had to be careful how much he gave him.

"This discrepancy," Adam said. "How large is it?"

"Very," Len Gilman said.

"In terms of . . ."

"Sorry, that's confidential."

"You can't seriously believe that Corinne would do anything—"

"Right now," Len Gilman said, "we just need to talk to her."

Adam stayed silent.

"Where is she, Adam?"

He couldn't tell them, of course. He couldn't even try to explain. The attorney in him took over. How many times had he warned his own client not to talk? How many convictions had he nailed because some idiot tried to talk his way out of it?

"Adam?"

"I think you guys better leave now."

CHAPTER 28

DAN Molino tried not to cry as he watched his son Kenny line up for the forty-yard dash.

Kenny was a high school senior and one of the top football prospects in the state. He had a breakout senior year, gaining notice and respect among the big-time scouts, and now here he was, warming up for the final combine event. Dan stood in the bleachers, feeling that familiar rush, that parental high, as he watched his big son—Kenny was 285 pounds now—getting ready to put his feet in the starting blocks. Dan was a big guy too, six-two, two forty. He'd also played some ball back in the day, All-State linebacker, but he'd been a step too slow and a size too small to go Division I. He started up his own business in freelance furniture delivery twenty-five years ago, and now Dan owned two trucks and had nine guys working for him. The big stores, they often had their own delivery fleet. Dan specialized in taking care of the little mom-and-pop shops, though there seemed to be less and less of them every day. The big chains were squeezing them out, just as the big boys like UPS and FedEx were squeezing him.

Still, Dan made a living. A few of those big-chain mattress stores had recently decided to cut back on their own fleet. Found it cheaper to hire a local guy like Dan. It helped. So, okay, Dan wasn't killing it, but he was doing fine. He and Carly had a nice place in Sparta off the lake. They had three kids. Ronald was the youngest. He was twelve. Karen was a freshman, getting to that stage when the sass and puberty kicked in and the boys start noticing. Dan hoped that he'd survive it. And then there was Kenny, his firstborn, the high school senior who was poised to get a full ride to a major college football program. Alabama and Ohio State were showing interest already.

If Kenny could just nail this forty-yard dash.

Watching his son, Dan felt his eyes water up. Always happened. It was kind of embarrassing, the way he'd react like this. Couldn't help it, though. He'd started wearing sunglasses to Kenny's high school games so no one would see, but that hadn't helped when they were inside and Kenny was getting some award, like when they named him MVP at the team dinner and Dan's sitting there, and boom, there it came, the eyes watering up, sometimes even a tear or two running down the cheek. When someone would notice, Dan would say allergies or that he had a cold or some such thing. Who knows? Maybe they bought that line. Carly loved this part of him, calling him her sensitive Teddy Bear or giving him a big hug. Whatever else Dan had done, whatever mistakes he'd made in his life, he had hit the biggest bottom-of-the-ninth homer when Carly Applegate had chosen him to be her life partner.

In truth, Dan didn't think that Carly had been quite as lucky. Eddie Thompson had liked her, back in the day. Eddie's family got in early on McDonald's chains, made a fortune. They were always in the town paper now, Eddie and his wife, Melinda, doing some charity thing or whatever. Carly never said anything, but Dan knew it bugged her. Or maybe that was just Dan's own issues. He didn't know anymore. Dan only knew that when he saw his kids do something special, like play football or win awards, his eyes watered up. He was an easy cry and he tried to hide that, but Carly knew the truth and loved him for it.

Dan was wearing sunglasses today. That was for sure.

With the big-time scouts keeping a watchful eye, Kenny had done really well in the other tests—the vertical jump, the 7-on-7, that trench warfare thing. Still, the forty-yard dash would clinch it for him. A full ride to some big-time university. Ohio State, Penn State, Alabama, maybe even— oh man, it was almost too much to even let himself think about it—Notre Dame. The Notre Dame scout was here, and Dan couldn't help noticing that the guy had been keeping tabs on Kenny.

Just one last dash. Just beat 5.2 and Kenny was golden. That was what they said. If a prospect ran slower than that, the scouts lost interest, even if he was great at everything else. They wanted a 5.2 or better. If Kenny did that, if Kenny could just run this one race at his best time . . .

"You know, don't you?"

The unfamiliar voice startled him for a second, but Dan just figured that the guy hadn't been talking to him. Still, when he sneaked a look, he could see some stranger was staring directly into Dan's sunglassed eyes.

Little guy, Dan thought, but then again, everyone looked little to Dan. Not short. Just small. Small hands, thin arms, almost frail. The guy who was staring at him now stuck out here because it was so clear he didn't belong. There was nothing football about him. Too little. Too nerdy. Big baseball cap pulled down too low. And that soft, friendly smile.

"You talking to me?" Dan asked.

"Yes."

"I'm kinda busy here."

The guy kept smiling as Dan slowly turned back toward the track. On the field, Kenny was putting his feet in the blocks. Dan watched and waited for his personal waterworks to begin.

But for once, his eyes stayed dry.

Dan risked a glance back. The guy was still smiling and staring.

"What's your problem?"

"It can wait till after the race, Dan."

"What can wait? How do you know my—?"

"Shhh, let's see how he does."

On the field, someone shouted, "On your mark, get set," and then the gun went off. Dan's head snapped back toward his son. Kenny got a good jump off the start and began pounding down his lane like a runaway truck. Dan smiled. Try getting in the way of that, he thought. Kenny would mow you down like a blade of grass.

The race lasted only scant seconds, but it felt much longer. One of Dan's new drivers, some kid working off a student loan, sent an article that said time slows down when you're having new experiences. Well, this was new. Maybe that's why the seconds ticked away so slowly. Dan was watching his boy heading for a personal-best time in the forty and, in doing so, locking in a full ride to someplace special, someplace Dan could never have gone, and when Kenny crossed the finish line with a record time of 5.07, Dan knew that the tears would start coming.

Except they didn't.

"Great time," the little guy said. "You must be so proud."

"You bet I am."

Dan faced the stranger straight-on now. Screw this guy. This was one of the greatest moments—maybe *the* greatest—of Dan's life and he'd be damned if he'd let some dork get in that way. "Do I know you?"

"No."

"You a scout?"

The stranger smiled. "Do I look like a scout, Dan?"

"How do you know my name?"

"I know lots of things. Here."

The stranger held out a manila envelope.

"What's this?"

"You know, don't you?"

"I don't know who the hell you think—"

"It's just hard to believe no one has ever raised this with you before."

"Raised what?"

"I mean, look at your son."

Dan spun back toward the track. Kenny had this huge smile on his face, looking toward the sideline for his father's approval. Now Dan's tears started to come. He waved, and his boy, who didn't go out carousing at night, who didn't drink or smoke pot or hang out with a bad crowd, who still—and yeah, no one believed it—preferred hanging out with his old man, watching the game or some movie on Netflix, waved back.

"His weight was, what, two thirty last year," the stranger said. "He put on fifty-five pounds and no one noticed?"

Dan frowned, even as he felt his heart drop. "It's called puberty, asshole. It's called working out hard."

"No, Dan. It's called Winstrol. It's called a PED."

"A what?"

"Performance-enhancing drug. Better known to the layman as steroids."

Dan turned and moved right up into the little stranger's face. The stranger just kept smiling. "What did you say?"

"Don't make me repeat myself, Dan. It's all in that manila folder. Your son went to Silk Road. You know what that is? The Deep Web? The online underworld economy? Bitcoin? I don't know if you gave Kenny your blessing or if your son paid for it on his own, but you know the truth, don't you?"

Dan just stood there.

"What do you think all these scouts are going to say when that file goes public?"

"You're full of it. You're making this up. This is all—"

"Ten thousand dollars, Dan."

"What?"

"I don't want to go into this in detail right now. You'll see all the proof in that manila envelope. Kenny started with Winstrol. That was his main PED, but he also took Anadrol and Deca Durabolin. You'll see how often he bought it, his method of payment, even the IP address on your home computer. Kenny started taking them junior year, so all those trophies, all those victories, all those stats . . . well, if the truth comes out, they all go away, Dan. All those congratulatory slaps on the back when you go into O'Malley's Pub, all those well-wishers, all those townspeople who think so highly of the nice boy you raised—what are they going to think of you when they find out your son cheated? What are they going to think of Carly?"

Dan put his finger on the little guy's chest. "Are you threatening me?"

"No, Dan. I'm asking for ten thousand dollars. A one-time payment. You know I could demand a lot more, what with how much college costs nowadays. So consider yourself lucky."

Then the voice that always brought the tears sounded to his right: "Dad?"

Kenny was jogging over with a look of joy and hope on his face. Dan just froze and stared at his son, unable to move for a moment.

"I'm going to leave you now, Dan. All the information is in that manila envelope I just gave you. Look at it when you get home. What happens tomorrow is up to you, but for right now"—the stranger gestured toward Kenny coming toward them—"why don't you enjoy this special moment with your son?"

CHAPTER 29

THE American Legion Hall was close to the relative bustle of downtown Cedarfield. This made it a tempting place to park when the limited metered spots on the streets filled up. To combat this, the American Legion powers that be hired a local guy, John Bonner, to "guard" the lot. Bonner had grown up in this town—had even been captain of the basketball team his senior year—but somewhere along the way, mental health issues began to gnaw at his edges before they moved inside and settled in for the long haul. Now Bonner was the closest thing to what Cedarfield might call a homeless guy. He spent his nights at Pines Mental Health and his days shuffling around town muttering to himself about various political conspiracies involving the current mayor and Stonewall Jackson. Some of Bonner's old classmates at Cedarfield High felt bad about his predicament and wanted to help. Rex Davies, the president of the American Legion, came up with the idea of giving Bonner the lot job just so he'd stop wandering so much.

Bonner, Adam knew, took his new job seriously. Too seriously. With his natural tendency toward OCD, he kept an extensive notebook that contained a potent blend of vague paranoid ramblings and ultra specifics about the makes, colors, and license plates of every vehicle that entered his lot. When you pulled in to park for something other than American Legion Hall business, Bonner would either warn you off, sometimes with a little too much gusto, or would intentionally let you illegally park, make sure that you had indeed gone to the Stop & Shop or Backyard Living instead of the hall, and then he'd call his old teammate Rex Davies, who coincidentally owned a body shop and car towing service.

Everything's a racket.

Bonner eyed Adam suspiciously as he pulled into the American Legion lot. He wore, as he always did, a blue blazer with too many buttons so that it looked like something used in a Civil War reenactment, and a red-and-white checkered tablecloth-cum-shirt. His pants were frayed at the cuffs, and a pair of laceless Chucks adorned his feet.

Adam had realized that he could no longer afford to sit back and wait for Corinne's return. There were enough lies and deception to go around, he thought, but whatever it was that had gone terribly wrong in the past few days had started here, at the American Legion Hall, when the stranger told him about that damned website.

"Hey, Bonner."

Bonner may have recognized him, may have not. "Hey," he said cautiously.

Adam put the car in park and got out. "I got a problem."

Bonner wriggled eyebrows so bushy they reminded Adam of Ryan's gerbils. "Oh?"

"I'm hoping you can help me."

"You like buffalo wings?"

Adam nodded. "Sure." Supposedly, Bonner had been

a genius before his illness, but wasn't that what they always say about someone with serious mental health issues? "You want me to get you some from Bub's?"

Bonner looked aghast. "Bub's is shit!"

"Right, sorry."

"Ah, go away." He waved a hand at Adam. "You don't know nothing, man."

"Sorry. Really. Look, I need your help."

"Lots of people need my help. But I can't be everywhere, now, can I?"

"No. But you can be here, right?"

"Huh?"

"In this lot. You can help with a problem in this lot. You can be here."

Bonner lowered his bushy eyebrows to the point where Adam couldn't see his eyes. "A problem? In my lot?"

"Yes. See, I was here the other night."

"For the lacrosse draft," Bonner said. "I know."

The sudden recollection should have startled Adam, but for some reason, it didn't. "Right, so anyway, my car got sideswiped by some out-of-towners."

"What?"

"Did some pretty serious damage."

"In my lot?"

"Yeah. Young out-of-towners, I think. They were driving a gray Honda Accord."

Bonner's face reddened at the injustice. "You get the plate number?"

"No, that's what I was hoping you could give me. So I can file a claim. They left at approximately ten fifteen."

"Oh, right, I remember them." Bonner took out his giant notebook and started paging through rapidly. "That was Monday."

"Yes."

He flipped more pages, his pace growing more and more frantic. Adam glanced over Bonner's shoulder. Every page in the thick notebook was filled from top to bottom, from far left to far right, with tiny letters. Bonner kept turning pages at a furious clip.

Then suddenly, Bonner stopped.

"You found it?"

A slow grin came to Bonner's face. "Hey, Adam?"

"What?"

Bonner turned the grin toward him. Then he did the gerbil wriggle again and said, "You got two hundred bucks on you?"

"Two hundred?"

"Because you're lying to me."

Adam tried to look perplexed. "What are you talking about?"

Bonner slammed the notebook closed. "Because, you see, I was here. I would have heard your car getting hit."

Adam was about to counter when Bonner held up his palm.

"And before you tell me it was late or it was noisy or it was barely a scratch, don't forget that your car is sitting right over there. It's got no damage. And before you tell me you were driving your wife's car or some other lie"—Bonner held up the notebook, still grinning—"I got the details of that night right here."

Caught. Caught in a clumsy lie by Bonner.

"So the way I see it," Bonner continued, "you want that guy's license plate number for another reason. He and that cute blonde he was with. Yeah, yeah, I remember them because the rest of you clowns I've seen a million times.

They were strangers. Didn't belong. I wondered why they were here." He grinned again. "Now I know."

Adam thought about saying a dozen things, but he settled on the simplest: "Two hundred dollars, you say?"

"It's a fair price. Oh, and I don't take checks. Or quarters."

CHAPTER 30

OLD Man Rinsky said, "The car is a rental."

They were in the hi-tech breakfast nook. Rinsky was all in beige today—beige corduroys, beige wool shirt, beige vest. Eunice was at the kitchen table, dressed for a garden party, having tea. Her makeup looked as though it'd been applied with a paintball gun. She had said, "Good morning, Norman," when Adam came in. He had debated correcting her when Rinsky stopped him. "Don't," he'd said. "It's called validation therapy. Let her run with it."

"Any idea who rented the car on Monday?" Adam asked.

"Got it right here." Rinsky squinted at the screen. "The name she used was Lauren Barna, but that's a pseudonym. I did some digging and Barna is actually a woman named Ingrid Prisby. She lives in Austin, Texas." His reading glasses were on a chain. He let them drop to his chest and turned around. "The name mean anything to you?"

"No."

"Might take a little while, but I could run a background check on her."

"That would be helpful."

"No problem."

So now what? He couldn't just fly off to Austin. Should he get the woman's phone number and call her, and say what exactly? *Hi, my name is Adam Price, and you and some guy in a baseball cap told me a secret about my wife....*

"Adam?"

He looked up.

Rinsky interlaced his fingers and rested them on his paunch. "You don't have to tell me what this is about. You know that, right?"

"I do."

"But just so we're clear, anything you tell me doesn't leave this house. You know that too, right?"

"Sorry, but you're the one with the privilege here," Adam said, "not me."

"Yeah, but I'm an old man. I have a bad memory."

"Oh, I doubt that."

Rinsky smiled. "Suit yourself."

"No, no. Actually, if it's not too much of a burden, I'd really like to get your take on this."

"I'm all ears."

Adam wasn't sure how much of the story he would tell Rinsky, but the old cop was a good listener. Back in the day, he must have done an Oscar-buzzed "good cop" because Adam couldn't shut himself up. He ended up telling him the entire story, from the moment the stranger walked into that American Legion Hall right up until now.

When Adam finished, the two men sat in silence. Eunice drank her tea.

"Do you think I should tell the police?" Adam asked.

Rinsky frowned. "You were a prosecutor, right?"

"Right."

"So you know better."

Adam nodded.

"You're the husband," he said as though that explained everything. "You just learned that your wife betrayed you in a pretty horrible way. Now she's run off. Tell me, Mr. Prosecutor, what would you think?"

"That I did something to her."

"That'd be number one. Number two would be that your wife—what's her name again?"

"Corinne."

"Right, Corinne. Number two would be that Corinne stole this money from that sports league or whatever so she could run away from you. You'd also have to tell that local cop about her faking the pregnancy. He's married?"

"Yes."

"So that'll be blabbed all over town before you know it. Not that that matters in light of the other stuff. But let's face it. The cops will either think you killed your wife or that she's a thief."

Rinsky had confirmed exactly what Adam had already thought.

"So what do I do?"

Rinsky lifted his reading glasses back to his face. "Show me that text your wife sent you before she took off."

Adam found it. He handed Rinsky the phone and read the message once again over the old man's shoulder:

MAYBE WE NEED SOME TIME APART. YOU TAKE CARE OF THE KIDS. DON'T TRY TO CONTACT ME. IT WILL BE OKAY.

Then:

JUST GIVE ME A FEW DAYS. PLEASE.

Rinsky read it, shrugged, took off the glasses. "What can you do? Far as you know, your wife needs some time away from you. She asked you not to contact her. So that's what you're doing."

"I can't sit around and do nothing."

"No, you can't. But if the cops ask, well, there's your answer."

"Why would the cops ask me that?"

"Got me. Meanwhile, you are doing all you can. You got that license plate number and you came to me. You did right on both counts. Chances are, your Corinne will just come home on her own soon. But either way, you're right—we need to try to find her first. I'll try to dig into this Ingrid Prisby. Maybe there's a clue there."

"Okay, thanks. I appreciate that."

"Adam?"

"Yeah?"

"Odds are, your Corinne stole this money. You know that."

"If she did, she had a reason."

"Like she needed to run away. Or to pay off this blackmailer."

"Or something we aren't thinking of yet."

"Whatever it is," Rinsky said, "you don't want to give the cops anything that can incriminate her."

"I know."

"You said she was in Pittsburgh?"

"That's what we saw on that phone locator, yeah."

"You know anybody there?"

"No." He looked over at Eunice. She smiled at him and lifted her tea. A perfectly normal domestic scene to an outside observer, but when you know her condition . . .

A memory hit Adam.

"What?"

"The morning before she disappeared, I came downstairs. The boys were at the breakfast table, but Corinne was in the backyard talking on her phone. When she saw me, she hung up."

"Any idea who she called?"

"No, but I can look it up on the Web."

Old Man Rinsky stood up and gestured for Adam to have a seat. Adam took it and brought up the website for Verizon. He typed in the phone number and the password. He knew it by heart, not because he had a great memory, but because for things like this, he and Corinne always used the same approximate password. The word they used was BARISTA, all caps, always. Why? Because they had decided to come up with a password while sitting in a coffee shop and started looking around for a random word and, voilà, there was a barista. The word was perfect because it had absolutely no connection to them. If the password needed to be longer than seven characters, the password was BARISTABARISTA. If the password required numbers, not just letters, it was BARISTA77.

Like that.

Adam got the password right on his second try— BARISTA77.

He clicked on the various links and reached her recent outgoing calls first. He'd hoped that maybe he'd get lucky, that maybe he'd see that she'd called someone a few hours ago or late last night. Nothing doing. In fact, the last call she'd made had been the one he was now searching for—a call made at 7:53 A.M. the morning she ran off.

The call had lasted only three minutes.

She had been outside in the backyard, talking softly, and hung up as he'd approached. He had pushed it, but Corinne had refused to tell him who was on the phone. But now . . .

Adam's eyes traveled right to the phone number on the screen. He froze and stared.

"You recognize the number?" Old Man Rinsky asked.

"Yeah, I do."

CHAPTER 31

KUNTZ dumped both guns into the Hudson River. He had plenty more, no big deal.

He took the A train to 168th Street. He got out on Broadway and walked three blocks down to the entrance of the hospital that used to be called Columbia Presbyterian. Now it was known as Morgan Stanley Children's Hospital of New York-Presbyterian.

Morgan Stanley. Yeah, when you think of health care for children, the first name that comes to your mind is the multinational financial giant Morgan Stanley.

But money talks. Money is as money does.

Kuntz didn't bother showing his ID. The security guards at the desk knew him too well from his too frequent visits. They also knew he'd once been NYPD. Some, maybe most, even knew why he'd been forced to leave. It had been in all the papers. The libtards in the media had crucified him — wanting him not only to lose his job and livelihood but even wanting him locked up on murder charges — but the guys on the street backed him. They got that Kuntz was being railroaded.

They got the truth.

The case had been in the papers. Some big black guy

resisting arrest. He'd been caught shoplifting at a grocery store on Ninety-Third, and when the Korean owner confronted him, the big black guy pushed him down and threw a kick. Kuntz and his partner, Scooter, cornered the guy. The guy didn't care. He growled and put it simply: "I ain't goin' wit' you. I just needed a pack of smokes." The big black guy started to walk away. Just like that. Two cops there, he'd just committed a crime, and he was just going to do as he pleased. When Scooter stepped in his way, the big black guy pushed him and kept walking.

So Kuntz took him down hard.

How was he supposed to know the big guy had some kind of health condition? Seriously. Are you really supposed to let a criminal walk away like that? What do you do when a thug won't listen to you? Do you try to take him down nicely? Maybe do something that puts your life or your partner's life in jeopardy?

What dumb assholes made these rules?

Long story short: The guy died and the libtard media had an orgasm. That dyke bitch on cable started it up. She called Kuntz a racist killer. Sharpton started with the marches. You know the drill. Didn't matter how clean Kuntz's record was or how many citations for bravery he'd received or how he volunteered with black kids in Harlem. Didn't matter that he had his own personal problems, including a ten-year-old boy with bone cancer. None of that meant a damn thing.

He was now a racist murderer—as evil as any of the scum he'd ever busted.

Kuntz took the elevator to the seventh floor. He nodded at the nurses' station as he hurried toward room 715. Barb was sitting in that same chair. She turned toward him and gave him a weary smile. There were dark circles under her eyes. Her hair looked as though it'd taken a late bus to get here. But when she smiled at him, that was still all he could see.

His son was sleeping.

"Hey," he whispered.

"Hey," Barb whispered back.

"How's Robby?"

Barb shrugged. Kuntz walked toward his son's bed and stared down at the boy. It broke his heart. It gave him resolve.

"Why don't you go home for a little while?" he said to his wife. "Relax a little."

"I will in a few," Barb replied. "Sit and talk with me."

You often hear that the media is a parasite, but rarely was it truer than in the case of John Kuntz. They swarmed and devoured until there was nothing left. He lost his job. He lost his pension and his benefits. But worst of all, he could no longer afford to give his son the best treatment available. That had been toughest on him. Whatever else a father is in this life—cop, fireman, Indian chief—he provides for his family. He does not sit by idly watching his son in pain without doing all he can to alleviate it in some way.

And then, when he was at his lowest, John Kuntz found salvation.

Isn't that always the way?

A friend of a friend hooked up Kuntz with a young Ivy Leaguer named Larry Powers, who had developed some new phone app that made it easier to find Christian guys to do home repair. Something like that. Charity and Construction, that was the pitch. The truth was, Kuntz didn't really care about the business angle of it. His job was to run both personal and company security—protect the key employees and all trade secrets—and so that was his single focus.

He was good at it.

The business, it was explained to him, was a start-up, and so the initial pay was crap. But still it was something, a job, a way to hold his head up. It was also more about the promise too. He was given stock options. Risky, sure, but that was how great fortunes were made. There was a back end—a big, juicy back end—if things went very well.

And they did.

The app caught on in a way no one had anticipated, and now, after three years, Bank of America had underwritten their IPO—initial public offering—and if things went just okay (not super great, just okay), two months from now, when the company started trading on the stock market, John Kuntz's stake would be worth approximately seventeen million dollars.

Let that number just sink in for a second. Seventeen million dollars.

Forget a comeback. Forget salvation. With that kind of money, he'd be able to afford the best doctors in the world for his son. He'd get Robby home care and the best of everything. He'd be able to get his other kids—Kari and Harry—into good schools, quality places, and maybe set them up in their own businesses one day. He'd get Barb some help around the house, maybe even take her away on a vacation. The Bahamas maybe. She was always looking at ads for that Atlantis hotel, and they hadn't gone anywhere since that three-day Carnival cruise six years ago.

Seventeen million dollars. All their dreams were about to come true.

Now, once again, someone was trying to take it all away from him.

And from his family.

CHAPTER 32

ADAM drove past MetLife Stadium, home of both the New York Giants and New York Jets. He parked in an office-building lot about a quarter of a mile down the road. The building, like everything around it, was on old swampland. The smell was pure New Jersey lore and the reason for much of the state's misconception. The odor was part swamp (obviously), part chemical from what-ever had been used to drain the swamp, and part dorm bong that never got rinsed out.

In sum, seriously funky.

The 1970s-era office building looked as though some-one had taken the Brady Bunch's house as inspiration. There was a lot of brown and the kind of rubberized flooring that might have been snapped into place. Adam knocked on the door of a ground-level office overlook-ing the loading dock.

Tripp Evans opened it. "Adam?"

"Why did my wife call you?"

It was odd to see Tripp out of his normal element. In town he was popular and well-liked and important within the small worlds he inhabited. Here he looked strikingly ordinary. Adam knew Tripp's story vaguely. When Corinne was growing up in Cedarfield, Tripp's father had owned Evans Sporting Goods, located in the center of town where Rite Aid now was. For thirty years, Evans was the place where all the kids in town got their sports equipment. They also sold Cedarfield varsity jackets and practice gear for the high school teams. They opened two other stores in neighboring towns. When Tripp graduated college, he came home and ran the marketing. He made Sunday circulars and came up with special events to keep Evans relevant. He paid to have local pro athletes come in and sign autographs and greet customers. Times were good.

And then, like for most mom-and-pop operations, it all went south.

Herman's World of Sporting Goods came in. Then Modell's opened on the highway, and Dick's and a few others. The family business slowly withered and died. Tripp had landed on his feet, though. His track record helped him nab a position at a big Madison Avenue advertising firm, but the rest of his family suffered greatly. A few years ago, Tripp moved out to the suburbs to open his own boutique firm, to quote Bruce Springsteen, here in the swamps of Jersey.

"Do you want to sit down and talk?" Tripp asked.

"Sure."

"There's a coffee shop next door. Let's take a stroll."

Adam was about to argue—he wasn't in the mood for a stroll—but Tripp started on his way.

Tripp Evans wore an off-white short-sleeved dress shirt flimsy enough to see the V-neck tee underneath. His suit pants were the brown of a middle school principal's. His shoes looked too big for his feet—not orthopedics but one of those comfortable, less expensive brands that aimed for faux formal. In town, Adam was used to seeing Tripp in his clearly more comfortable coaching gear—the polo shirts with the Cedarfield Lacrosse logo, the crisp khakis, the baseball cap with the stiff brim, the whistle around his neck.

The difference was startling.

The coffee shop was an old-school greasy spoon, complete with a waitress who kept her pencil in her hair bun. They both ordered coffees. Just coffees. This wasn't the type of place that served macchiatos or lattes.

Tripp placed his hands on the sticky table. "You want to tell me what's going on?"

"My wife called you."

"How do you know this?"

"I checked the phone records."

"You checked . . ." Tripp's eyebrows jumped up a bit at that. "Are you serious?"

"Why did she call you?"

"Why do you think?" Tripp countered.

"Was it about this whole stolen-money thing?"

"Of course it was about this stolen-money thing. What else would it be?"

Tripp waited for a reply. Adam didn't give him one.

"So what did she say to you?"

The waitress came by, dropping the coffees with a thud that caused some to splash onto the saucer.

"She said that she needed more time. I told her I'd stalled long enough."

"Meaning?"

"The other board members were growing impatient. Some wanted to confront her more aggressively. A few wanted to go to the police right away on a more official basis."

"So how long has this been going on?" Adam asked.

"What, the investigation?"

"Yes."

Tripp put some sugar in his coffee. "A month or so."

"A month?"

"Yes."

"How come you never said anything to me?"

"I almost did. Draft night at the American Legion Hall. When you went nuts on Bob, I thought that maybe you already knew."

"I had no idea."

"Yeah, I get that now."

"You could have said something to me, Tripp."

"I could have," he agreed. "Except for one thing."

"What?"

"Corinne asked me not to."

Adam stayed perfectly still. Then he said: "I just want to make sure I understand."

"Let me see if I can help, then. Corinne knew that we were looking at her for the theft, and she made it clear that we shouldn't tell you," Tripp said. "You understand just fine."

Adam just sat back.

"So what did Corinne say that morning when you called?"

"She asked me for more time."

"Did you give it to her?"

"No. I told her time was up. I had tried to hold the board back long enough."

"When you say the board—"

"All of them. But mostly Bob, Cal, and Len."

"How did Corinne respond?"

"She asked—no, I think a better word might be

begged—she begged for another week. She said she had a way to prove she was completely innocent, but she needed more time."

"Did you believe her?"

"Truth?"

"Preferably."

"No, not anymore."

"What did you think?"

"I thought she was trying to find a way to pay it back. She knew we didn't want to press charges. We just wanted it to be made whole. So yeah, I figured that she was contacting relatives or friends or something to raise the money."

"Why wouldn't she come to me?"

Tripp didn't reply. He just sipped his coffee.

"Tripp?"

"I can't answer that."

"This makes no sense."

Tripp just kept sipping his coffee.

"How long have you known my wife, Tripp?"

"You know the answer. We both grew up in Cedarfield. She was two years behind me—the same year as my Becky."

"Then you know. She wouldn't do this."

Tripp stared into his coffee. "I thought that for a long time."

"So what changed your mind?"

"Come on, Adam. You used to be a prosecutor. I don't think Corinne started out to steal. You know how it is. When you hear about the sweet old lady stealing from the church tithing or, heck, the sports board member embezzling, it isn't like they set out to do it. You come in with the best of intentions, right? But it creeps up on you."

"Not Corinne."

"Not anybody. That's what we always think. We're always shocked, aren't we?"

Adam could see that Tripp was about to start into some philosophical spiel. For a moment, Adam debated stopping him, but maybe he should let go. Maybe the more Tripp talked, the more Adam would learn.

"But, let's say, for example, you stay up late at night to schedule the lacrosse practice. You're working really hard and maybe you're in a diner, like this, so you order a coffee, just like the ones we have in our hands, and maybe you forgot your wallet in the car and figure, what the hell, the organization should pay for it anyway. A legitimate expense, am I right?"

Adam didn't reply.

"And then a few weeks later, some referee doesn't show up at a game in, say, Toms River, and you lose three hours of time covering for him, so hey, the least the organization can do is pay for your gas on the ride down. Then maybe it's a dinner because you're far away from home and the game ran late. Then you need to pay for the pizzas for the coaches when the board meeting makes you all miss dinner. Then you need to hire local teens to ref the little kids' games, so you make sure your teen gets the job. Hey, why not? Who better? Shouldn't your family benefit from all this volunteering you're doing?"

Adam just waited.

"So you keep sliding like that. That's how it starts. And then one day you're behind on a car payment and what do you know—your organization has a big surplus. Because of you. So you borrow some money. No big deal, you'll pay it back. So who are you hurting? No one. That's what you fool yourself into believing."

Tripp stopped and looked at Adam.

"You can't be serious," Adam said.

"As a heart attack, my friend." Tripp made a project of looking at his watch. He threw some bills on the table and stood up. "And who knows? Maybe we're all wrong about Corinne."

"You are."

"That would thrill me to no end."

"She asked for a little more time," Adam said. "Can you just give it to her?"

Tripp quietly sighed and hitched up his pants a bit. "I can try."

CHAPTER 33

AUDREY Fine finally said something relevant. And that led to Johanna's first real lead.

Police Chief Johanna Griffin had been right about the county guys. They had put on their spouse blinders and zoomed in on Marty Dann for the murder of his wife, Heidi. Even the fact that poor Marty had a rock-solid alibi for the timing of the killing hadn't dissuaded them. Yet. They had assumed a "professional hit job" from the start, so now they were digging into poor Marty's phone records and texts and e-mails. They were asking around the offices of TTI Floor Care about his recent behavior, about his contacts, about where he went out for drinks or lunch, that kind of thing, hoping to find some connection between Marty and a possible hit man.

Lunch was the key.

Not where Marty had lunch, though. That's where the county boys had messed up again.

But where Heidi ate lunch.

Johanna knew about Heidi's weekly lunch with the girls. She had even gone a time or two. At first, Johanna had dismissed it as indulgent, as a privileged waste of time. There was some of that. But these were also women who wanted to bond with other women. These were women who made it a priority to make their lunch hour last a little longer so that they could share time with friends and connect to something other than their own family or career.

What was wrong with that?

This week, the lunch had taken place at Red Lobster and included Audrey Fine, Katey Brannum, Stephanie Keiles, and Heidi. No one noticed anything unusual. According to all of them, Heidi, fewer than twenty-four hours from being murdered in her home, had been her usual ebullient self. It was an odd thing talking to these other women. All of them were beyond devastated. All of them had felt that they had lost their closest friend in Heidi, the one person whom they could confide in, the one who was the strongest among their friends.

Johanna felt that way too. Yep, Heidi was magic. She was one of those people who made all those around her feel somehow better about themselves.

How, Johanna wondered, does one bullet take out a spirit like that?

So Johanna met with the entire lunch group and listened to them give her nothing. She was about to call it a day and see if she could uncover some other lead, something else the county boys wouldn't consider, when Audrey remembered something.

"Heidi was talking to a young couple in the parking lot."

Johanna had been drifting off, lost in a memory. Twenty years ago, after much trial and error, Johanna had gotten "miracle" pregnant through IVF. Heidi had been with her at the ob-gyn when she'd gotten the news. And Heidi had been the first person Johanna had called when she'd miscarried. Heidi had driven over. Johanna slipped into the passenger seat and told her the news. The two women sat in the car and cried together for a long time. Johanna would never forget the way Heidi lowered her head onto the steering wheel, her hair spread out like a fan, and cried for Johanna's loss. Somehow they both knew.

There would be no more miracles. This pregnancy had been Johanna's only chance. She and Ricky ended up never having any children.

"Wait," Johanna said. "What young couple?"

"We all said our good-byes and we got in our cars. I started pulling out onto Orange Place, but this truck zoomed by so fast, I thought it'd take my front grille off. I looked in the rearview mirror, and I saw Heidi talking to this young couple."

"Could you describe them?"

"Not really. The girl had blond hair. The guy had a baseball cap on. I figured that they were asking her directions or something."

Audrey remembered nothing else. Why would she? But the entire world, especially the parking lots of chain stores and restaurants, had video cameras. Getting the warrant would take time, so Johanna just went to Red Lobster on her own. The head of security put the video on a DVD for her, which felt a little old-school, and asked for it to be returned. "Policy," he said to Johanna. "We need it back."

"No problem."

The Beachwood police station had a DVD player. Johanna hurried in to her office, closed the door, and jammed the DVD into the slot. The screen came to life. The security guy knew his stuff. Two seconds into the video, Heidi appeared from the right-hand corner. Johanna gasped out loud at the sight. Something about seeing her dead friend, alive, teetering as she did on those heels, made the tragedy too real.

Heidi was dead. Gone forever.

There was no sound on the tape. Heidi kept walking. Suddenly, she stopped and looked up. There was a man in a baseball cap and a blond woman. They did indeed look young. Later, the second and the third and the fourth time Johanna watched the tape, she would try to make out their facial features more, but at this height and this angle, there wasn't much to see. Eventually, she would send it to county and let them get their computer guys and techno-whizzes to get whatever they could from the tape.

But not just yet.

At first, watching silently, it did indeed appear as though the young couple was asking for directions. That might make sense to a casual observer. But as time passed, Johanna felt the room chill. The conversation was taking much too long for this to just be about directions, for one thing. But more than that, Johanna knew her friend. She knew her mannerisms and her body language, and right now, even watching silently, Johanna could see that they were both all wrong.

As the conversation continued, Johanna grew more and more still. At one point, Johanna was sure that she even saw her friend's legs buckle. A minute later, the young couple got into their car and drove away. For almost a full minute, Heidi just stood in the lot, dazed, lost, before she got into her car. From her angle, Johanna could no longer see her friend. But time passed. Ten seconds. Twenty, thirty. Then, suddenly, there was movement in the front windshield. Johanna squinted and moved closer. It was hard to see, hard to make out, but Johanna recognized it now.

Heidi's hair spread out like a fan.

Oh no. . . .

Heidi had lowered her head to the steering wheel, the same way she had done twenty years ago when Johanna had told her about the miscarriage.

She was, Johanna was certain, crying.

"What the hell did they say to you?" Johanna asked out loud.

She backed up the tape now and watched the young couple pull out of the parking lot. She slowed it down and then hit the pause button. She zoomed in, picked up her phone, and dialed in the number.

"Hey, Norbert," she said, "I need you to run a license plate for me right away."

CHAPTER 34

THOMAS was waiting for his father in the kitchen.

"Any word on Mom?"

Adam had hoped that neither of his sons would be home yet. After spending the entire car ride home wondering what to do, an idea of sorts had emerged. He needed to get upstairs and do a little more research on the computer.

"She should be home any day now," Adam said. And then, to immediately get off the subject, he added, "Where's your brother?"

"Drum lesson. He walks there after school, but Mom usually picks him up."

"What time?"

"In forty-five minutes."

Adam nodded. "It's that place on Goffle Road, right?"

"Right."

"Okay, cool. Look, I have some work to do. Maybe we can run out to Café Amici for dinner after I pick up your brother, okay?"

"I'm walking over to the gym and lifting with Justin."

"Now?"

"Yeah."

"Well, you have to eat."

"I'll make something when I get back. Dad?"

"What?"

The two of them stood in the kitchen, father and son, the son closing in on manhood. Thomas was only an inch shorter than his father now, and with the way Thomas had been lifting weights and working out, Adam wondered whether his son could finally take him. Thomas had last challenged his father to a one-on-one game of basketball about six months earlier, and for the first time, Adam had to really try to squeak out an 11–8 victory. Now he wondered whether that score would be reversed, and how he'd feel about it.

"I'm worried," Thomas said.

"Don't be."

He said it as a parental reaction rather than anything of truth or substance.

"Why did Mom run off like this?"

"I told you. Look, Thomas, you're old enough to understand. Your mother and I love each other very much. But sometimes parents need a little distance."

"From each other," Thomas said with a small nod. "But not from Ryan and me."

"Well, yes and no. Sometimes we just need to get away from it all."

"Dad?"

"What?"

"I don't buy it," Thomas said. "I don't want to sound full of myself or anything, and yeah, I get it. You guys have your own lives. You aren't all about us. So maybe I could understand Mom needing to, I don't know, get away or blow off some steam or whatever. But Mom's a mom. You know what I mean? She would tell us first, or if she did it like at the last second? She'd contact us or something. She'd answer our texts. She'd tell us not to worry. Mom is a lot of things, but first off, sorry, she's our mom."

Adam wasn't sure what to say to that, so he said something dumb: "It's going to be okay."

"What does that mean?"

"She told me to take care of you guys and to give her a few days. She asked me not to contact her."

"Why?"

"I don't know."

"I'm really scared," Thomas said. And now the almost-man was back to sounding like the little boy. It was the father's job to assuage that feeling. Thomas was right. Corinne was a mother first and foremost—and he, Adam, was a father. You protect your children.

"It's going to be okay," he said, hearing the hollow in his own voice.

Thomas shook his head, the maturity returning as fast as it had fled. "No, Dad, it's not." He turned, wiped the tears off his face, and started for the door. "I gotta go meet Justin."

Adam was about to call him back, but what good would that do? He didn't have any words of comfort, and perhaps, if nothing else, being with his friend might distract his son. The solution—the only real comfort here—would be to find Corinne. Adam needed to dig in more, figure out what was going on, get his sons some real answers. So he let Thomas go and headed up the stairs. There was still time before drum lesson pickup.

Once again he briefly debated getting the police involved. He didn't really fear anymore that they'd think he did something to his wife—let them—but he knew from experience that the police understandably deal in facts. Fact One: Corinne and Adam had a fight. Fact Two: Corinne had already texted Adam, telling him that she wanted a few days away and not to contact her.

Would the police need a Fact Three?

He sat down at the computer. At Old Man Rinsky's, Adam had quickly checked Corinne's recent mobile phone records. Now he wanted to get a more detailed look at her calling and texting pattern. Would the stranger or this Ingrid Prisby have called or texted Corinne? It seemed a long shot—hadn't the stranger simply approached him without warning?—but there was a chance that Corinne's phone records might produce some kind of clue.

But it didn't take him long to realize that there was nothing to mine. His wife was, it seemed according to recent communications, an open book. There were no surprises. Most numbers he knew from memory—calls and texts to him, to the boys, to friends, to fellow teachers, to lacrosse board members, and that was about it. There were a few other calls sprinkled in, but they were to restaurants for reservations, the dry cleaner about a pickup, that kind of thing.

No clue.

Adam sat and thought about what to do. Yes, Corinne was an open book. That was how it seemed according to her recent texts and phone calls.

The key word: *recent*.

He flashed back to the surprise on his Visa card—the charge to Novelty Funsy from two years ago.

Corinne had been much more of a surprise back then, no?

Something had precipitated that purchase. But what? You don't one day just decide to fake a pregnancy. Something happened. She had called someone. Or someone had called her. Or texted.

Something.

It took Adam a few minutes to find the old archives dating back two years, but he did. He knew that Corinne had made her first order from Fake-A-Pregnancy in February. So he started there. He traced through the phone records, scanning up the screen rather than down.

At first, all he found were the usual suspects—calls and texts to him, the boys, friends, fellow teachers. . . .

And then, when Adam saw a familiar number, his heart sank.

CHAPTER 35

SALLY Perryman sat alone at the far end of the bar, sipping a beer and reading the *New York Post*. She had on a white blouse and a gray pencil skirt. Her hair was pulled back in a ponytail. She'd put her coat on the stool next to her, saving it for him. As Adam moved closer, she moved the coat without looking up from the paper. Adam slid onto the stool.

"Been a long time," she said.

Sally still hadn't looked up from the paper.

"It has," he said. "How's work?"

"Busy, lot of clients." She finally met his eye. He felt a gentle pow and held on. "But you didn't call for that."

"No."

It was one of those moments when the noise fades away and the rest of the world becomes background and it's him and her and nothing else.

"Adam?"

"What?"

"I can't handle a big thing here. Just tell me what you want."

"Did my wife ever call you?"

Sally blinked as if the question, too, had been a bit of a pow. "When?"

"Ever."

She turned toward her beer. "Yeah," she said. "Once."

They were in one of those noisy chain-restaurant bars, the kind that majors in deep-fried appetizers and has a million TV screens playing maybe two sporting events. The bartender came over and made a big production of introducing himself. Adam quickly ordered a beer to get him to leave.

"When?" he asked.

"Two years ago, I guess. During the case."

"You never told me."

"It was just once."

"Still."

"What difference does it make now, Adam?"

"What did she say?"

"She knew you'd been to my house."

Adam almost asked how, but of course, he knew the answer, didn't he? She'd put a tracking app on all the phones. She could check at any time to see the boys' location.

Or his.

"What else?"

"She wanted to know why you were there."

"What did you tell her?"

"That it was work," Sally Perryman said.

"You told her it was nothing, right?"

"It was nothing, Adam. We were obsessed with that case." Then: "But it was almost something."

"Almost doesn't count."

A sad smile came to Sally's lips. "I think to your wife it probably does."

"Did she believe you?"

Sally shrugged. "I never heard from her again."

He sat there and looked at her. He opened his mouth, not sure what he would say, but she stopped him with her open palm. "Don't."

She was right. He slid away from the counter and headed outside.

CHAPTER 36

AS the stranger entered the garage, he thought, as he did nearly every time he came here, about all the famous companies that purportedly started in just this way. Steve Jobs and Steve Wozniak started Apple (why not call the company the Steves?) by selling fifty units of Wozniak's new Apple I computer out of a garage in Cupertino, California. Jeff Bezos began Amazon as an online bookseller out of his garage in Bellevue, Washington. Google, Disney, Mattel, Hewlett-Packard, Harley-Davidson, all began life, if legend is to be believed, out of tiny, indistinct garages.

"Any word on Dan Molino?" the stranger asked.

There were three of them in the garage, all sitting in front of powerful computers with large monitors. Four Wi-Fi routers sat on the shelf next to paint cans Eduardo's dad had put out here more than a decade ago. Eduardo, who was easily the best of them when it came to the technological aspects of what they did, had set up a system whereby the Wi-Fi not only went out and bounced all over the world, making them as anonymous as the Internet gets, but even if someone somehow tracked it back to them, the routers would automatically trip into action and move them to another host. In truth, the stranger didn't get it all. But he didn't have to.

"He paid," Eduardo said.

Eduardo sported stringy hair that always needed a cut and the kind of unshaven look that made him look more greasy than hip. He was an old-school hacker who enjoyed the chase as much as the moral indignation or cash.

Next to him was Gabrielle, a single mother of two and the oldest of them by far at forty-four. Two decades ago, she'd started out as a phone-sex operator. The idea was to keep the guy on the line for as long as possible, charging his phone $3.99 per minute. More recently, in a similar vein, Gabrielle had posed as various hot housewives on a "no strings attached" hookup site. Her job was to coax a new client (read: dupe) into thinking sex was imminent until his free trial was over and he committed to a full-year subscription on his credit card.

Merton, their most recent colleague, was nineteen, thin, heavily tattooed, with a shaved head and bright blue eyes just south of sane. He wore baggy jeans with chains coming out of the pocket that hinted at either biking or bondage, it was hard to tell which. He cleaned his fingernails with a switchblade and spent his free time volunteering for a televangelist who did his services out of a twelve-thousand-seat arena. Ingrid had brought Merton in from her job at a website for a company called the Five.

Merton turned toward the stranger. "You look disappointed."

"He'll get away with it now."

"With what, taking steroids to play big-time football?

Big deal. Probably eighty percent of those kids are on some kind of juice."

Eduardo agreed. "We stick to our principles, Chris."

"Yeah," the stranger said. "I know."

"Your principles, really."

The stranger, whose real name was Chris Taylor, nodded. Chris was the founder of this movement, even if this was Eduardo's garage. Eduardo had been first in with him. The enterprise started as a lark, as an attempt to right wrongs. Soon, Chris realized, their movement could be both a profitable company and a source for doing good. But in order to do that, in order to not let one take over the other, they all had to stick to their founding principles.

"So what's wrong?" Gabrielle asked him.

"What makes you think something's wrong?"

"You don't come here unless there's a problem."

That was true enough.

Eduardo sat back. "Were there any issues with Dan Molino or his son?"

"Yes and no."

"We got the money," Merton said. "It couldn't have been that bad."

"Yeah, but I had to handle it alone."

"So?"

"So Ingrid was supposed to be there."

They all looked at one another. Gabrielle broke the silence. "She probably figured that a woman would stand out at a football tryout."

"Could be," Chris said. "Have any of you heard from her?"

Eduardo and Gabrielle shook their heads. Merton stood and said, "Wait, when did you talk to her last?"

"In Ohio. When we approached Heidi Dann."

"And she was supposed to meet you at the football tryouts?"

"That's what she said. We followed protocol, so we traveled separately and had no communication."

Eduardo started typing again. "Hold up, Chris. Let me check something."

Chris. It was almost odd to hear someone speak his name. The past few weeks, he'd been anonymous, the stranger, and no one called him by name. Even with Ingrid, the protocol had been clear: no names. Anonymous. There was irony in that, of course. The people he approached had assumed and craved anonymity, not realizing that in truth, it didn't exist for them.

For Chris—for the stranger—it did.

"According to the schedule," Eduardo said, staring at the screen, "Ingrid was supposed to drive to Philadelphia and drop off the rental car yesterday. Let me check and see. . . ." He looked up. "Damn."

"What?"

"She never returned the car."

The room chilled.

"We need to call her," Merton said.

"It's risky," Eduardo said. "If she's been compromised, her mobile might be in the wrong hands."

"We need to break protocol," Chris said.

"Carefully," Gabrielle added.

Eduardo nodded. "Let me call her via Viber and knock the connection through two IPs in Bulgaria. It should only take me five minutes."

It took more like three.

The phone rang. Once, twice, and then on the third

ring, the phone picked up. They expected to hear Ingrid's voice. But they didn't.

A man's voice asked, "Who is this calling, please?"

Eduardo quickly disconnected the call. The four of them stood still for a moment, the garage completely silent. Then the stranger—Chris Taylor—said what they were all thinking.

"We've been compromised."

CHAPTER 37

THEY had done nothing wrong.

Sally Perryman had been a junior partner in the firm assigned to be Adam's first chair for a time-consuming case involving the immigrant owners of a Greek diner. The owners had been happily and profitably working in the same location in Harrison for forty years, until a big hedge fund had built a new office tower down the street, causing the powers that be to conclude that the road leading to the tower would have to be widened to accommodate the new traffic. That meant bulldozing the diner. Adam and Sally were up against the government and bankers and, in the end, deep corruption.

Sometimes you can't wait to wake up and get to work in the morning and you hate the day to end. You get consumed. You eat, drink, sleep the case. This was one of those times. You grow close to those who stand with you in what you start to see as a glorious, hard-fought quest.

He and Sally Perryman had grown close.

Very close.

But there hadn't been anything physical—not so much as a kiss. Lines hadn't been crossed, but they'd been approached and challenged and perhaps even stepped on, though never over. There comes a stage, Adam had learned, where you are standing near that line, teetering, one life on one side, one life on the other, and at some point, you either cross it or something has to wither and die. In this case, something died. Two months after the case ended, Sally Perryman took another job with a law firm in Livingston.

It was over.

But Corinne had called Sally.

Why? The answer seemed obvious. Adam tried to think it through, tried to come up with theories and hypotheses that could possibly explain what had happened to Corinne. A few of the pieces maybe came together. The picture beginning to emerge was not pleasant.

It was past midnight. The boys were in bed. This house had a grieving quality to it now. Part of Adam wanted the boys to express their fears, but right now, most of him just wanted them to block, to just get through another day or two, until Corinne came home. In the end, that was the only thing that would make this right.

He had to find Corinne.

Old Man Rinksy had sent him the preliminary information on Ingrid Prisby. So far, there was nothing noteworthy or spectacular. She lived in Austin, had graduated eight years ago from Rice University in Houston, had worked for two Internet start-ups. Rinsky had gotten a home phone number. It went immediately into a message machine set to a robotic default voice. Adam left a message asking Ingrid to call him. Rinsky had also provided the home phone number and address of Ingrid's mother. Adam considered calling her but wondered how to approach her. It was late. He decided to sleep on that.

So now what?

Ingrid Prisby had a Facebook page. He wondered

whether that might provide more clues. Adam had his own Facebook page but rarely checked it. He and Corinne had set ones up a few years back when Corinne, feeling nostalgic, had read an article on how social media was a great way for people their age to rediscover old friends. The past held little draw for Adam, but he'd gone along with it. He'd barely touched his page since throwing up a profile picture. Corinne started off a little more enthusiastic about the whole social media thing, but he doubted that she'd ever gone on it more than two or three times in a week.

But who knew for sure?

He flashed back to sitting in this very room with Corinne when they had first created their Facebook profiles. They began searching and "friending" family and neighbors. Adam had gone through the photographs his college buddies had posted—their grinning family shots on the beach, the Christmas dinners, the kids' sports, the ski vacation in Aspen, the tan wife wrapping her arms around the smiling husband, that kind of thing.

"Everyone looks happy," he'd said to Corinne.

"Oh, not you too."

"What?"

"Everyone looks happy on Facebook," Corinne said. "It's like a compilation of your life's greatest hits." Her voice had an edge to it now. "It's not reality, Adam."

"I didn't say it was. I said everyone *looks* happy. That was kinda my point. If you judge the world by Facebook, you wonder why so many people take Prozac."

Corinne had grown quiet after that. Adam had pretty much laughed it off and moved on, but now, years later, looking through his newly cleaned goggles of hindsight, so many things took on a darker, uglier hue.

He spent almost an hour on Ingrid Prisby's Facebook page. First he checked her relationship status—maybe he'd get lucky and the stranger was her husband or boyfriend—but Ingrid listed herself as single. He clicked through her list of 188 friends, hoping to find the stranger among them. No luck. He looked for familiar names or faces, someone from his or Corinne's past. He found none. He started down Ingrid's page, looking through her status updates. There was nothing that hinted at the stranger or pregnancy faking or any of that. He tried to scrutinize her photographs in a critical way. The vibe he got off her was a positive one. Ingrid Prisby looked happy in the party pictures, drinking and letting go and all that, but she looked far happier in those photos where she volunteered. And she volunteered a lot: soup kitchens, Red Cross, USO, Junior Achievement. He noticed something else about her. All her pics were group shots, never solos, never portraits, never selfies.

But these observations brought him no closer to finding Corinne.

He was missing something.

It was getting late, but Adam kept plugging away. First off, how did Ingrid know the stranger? They had to be close in some way. He thought about Suzanne Hope and how she'd been blackmailed over faking her pregnancy. The most likely scenario was that Corinne had been blackmailed too. Neither woman had paid the blackmail money. . . .

Or was that true? He knew that Suzanne hadn't paid it. She told him as much. But maybe Corinne had paid. He sat back and thought about that for a second. If Corinne had stolen the lacrosse money—and he still didn't believe it—but if she had, maybe she had done so to pay for their silence.

And maybe they were just the kind of blackmailers who told anyway.

Was that likely?

No way of knowing. Concentrate on the question at hand: How did Ingrid and the stranger know each other? There were several possibilities, of course, so he put them in order from most to least likely.

Most likely: work. Ingrid had worked for several Internet companies. Whoever was behind this probably worked for Fake-A-Pregnancy.com or specialized in the Web—hacking or whatnot—or both.

Second most likely: They met in college. They both seemed about the right age to have met on a campus and remained friendly. So maybe the answer lay at Rice University.

Third most likely: Both were from Austin, Texas.

Did this make sense? He didn't know, but Adam went back through her friends, keeping an eye out for people who also worked on the Internet. There was a fair amount. He checked their pages. Some were blocked or had limited access, but most people don't go on Facebook to hide. Time passed. Then he looked through her friends' friends who worked on the Internet. And even friends of those friends. He checked out profiles and work histories, and at 4:48 A.M.—he saw the time on the little digital clock on the top bar on his computer—Adam finally struck gold.

The first clue had come from the Fake-A-Pregnancy website. Under the CONTACT US link, the company listed a mailing address in Revere, Massachusetts. Adam Googled the address and found a match—a business conglomerate called Downing Place that operated various start-ups and Web pages.

Now he had something.

Scouring again through Ingrid's friends, he found someone who listed his employer as Downing Place. He clicked on his profile page. There was nothing much there, but the guy had two friends who also worked at Downing. So he clicked on their pages—and so on, until he arrived at a page belonging to a woman named Gabrielle Dunbar.

According to her ABOUT page, Gabrielle Dunbar studied business at New Jersey's Ocean County College and in the past had attended Fair Lawn High School. She did not list a current or past employer—nothing about Downing Place or any other website—and she had not posted anything on her page in the past eight months.

What had drawn his eye was the fact that she had three "friends" who listed Downing Place as their employer. It also stated that Gabrielle Dunbar lived in Revere, Massachusetts.

So he started clicking on her page, scanning through her photo albums, when he stumbled across a picture from three years ago. It was in an album called "Mobile Uploads" and captioned simply HOLIDAY PARTY. It was one of those quickly-round-up-before-we-all-get-too-wasted office-party pics, where someone good-naturedly asks everyone to pose for a group shot and then e-mails it or posts it to their pages. The party was held at a wood-paneled restaurant or bar. There were probably twenty or maybe thirty people in the picture, many red-faced and red-eyed from both the camera flash and the alcohol.

And there, on the far left with a beer in his hand, not looking at the camera—probably not even realizing the photograph was being taken—was the stranger.

CHAPTER 38

JOHANNA Griffin had two Havanese dogs named Starsky and Hutch. At first she didn't want to get Havaneses. They were considered a toy breed, and Johanna had grown up with Great Danes and considered small dogs, please forgive her, semirodents. But Ricky had insisted and damned if he wasn't right. Johanna had owned dogs all her life, and these two were as lovable as all get-out.

Normally, Johanna liked taking Starsky and Hutch for a walk early in the morning. She prided herself on being a good sleeper. Whatever horror or issues might be plaguing her daily life, she never let them past her bedroom door. That was her rule. Worry it all to death in the kitchen or living room—but when you crossed that portal, you flicked a switch. That was it. The problems were gone.

But two things had been robbing her of sleep. One was Ricky. Maybe it was because he'd put on a few pounds or maybe it was just age, but his once tolerable snoring had become a constant, grating buzz saw. He had tried various remedies—a strip, a pillow, some over-the-counter medication—but none had worked. It had reached the stage where they'd been debating separate sleeping quarters, but that felt too much like a white flag to Johanna. She'd just have to plow through it until a solution popped up.

Second, of course, was Heidi.

Her friend visited Johanna in her sleep. It wasn't in a gory, bloody way. Heidi didn't turn into a ghostly figure or whisper, "Avenge me." Nothing like that. Johanna really couldn't say what exactly occurred in her Heidi-centric dreams. The dreams felt normal, like real life, and Heidi was there and laughing and smiling and they were having a good time, and then at some point, Johanna remembered what had happened, that Heidi had, in fact, been murdered. Then panic would take hold of Johanna. The dream would start ending, and Johanna would reach out and desperately try to grab her friend, as though she could keep Heidi there, alive—as though Johanna, if she tried hard enough, could undo the murder and Heidi would be okay.

Johanna would wake up with cheeks wet from tears.

So lately, to change it up, she had taken Starsky and Hutch for late-night walks. Johanna tried to enjoy the solitude, but the roads were dark and, even with the streetlights, she always feared that she'd hit a patch of uneven sidewalk and fall. Her dad had taken a fall when he was seventy-four and never fully recovered. You hear that a lot. So as she walked, Johanna kept her eyes glued to the ground. Right now, as she hit a particularly dark patch, she took out her smartphone and used the flashlight app.

Her phone buzzed in her hand. At this late hour, it would have to be Ricky. He'd probably woken up and either wondered when she'd be getting back or decided that maybe with all that weight he was gaining, he could use a little exercise and would want to join the dog walk. That was okay by her. She had just started out, so circling back with Starsky and Hutch wouldn't be a problem.

She put both leashes in her left hand and put the phone to her ear. She didn't check the caller ID. She simply hit the answer button and said, "Hello?"

"Chief?"

She could tell from the voice that this wasn't a casual call. She stopped. Both dogs stopped too.

"Is that you, Norbert?"

"Yeah, sorry about the hour, but . . ."

"What's wrong?"

"I checked on that license plate for you. I had to do some digging, but it looks like it was a car rented to a woman whose real name is Ingrid Prisby."

Silence.

"And?" she prompted.

"And it's bad," Norbert said. "Really, really bad."

CHAPTER 39

ADAM called Andy Gribbel early in the morning. Gribbel moaned out a "What?"

"Sorry, didn't mean to wake you up."

"It's six in the morning," Gribbel said.

"Sorry."

"The band had a gig late last night. Then there were hot groupies at the after-party. You know how it is."

"Yeah. Listen, do you know anything about Facebook?"

"You kidding? Of course I do. Band has a fan page. We have, like, almost eighty followers."

"Great. I'm forwarding you a Facebook link. Four people are in it. See if you can get me addresses on any of them and find out anything else you can about the picture—where it was taken, who else is in it, anything."

"Priority?"

"Top. I need the info yesterday."

"Got it. Hey, we did a killer version of 'The Night Chicago Died' last night. Not a dry eye in the house."

"You can't imagine how much this means to me right now," Adam said.

"Wow, this is that important?"

"More."

"On it."

Adam hung up and got out of bed. He woke up the boys at seven and took a long, hot shower. It felt good. He got dressed and checked the time. The boys should be downstairs now.

"Ryan? Thomas?"

It was Thomas who replied. "Yeah, yeah, we're up."

Adam's mobile phone buzzed. It was Gribbel. "Hello?"

"We got lucky."

"How's that?"

"That link you sent. It came from the profile page of a woman named Gabrielle Dunbar."

"Right, what about it?"

"She doesn't live in Revere anymore. She moved back home."

"Fair Lawn?"

"You got it."

Fair Lawn was only a half hour from Cedarfield.

"I just texted you her address."

"Thanks, Andy."

"No problem. You going to see her this morning?"

"Yes."

"Let me know if you need me."

"Thanks."

Adam hung up. He started down the corridor when he heard a noise coming from Ryan's bedroom. Adam moved closer to the shut door and placed his ear against it. Through the wood, he could hear his son's muffled sobs. The sound was like shattered glass rolling across his heart. Adam rapped his knuckles on the door, braced himself, and turned the knob.

Ryan was sitting up in bed sobbing like a little boy,

which, in a sense, he still was. Adam stayed in the doorway. The pain inside him, fueled by helplessness, grew.

"Ryan?"

Tears made everyone look smaller and frailer and so damn young. Ryan's chest hitched, but he still managed to say, "I miss Mommy."

"I know you do, pal."

For a second, a bolt of anger boomed through him— anger at Corinne for running away, for not staying in touch, for faking that damn pregnancy, for stealing the money, for all of it. Forget what she had done to Adam. That wasn't an issue. But hurting the boys like this ... that would be far harder to forgive.

"Why isn't she answering my texts?" Ryan cried. "Why isn't she home with us?"

He was about to offer up more platitudes about her being busy and needing time and all that. But the platitudes were lies. The platitudes just made it worse. So this time, Adam settled for the truth.

"I don't know."

That answer seemed oddly to soothe Ryan a little. The sobs didn't suddenly stop, but they did begin to decelerate toward something more akin to sniffles. Adam came over and sat on the bed with Ryan. He was going to put his arm around his son, but somehow that felt like the wrong move. So he just sat beside him and let him know he was there. It seemed enough.

A moment later, Thomas came to the doorway. All three of them were together now—"my boys," as Corinne always called them, joking that Adam was just her biggest child. They stayed in the room, unmoving, and Adam realized something simple but somehow profound: Corinne loved her life. She loved her family. She loved the world she had fought so hard to create. She loved living in this town where she'd started out, in this neighborhood she cherished, in this home she shared with her boys.

So what had gone wrong?

All three of them heard the car door slam. Ryan's head snapped toward the window. Adam instinctively went into protective mode, getting to the window fast and positioning his body in such a way as to block his boys' view. The block didn't last long. The two boys came up to him, each on one side, and looked down. No one cried out. No one gasped. No one said a word.

It was a police car.

One of the officers was Len Gilman, which made no sense because the side of the vehicle read ESSEX COUNTY POLICE. Len worked for the town of Cedarfield.

Coming out of the driver's side was a county officer in full uniform.

Ryan said, "Dad?"

Corinne is dead.

It was a flash, no more than that. But wasn't that the obvious answer here? Your wife goes missing. She doesn't communicate with you or even her children. Now two cops, one a family friend, one from the county, show up at his doorstep with grim faces. And really, wasn't that the logical assumption all along—that Corinne was dead and lying in a ditch somewhere and these grim-faced men were there to deliver that news and then he'd have to pick up the pieces and carry on and grieve and be brave for the boys?

He turned and started down the stairs. The boys fell in line behind him, Thomas first, then Ryan. It was almost as though there had been an unspoken adhesion, a bond formed by the three survivors to stand together and take the oncoming blow. By the time Len Gilman rang the bell, Adam was already turning the knob to open the door.

Len startled back and blinked.

"Adam?"

Adam stood there, the door half-opened. Len looked behind him and spotted the boys.

"I thought they'd be at practice by now."

"They were just about to leave," Adam said.

"Okay, maybe you could let them go and then we could—"

"What's going on?"

"It's better if we talk at the precinct." Then, clearly for the benefit of the boys, Len added, "Everything is fine, boys. We just have some questions."

Len met Adam's eye. Adam was having none of it. If the news was bad—if it was going to devastate them—it would be just as devastating if they heard now or after practice.

"Does this have something to do with Corinne?" Adam asked.

"No, I don't think so."

"Don't think?"

"Please, Adam." He could hear the plea in Len's voice now. "Get the boys off to practice and come with us."

CHAPTER 40

KUNTZ spent the night in his son's hospital room, semi-sleeping on a chair that half folded out into what no one would really call a bed. When the nurse saw him trying to stretch his stiff back in the morning, she said, "Not very comfortable, is it?"

"Did you guys order these from Guantánamo?"

The nurse smiled at him and took Robby's vital signs—temperature, heart rate, blood pressure. They did that every four hours, awake or asleep. His little boy was so used to it, he barely stirred. A little boy should never get used to something like that. Never.

Kuntz sat by his son's bedside and let the familiar horror of helplessness wash over him. The nurse saw the distress on his face. They all did, but they were wise enough not to patronize or soothe with comforting lies. She merely said, "I'll be back in a bit." He appreciated that.

Kuntz checked his texts. There were several urgent ones from Larry. Kuntz had expected as much. He waited for Barb to arrive. He kissed her on the forehead and said, "Gotta go for a bit. Business."

Barb nodded, not asking for or needing details.

Kuntz grabbed a taxi and headed to the apartment on

Park Avenue. Larry Powers's pretty wife, Laurie, answered the door. Kuntz never understood cheating on your wife. Your wife was the woman you loved more than anything in the world, your only true companion, a part of you. You either love her with all your heart or you don't—and if you don't, it was time to move along, little doggie.

Laurie Powers always had a ready smile. She wore a pearl strand necklace and a simple black dress that looked expensive—or maybe it was Laurie who looked expensive. Laurie Powers had come from old-world money, and even if she wore a muumuu, you'd probably be able to see that.

"He's expecting you," she said. "He's in the study."

"Thanks."

"John?"

Kuntz turned toward her.

"Is something wrong?"

"I don't think so, Mrs. Powers."

"Laurie."

"Okay," he said. "And how about you, Laurie?"

"What about me?"

"Are you okay?"

She tucked her hair behind her ear. "I'm fine. But Larry . . . he hasn't been himself. I know it's your job to protect him."

"And I will. Don't give it another thought, Laurie."

"Thank you, John."

Here is one of life's little shortcuts: If someone is meeting you in their "study," they have money. Normal people have a home office or a family room or maybe a man cave. Rich people have studies. This one was particularly opulent, loaded up with leather-bound books and wooden globes and Oriental rugs. It looked like someplace Bruce Wayne would hang out before heading down to the Bat-cave.

Larry Powers sat in a burgundy leather wing chair. He held a glass filled with what looked like cognac. He'd been crying.

"John?"

Kuntz came over and took the glass from his hand. He checked the bottle and saw that too much of it was gone. "You can't be drinking like this."

"Where have you been?"

"I've been taking care of our problem."

The problem was both devastating and simple. Because of the somewhat religious connection to their product, the bank issuing the IPO had insisted on moral clauses, including one involving adultery. In short, if it got out that Larry Powers frequented a sugar babies website and had, in fact, used it to secure the sexual services of college students, bye-bye, IPO. Bye-bye, seventeen million dollars. Bye-bye, best health care for Robby. Bye-bye, trip to the Bahamas with Barb.

Bye-bye to it all.

"I got an e-mail from Kimberly," Larry said.

He started crying again.

"What did it say?"

"Her mother was murdered."

"She told you that?"

"Of course, she told me. Jesus, John, I know you—"

"Quiet."

The tone in his voice stopped Larry like a slap across the face.

"Just listen to me."

"It didn't have to be this way, John. We could have

started again. There might have been other opportunities. We would have been okay."

Kuntz just stared at him. Right, sure. Other opportunities. Easy for him to say. Larry's father had been a bond trader, made nice cash his whole life, sent his kid to an Ivy League school. Laurie came from huge money. Neither of them had a friggin' clue.

"We could have—"

"Stop talking, Larry."

He did so.

"What exactly did Kimberly say to you?"

"Not say. It was by e-mail. I told you. We never talk on the phone. And it's not my real e-mail. It's via my sugar babies account."

"Okay, good. What did her e-mail say?"

"That her mother had been killed. She thought it was some kind of breaking and entering."

"Probably was," Kuntz said.

Silence.

Then Larry sat up and said, "Kimberly isn't a threat. She doesn't even know my name."

Kuntz had already gone through the pros and cons of silencing Heidi's daughter, Kimberly, but in the end, he decided it would be more dangerous to kill her. Right now, the police would have absolutely no need to connect Heidi Dann's murder to Ingrid Prisby's. They were separated by more than four hundred miles. He had even used two different guns. But if suddenly something also happened to Heidi's daughter, that would draw too much attention.

Larry claimed that he did not use his real name with Kimberly. The site did a fairly good job of keeping the men's identities a secret. Sure, Kimberly might recognize him if his picture ended up in the paper, but they'd already decided to now make Larry the shy CEO and let the president do all the press when the IPO officially came out. And if she did make trouble later on, well, Kuntz would figure a way to handle it then.

Larry stood and started doing a drunk-stagger pace. "How did these people know about me?" he whined. "The site is anonymous."

"You had to pay for the services, right?"

"Yes, sure, with a credit card."

"Someone has to run the card, Larry. That's how they knew."

"And someone told Kimberly's mom about this?"

"Yes."

"Why?"

"Why do you think, Larry?"

"Blackmail?"

"Bingo."

"So let's just pay them."

Kuntz had considered that, but one, they hadn't yet approached them for anything, and two, it left too many loose ends. Blackmailers, especially ones who had a certain brand of fanaticism, were not reliable or trustworthy. He hadn't known enough about the threat when he first arrived in Ohio. What he did know was that Heidi Dann had been devastated by the news that her daughter had taken up something akin to prostitution. She knew the aliases of the johns, but luckily, she hadn't discussed that with her daughter. After some persuasion, Heidi had told Kuntz about the young couple approaching her outside Red Lobster. Kuntz had flashed his credentials at some kid who worked in the restaurant's security office, gotten the video of the young couple talking to Heidi, written down the license plate.

From there, it'd been easy. He got the name Lauren Barna from the rental car agency and connected it to Ingrid Prisby. Then he ran a trace on her credit card and found her staying at a motel near the Delaware Water Gap.

"So is that it?" Larry asked. "It's over, right?"

"Not yet."

"No more bloodshed. Please? I don't care if we lose the IPO. You can't hurt anyone else."

"You hurt your wife."

"What?"

"Cheating on her. You hurt her, right?"

Larry opened his mouth, closed it, tried again. "But . . . I mean, she's not dead. You can't compare the two."

"Sure I can. You hurt someone you love, yet you worry about strangers who are out to harm you."

"You're talking murder, John."

"I'm not talking anything, Larry. You are. I heard that Kimberly's mom died from a breaking and entering. That's a good thing, because if someone did her harm—say, someone who worked for you—that person could easily cut a deal and say he was just a hired hand. Are you following me?"

Larry said nothing.

"You got any other messes I need to clean up, Larry?"

"No," he said softly. "Nothing."

"Good. Because nothing is going to stop this IPO from coming together. You understand that?"

He nodded.

"Now stop drinking, Larry. Pull yourself together."

CHAPTER 41

WITH the two cops still standing at their door, Thomas and Ryan surprised Adam. They didn't protest or offer any resistance. They just quickly grabbed their stuff and got ready to go. They made a production of hugging and kissing their father good-bye. When Len Gilman smiled, slapped Ryan on the back, and said, "Your dad is just helping us with something," Adam managed not to roll his eyes. He told his boys not to worry and that he'd contact them the moment he knew what was up.

When the boys were gone, Adam walked down the path to the police cruiser. He wondered what the neighbors would think, but he really didn't give a crap. He tapped Len Gilman on the shoulder and said, "If this is about that stupid lacrosse money—"

"It's not," Len said, his voice a door slamming shut.

They didn't talk during the drive. Adam sat in the back. The other cop—young guy, hadn't introduced himself—drove, while Len Gilman sat in the passenger seat. Adam had figured they were headed to the Cedarfield police station on Godwin Road, but when they hit the highway, he realized that they were heading into Newark. They took Interstate 280 and pulled up to the county sheriff's office on West Market Street.

The car stopped. Len Gilman stepped out. Adam reached for the door handle, but there weren't any in the backseats of cop cars. He waited and let Len open the door for him. He stepped out. The car drove off.

"Since when do you work for the county?" Adam asked.

"They asked for a favor."

"What's going on, Len?"

"Just some questions, Adam. More than that, I can't tell you."

Len led him through the door and down a corridor. They entered an interrogation room.

"Have a seat."

"Len?"

"What?"

"I've been on the other side of this, so do me a favor. Don't make me wait too long, okay? It won't make me cooperative."

"Duly noted," Len said, closing the door behind him.

But he didn't listen. After Adam had sat there alone for an hour, he got up and pounded on the door. Len Gilman opened it. Adam spread his arms and said, "Really?"

"We aren't playing with you," Len said. "We're just waiting for someone."

"Who?"

"Give us fifteen minutes."

"Fine, but let me take a piss."

"No problem. I'll escort—"

"No, Len, I'm here voluntarily. I'll go to the bathroom by myself like a big boy."

He did his business, came back, sat in the chair, played

with his smartphone. He checked his texts again. Andy Gribbel had taken care of clearing his morning schedule. Adam looked at the address for Gabrielle Dunbar. She lived right near the center of Fair Lawn.

Would she be able to lead him to the stranger?

The interrogation room door finally opened. Len Gilman came in first, followed by a woman Adam would guess was in her early fifties. Her pantsuit was a hue that could best be described as institutional green. Her shirt collar was too long and pointy. Her hair was what they called wash-and-wear—a sort of brown shag-mullet that reminded Adam of hockey players in the seventies.

"Sorry to keep you waiting," the woman said.

Her accent was slight, maybe Midwestern—definitely not New Jersey. She had a rawboned face, the kind that reminded you of farmhands and square dances.

"My name is Johanna Griffin."

She reached out with a big hand. He shook it.

"I'm Adam Price, but I assume you know that."

"Please sit."

They sat across the table from each other. Len Gilman leaned against a far corner, trying like all get-out to look casual.

"Thanks for coming in this morning," Johanna Griffin said.

"Who are you?" Adam asked.

"Pardon me?"

"I assume you have a rank or . . ."

"I'm a police chief," she said. Then, after giving it some thought, "From Beachwood."

"I don't know Beachwood."

"It's in Ohio. Near Cleveland."

Adam hadn't expected that. He sat and waited for her to continue.

Johanna Griffin put a briefcase on the desk and snapped it open. She reached inside, and as she pulled out a photograph, she asked, "Do you know this woman?"

She slid the photograph across the table. It was an unsmiling head shot against a plain backdrop, probably off a driver's license. It took Adam a second, no more, to recognize the blond woman. He had seen her only once and it was dark and from a distance and she'd been driving a car. But he knew right away.

Still he hesitated.

"Mr. Price?"

"I might know who she is."

"Might?"

"Yes."

"And who *might* she be?"

He wasn't sure what to say here. "Why are you asking me this?"

"It's just a question."

"Yeah, and I'm just an attorney. So tell me why you want to know."

Johanna smiled. "So that's how you want to play it."

"I'm not playing it any way. I just want to know—"

"Why we are asking. We will get to that." She pointed to the photograph. "Do you know her, yes or no?"

"We've never met."

"Oh wow," Johanna Griffin said.

"What?"

"Now you're going to play semantics games with us? Do you know who she is, yes or no?"

"I think I do."

"Super, terrific. Who is she?"

"You don't know?"

"This isn't about what we know, Adam. And really, I don't have time, so let's cut to it. Her name is Ingrid Prisby. You paid John Bonner, a parking attendant at an American Legion Hall, two hundred dollars to give you her license plate number. You had that number traced by a retired police detective named Michael Rinsky. Do you want to tell us why you did all that?"

Adam said nothing.

"What's your connection to Ingrid Prisby?"

"No connection," he said carefully. "I just wanted to ask her something."

"Ask her what?"

Adam felt his head spin.

"Adam?"

It didn't escape his notice that she had moved from calling him Mr. Price to the more informal Adam. He glanced toward the corner. Len Gilman had his arms folded. His face was impassive.

"I was hoping she could help me with a confidential matter."

"Forget confidential, Adam." She reached into her briefcase again and produced another photograph. "Do you know this woman?"

She put down a picture of a smiling woman who looked to be about Johanna Griffin's age. Adam shook his head.

"No, I don't know her."

"Are you sure?"

"I don't recognize her."

"Her name is Heidi Dann." Johanna Griffin's voice was a little off now. "Does that name mean anything to you?"

"No."

Johanna locked eyes with him. "Be sure, Adam."

"I am. I don't know this woman. I don't recognize her name."

"Where's your wife?"

The sudden change of topics threw him.

"Adam?"

"What does my wife have to do with any of this?"

"You're full of questions, aren't you?" There was steel in her voice now. "That's getting really annoying. I understand that your wife is suspected of stealing a lot of money."

Adam glanced back toward Len. Still impassive. "Is that what this is about? False allegations?"

"Where is she?"

Adam considered his next move carefully. "She's traveling."

"Where?"

"She didn't say. What the hell is going on here?"

"I want to know—"

"I don't really care what you want to know. Am I under arrest?"

"No."

"So I can get up and go at any time, correct?"

Johanna Griffin glared at him. "That is right, yes."

"Just so we're clear, Chief Griffin."

"We are."

Adam sat up a little straighter, trying to press the advantage. "And now you're asking me about my wife. So either tell me what's going on right now or . . ."

Johanna Griffin took out another photograph.

She slid the photograph across the table without saying a word. Adam froze. He stared down at the photograph. No one moved. No one spoke. Adam felt his world teeter. He tried to right himself, tried to speak.

"Is this . . . ?"

"Ingrid Prisby?" Johanna finished for him. "Yes, Adam, that's Ingrid Prisby, the woman you *might* know."

Adam was having trouble breathing.

"According to the coroner, the cause of death was a bullet to the brain. But before that, what you're seeing there? In case you're wondering, we believe that the killer did that to her with a box cutter. We don't know how long she suffered."

Adam couldn't look away.

Johanna Griffin produced another photograph. "Heidi Dann was shot in the kneecap first. We don't know how long the killer tortured her either, but eventually, the same thing. A bullet to the brain."

Adam managed to swallow. "And you think . . . ?"

"We don't know what to think. We want to know what you know about this."

He shook his head. "Nothing."

"Really? Let me run down the chronology for you, then. Ingrid Prisby of Austin, Texas, flew into Newark airport from Houston. She stayed for one night alone at the Court-yard Marriott by the airport. While here, she rented a car and drove to the American Legion Hall in Cedarfield. There was a man in the car with her. That man talked to you inside the American Legion Hall. We don't know what was said, but we do know that sometime later, you paid off a parking attendant to get her license plate and presum-ably you tracked the two of them down. Meanwhile, Ingrid drove that same rental car all the way to Beachwood, Ohio, where she had a conversation with this woman."

With a shaking hand, with something that looked like barely controlled rage, Johanna Griffin put her finger on the photograph of Heidi Dann.

"Sometime after that, this woman, Heidi Dann, was

shot in the kneecap and then in the head. In her own home. Not long after—we are still putting the timetable together, but sometime between twelve and twenty-four hours later—Ingrid Prisby was mutilated and murdered in a motel room in Columbia, New Jersey, right near the Delaware Water Gap."

She sat back.

"So how do you fit in, Adam?"

"You can't possibly . . ."

But they did.

Adam needed time. He needed to get his head together and think it through and try to figure out what to do here.

"Does this have anything to do with your marriage?" Johanna Griffin asked.

He looked up. "What?"

"Len tells me you and Corinne had some difficulties a few years back."

Adam's eyes snapped to the corner. "Len?"

"Those were the rumors, Adam."

"So police work involves gossip?"

"Not just gossip," Johanna continued. "Who is Kristin Hoy?"

"What? She's my wife's close friend."

"And yours too, right? You two have been in communication a lot lately."

"Because—" He stopped himself.

"Because?"

Too much coming out too quickly. He wanted to trust the cops, but he just didn't. The cops had a theory here, and Adam knew that once a theory was formed, it was hard, if not impossible, to get them to see the facts and not twist them to suit what they already believed. Adam remembered how Old Man Rinsky had warned him not to talk to the police. The stakes had been upped, no question, but did that mean he had abandoned the idea of finding Corinne on his own?

He didn't know.

"Adam?"

"We were just talking about my wife."

"You and Kristin Hoy?"

"Yes."

"What about your wife?"

"About her recent . . . trip."

"Her trip. Oh, I see. You mean the one where she just left work in the middle of the day and never returned and now won't reply to your or your children's texts?"

"Corinne said she needed time," Adam said. "I assume, since you clearly went through my communications—and keep in mind I'm an attorney and some of the communications you intercepted could be construed as work product—you read that text too."

"Convenient."

"What?"

"Your wife's text to you. That whole thing about going away and not looking for her. Kinda gives a person time, don't you think?"

"What are you talking about?"

"Anyone could have sent that text, right? Even you."

"Why would I . . . ?"

He stopped.

"Ingrid Prisby was with a man at the American Legion Hall," Johanna said. "Who is he?"

"He never told me his name."

"What did he tell you?"

"It has nothing to do with this."

"Sure it does. Did he threaten you?"

"No."

"And you and Corinne have no marital issues, right?"

"I didn't say that. But it has nothing—"

"You want to tell us about meeting up with Sally Perryman last night?"

Silence.

"Is Sally Perryman another friend of your wife's?"

Adam stopped. He took deep breaths. Part of him wanted to come clean to Johanna Griffin. He really did. But right now, Johanna Griffin seemed hell-bent on nailing him or Corinne for whatever craziness was going on. He wanted to help. He wanted to know more about these murders, but he also knew the cardinal rule: You never have to take back words you don't say. He'd had a plan this morning. Go to Gabrielle Dunbar's house in Fair Lawn. Get the name of the stranger. He should stick with that plan. It wouldn't take long to drive there.

More important, it would give him a chance to think.

Adam stood. "I have to go."

"You're joking, right?"

"No. If you want my help, give me a few hours."

"There are two dead women here."

"I understand that," Adam said, moving toward the door. "But you're looking at this wrong anyway."

"How should we be looking at it?"

"The man who was traveling with Ingrid," Adam said, "the one at the American Legion Hall."

"What about him?"

"Do you know who he is?"

She glanced behind her at Len Gilman, then back at Adam. "No."

"No clue?"

"No clue."

Adam nodded. "He's the key to this. Find him."

CHAPTER 42

GABRIELLE Dunbar's house had probably been charming at one point, but over the years, the once-modest Cape Cod had been transformed into a bloated, character-less McMansion by additions and updates and purported "improvements." The newer architectural touches, like bay windows and turrets, distracted rather than enhanced—they gave the house an overly artificial feel.

Adam approached the ornate front door and rang a bell that played an elaborate tune. Not wanting to wait for the police to drive him back home, he'd used his Uber app to summon a car and get him here. Andy Gribbel was on his way to pick him up and take him to the office. Adam didn't expect this to take long.

Gabrielle answered the door. Adam recognized her from the Facebook photos. She had raven black hair so straight it had to be ironed. She had a welcoming smile on her face as she opened the door. The smile dissolved the moment she saw Adam.

"Can I help you?" she said.

Her voice had a quiver in it. She didn't open the screen door.

Adam dove in. "I'm sorry for just intruding like this,

but my name is Adam Price." He tried to hand her his business card, but the screen door was still closed. He slid it through the door. "I'm an attorney in Paramus."

Gabrielle stood there. The color was ebbing from her face.

"I'm working on an inheritance case and . . ." He held up his camera phone with the screen grab on it. He used his fingers to blow up the image, so she could see the stranger's face clearer. "Do you know this man?"

Gabrielle Dunbar slipped her fingers through the door and plucked out his business card. She stared at it for a long time. Then, finally, she turned her attention to the image on his iPhone. After a few seconds, she shook her head and said, "No."

"It was an office party, from the looks of it. Surely, you must—"

"I have to go now."

The quiver had grown toward something closer to panic or fear. She started to close the door.

"Ms. Dunbar?"

She hesitated.

Adam wasn't sure what to say exactly. He had spooked her. That was obvious to him. He had spooked her, and that meant that she had to know something.

"Please," he said. "I need to find this man."

"I told you. I don't know him."

"I think you do."

"Get off my property."

"My wife is missing."

"What?"

"My wife. This man did something, and now she's gone."

"I don't know what you're talking about. Please leave."

"Who is he? That's all I want to know. His name."

"I told you. I don't recognize him. Please, I have to go. I don't know anything."

The door started to close again.

"I won't stop looking. Tell him that. I won't stop until I find the truth."

"Get off my property, or I'll call the police."

She slammed the door shut.

GABRIELLE Dunbar paced for ten minutes, chanting the words *So Hum* over and over. She had learned this particular Sanskrit mantra at yoga. At the end of the class, her teacher would have them all lie on their backs in Corpse pose. She would have them close their eyes and repeat "So Hum" for five straight minutes. The first time the teacher had suggested this, Gabrielle had practically rolled her closed eyes. But then, somewhere around minute two or three, she began to feel the toxins of stress drain from her body.

"So . . . hum . . ."

She opened her eyes. It wasn't working. There were things she had to do first. Missy and Paul wouldn't be home from school for hours. That was good. That would give her time to prepare and pack. She grabbed her phone, scrolled through her favorites, hit the contact she called Douche Nozzle.

Two rings later, her ex answered. "Gabs?"

His nickname for her—he was the only one who called her that—still grated. When they first began dating, he started calling her "my Gabs" and she'd thought it was adorable in that way you do when you first fall in love and then, months later, the very sound of it made her gag.

"Can the kids stay with you?" she asked.

He didn't bother hiding his exasperation. "When?"

"I was thinking of dropping them off tonight."

"You're kidding, right? I've been asking you for extra visits—"

"And now I'm giving it to you. Can you take them tonight?"

"I'm in Chicago on business till the morning."

Damn it. "How about Whatshername?"

"You know her name, Gabs. Tami is here with me."

He had never taken Gabrielle on business trips, probably because he was meeting up with Tami or one of her predecessors. "Tami," Gabrielle repeated. "Does she dot the *i* or put a heart over it? I forget."

"Funny," he said. But it hadn't been, she knew. It had been stupid. There were much bigger fish to fry than a long-dead marriage. "We'll be back first thing in the morning."

"I'll drop them off then," she said.

"For how long?"

"A few days," she said. "I'll let you know."

"All okay, Gabs?"

"Peachy. Love to Tami."

Gabrielle hung up. She looked out the window. Part of her had known this day would come from the first time Chris Taylor had approached her. It was just a question of when. The whole enterprise had been enormously appealing, a win-win, revealing truths and making money, but she'd never forgotten the obvious: They were playing with fire. People will do anything to keep their secrets.

Even kill.

"So . . . hum . . ."

It still wasn't working. She headed up to her bedroom. Even though Gabrielle knew that she was alone in the house, she closed the door. She lay on her bed in a fetal position and started to suck her thumb. Embarrassing, but when the so-hums couldn't do the trick, reverting to something so primitive and infantile often did. She pulled up her knees tighter to her chest and let herself have a little cry. When she was done, she took out her mobile phone. She used a VPN for privacy. It wasn't foolproof, but for now, it would be enough. She read the business card again.

ADAM PRICE, ATTORNEY-AT-LAW

He had found her. And if he had found her, it made sense that he'd also been the one who found Ingrid.

To paraphrase that movie with Jack Nicholson, some people can't handle the truth.

Gabrielle reached into her bottom drawer and took out a Glock 19 Gen4 and laid it on the bed. Merton had given it to her, claiming it was the perfect handgun for women. He'd taken her out to a firing range in Randolph and taught her how to use it. It was loaded and ready to go. She'd been worried at first about keeping a loaded gun in the house with young children, but the possible threats had trumped standard home safety.

So what now?

Simple. Follow procedure. She snapped a photo of Adam Price's card with her iPhone. She attached the image to an e-mail and typed in two words before hitting SEND:

HE KNOWS

CHAPTER 43

ADAM left work early and drove to the new turf field at Cedarfield High School. The boys' lacrosse team was practicing. He parked down the block, out of sight, and watched his son Thomas from behind the bleachers. He had never done this before—watched a practice—and he probably couldn't articulate exactly what he was doing here. He just wanted to watch his son for a while. That's all. Adam remembered what Tripp Evans had said at the American Legion Hall the night this all started, how he couldn't believe how lucky those of them who lived in towns like this were:

"We're living the dream, you know."

Tripp was right, of course, but it was interesting how we described our personal paradise as a "dream." Dreams are fragile. Dreams don't last. One day you wake up and poof, the dream is gone. You stir and feel it pull away from you as you helplessly grab at the smoky remnants. But it's useless. The dream dissolves, gone forever. And standing there, watching his son play the game he loved, Adam couldn't help but feel that since the stranger's visit, they were all on the verge of waking up.

The coach blew the whistle and told everyone to take

a knee. They did so. A few minutes later, the boys took off their helmets and trudged back toward the locker room. Adam stepped out from behind the bleachers. Thomas stopped short when he saw him.

"Dad?"

"It's fine," Adam said. Then realizing that might be mis-interpreted to mean that Corinne was back, he added, "I mean, nothing new."

"Why are you here?"

"I got out of work early. I thought I'd give you a ride home."

"I need to shower first."

"No problem. I'll wait."

Thomas nodded and started back toward the locker room. Adam checked in on Ryan. He'd gone to Max's house straight from school. Adam texted him, asking whether he'd be ready to be picked up when Thomas was finished in or-der to save his old man another trip out. Ryan texted back "np," and it still took Adam a few moments to realize that meant "no problem."

In the car ten minutes later, Thomas asked him what the police wanted.

"It's really hard to explain right now," Adam said. "I'm not saying that to protect you, but for now, you're going to have to let me handle it."

"Does it have something to do with Mom?"

"I don't know."

Thomas didn't push it. They stopped and picked up Ryan. Ryan slipped into the backseat and said, "Oh, gross, what's that smell?"

"My lacrosse equipment," Thomas said.

"Nasty."

"Agreed," Adam said, lowering the windows. "How was school?"

"Good," Ryan said. Then: "Anything new on Mom?"

"Not yet." He debated saying more and then decided that some of the truth might offer comfort. "But the good news is, the police are involved now."

"What?"

"They're going to look for Mom too."

"The police," Ryan said. "Why?"

Adam gave a half shrug. "It's like Thomas said to me last night. This isn't like her. So they'll help us find her."

The boys, he was certain, would have follow-up questions, but as the car pulled onto their street, Ryan said, "Hey, who's that?"

Johanna Griffin sat on their front stoop. She stood as Adam turned into the driveway, smoothing out the institutional green pantsuit. She smiled and waved like a neighbor who'd stopped by to borrow sugar. Adam pulled the car to a stop as Johanna, still smiling, strolled casually and unthreateningly toward them.

"Hey, guys," she called out.

They all got out of the car. The boys looked wary.

"I'm Johanna," she said, shaking the boys' hands. Thomas and Ryan looked toward their father for answers.

"She's a police officer," he told them.

"Well, not officially when I'm here," Johanna said. "In Beachwood, Ohio, I'm known as Chief Griffin. But here, well, I'm out of my jurisdiction, so I'm just Johanna. Nice to meet you guys." She kept the smile up, but Adam knew it was just for show. The boys probably knew that too.

"Mind if I come in?" she asked Adam.

"Okay."

Thomas opened the back of the car and pulled out his lacrosse bag. Ryan strapped on a backpack ridiculously overstuffed with textbooks. As they headed toward the door, Johanna lingered behind. Adam stayed with her. When the boys were out of earshot, he simply said, "Why are you here?"

"We found your wife's car."

CHAPTER 44

ADAM and Johanna sat in the living room.

The boys were in the kitchen. Thomas had boiled up the water for pasta. Ryan microwaved a packet of frozen vegetables. It would hold them for now.

"So where did you find Corinne's car?" Adam asked.

"First off, I have to come clean."

"Meaning?"

"Meaning I meant what I said out there. I'm not a cop in New Jersey. Heck, I'm barely a cop back home. I don't do homicides. The county does them. And even if I did, I'm way out of my jurisdiction here."

"But they flew you out here to question me."

"No, I came out on my own dime. I knew a guy from Bergen who called a guy from Essex, and they extended me a courtesy by picking you up and bringing you in."

"Why are you telling me this?"

"Because the county guys back home heard about it and they got pissed. So I've been officially taken off the case."

"I'm not following. If this wasn't your case, why did you come out here at all?"

"Because one of the victims was a friend of mine."

Adam understood now. "That Heidi woman?"

"Yeah."

"I'm sorry for your loss."

"Thank you."

"So where was Corinne's car?"

"Nice change of subject," she said.

"You came to tell me."

"True."

"So?"

"At an airport hotel in Newark."

Adam made a face.

"What?"

"That makes no sense," he said.

"Why not?"

Adam explained about the locator app on the iPhone showing Corinne in Pittsburgh.

"She could have flown somewhere and rented a car," Johanna said.

"I'm not sure where you'd fly that you'd pick up a car and drive through Pittsburgh. And you said it was in a hotel parking lot?"

"Near the airport, right. We found it right before it got towed. I asked the tow company to deliver it back here, by the way. You should have it in an hour."

"I don't get something."

"What?"

"If she was taking a flight, Corinne would have just parked in the airport lot. That's what we always do."

"Not if she didn't want anyone to know where she was going. She might have figured that you'd look there."

He shook his head. "I'd look for her car in an airport parking lot? That makes no sense."

"Adam?"

"Yeah."

"I know you have no reason to trust me. But let's go off the record here for a second."

"You're a cop, not a reporter. You don't go off the record."

"Just listen to me, okay? Two women are dead. I won't go into how special Heidi was but . . . look, you need to come clean now. You need to tell me everything you know." She met his gaze and held it. "I promise you. I promise you on the soul of my dead friend that I won't use anything you say against you or your wife. I want justice for Heidi. That's all. Do you understand?"

Adam could feel himself squirming in his seat. "They can compel you to testify."

"They can try." She leaned forward. "Please help me."

He thought about it but not for long. There was no choice now. She was right. Two women were dead, and Corinne could be in serious trouble. He had no solid leads anymore, just an uneasy feeling about Gabrielle Dunbar.

"First," he said, "tell me what you know."

"I told you most of it."

"Tell me about how Ingrid Prisby is connected to your friend."

"Simple," Johanna said. "Ingrid and that guy showed up at a Red Lobster. They talked. The next day, Heidi was dead. A day after that, Ingrid was dead."

"Do you suspect the guy Ingrid was with?"

"I certainly think he can help us figure this out," Johanna said. "I assume they talked to you too, right? At that American Legion Hall."

"The guy did, yes."

"Did he tell you his name?"

Adam shook his head. "He just said he was the stranger."

"And after they left, you tried to find him. Or them. You got that parking lot attendant to give you their license plate. You tracked her down."

"I got her name," Adam said. "That was all."

"So what did the guy say to you at the American Legion Hall? This stranger?"

"He told me that my wife faked a pregnancy."

Johanna blinked twice. "Come again?"

Adam told her the story. Once he opened his mouth, it all just spilled out of him. When he was finished, Johanna asked him a question that seemed both obvious and surprising.

"Do you think it's true? Do you think she faked the pregnancy?"

"Yes."

Just like that. No hesitation. Not anymore. He had probably known the truth from the start—right from the moment the stranger first told him—but he'd needed the pieces to come together before he could voice it.

"Why?" Johanna asked.

"Why do I think it's true?"

"No, why do you think she'd do something like that?"

"Because I made her feel insecure."

She nodded. "That Sally Perryman woman?"

"Mostly, I guess. Corinne and I had grown distant. She feared losing me, feared losing all this. It doesn't matter."

"Actually, it might."

"How?"

"Humor me," Johanna said. "What was going on in your life when she went to that pregnancy-faking website?"

Adam couldn't see the point, but he also saw no reason not to tell her. "Like I said, we were growing apart. It's an old story, isn't it? We became all about the boys and the family logistics—who was going to do the food shopping, who was going to do the dishes, who was going to pay the bills. I mean, this is all such normal shit. Really. I was also going through a midlife crisis, I guess."

"You felt unappreciated?"

"I felt, I don't know, I felt like I wasn't a real man anymore. I know how that sounds. I was a provider and a father...."

Johanna Griffin nodded. "And suddenly there's this Sally Perryman paying you all kinds of attention."

"Not suddenly, but yeah, I start working on this great case with Sally, and she's beautiful and passionate and she looks at me the way Corinne used to look at me. I get how stupid it all sounds."

"Normal," Johanna said. "Not stupid."

Adam wondered whether she meant that or whether she was humoring him. "Anyway, I think Corinne was worried I'd leave. I didn't see it at the time, I guess, or maybe I didn't care, I don't know. But she had this tracker on my iPhone."

"The one that showed you she was in Pittsburgh?"

"Right."

"And you didn't know about it?"

He shook his head. "Not until Thomas showed me."

"Wow." Johanna shook her head. "So your wife was spying on you?"

"I don't know, maybe. That's what I think happened. I told her I was working late a bunch of times. Maybe she checked that tracker app and saw I was at Sally's more than I should have been."

"You didn't tell her where you were?"

He shook his head. "It was just work."

"So why not tell her?"

"Because, ironically enough, I didn't want her to worry. I knew how she'd react. Or maybe I knew on some level that it was wrong. We could have stayed in the office, but I liked being at her house."

"And Corinne found out."

"Yes."

"But nothing happened between you and Sally Perryman?"

"Right." Then thinking about it: "But maybe something was close to happening."

"What's that supposed to mean?"

"I don't know."

"Did you get physical? Second base? Third base?"

"What? No."

"You didn't kiss her?"

"No."

"So why the guilt?"

"Because I wanted to."

"Hell, I want to give Hugh Jackman a sponge bath. So what? You can't help what you want. You're human. Let it go."

He said nothing.

"So then your wife confronted Sally Perryman."

"She called her. I don't know if she confronted her."

"And Corinne never told you?"

"Right."

"She asked Sally what was going on, but she never did you that courtesy. That about right?"

"I guess."

"So then what?"

"Then, well, then Corinne got pregnant," Adam said.

"You mean, faked being pregnant."

"Right, whatever."

Johanna just shook her head and said, "Wow," again.

"It's not what you think."

"No, it's exactly what I think."

"The pregnancy startled me, you know? But in a good way. It brought me back. It reminded me of what was important. That's the other irony here. It worked. Corinne was right to do it."

"No, Adam. She wasn't right."

"It brought me back to reality."

"No, it didn't. She manipulated you. You'd probably have gotten back to reality anyway. And if you didn't, then maybe you weren't meant to. Sorry, but what Corinne did was bad. Really bad."

"I think maybe she felt desperate."

"That's not an excuse."

"This is her world. Her family. Her entire life. She fought so hard to build it, and it was being threatened."

Johanna shook her head. "You didn't do what she did, Adam. You know that."

"I'm guilty too."

"It isn't about guilt. You had a doubt. You had your head turned. You wondered about the what-if. You're not the first person to feel these things. You either find your way through it or you don't. But in the end, Corinne didn't give you that chance. She chose to trick you and live a lie. I'm not defending or condemning you. Every marriage is its own story. But you didn't see the light. You had someone shine a flashlight in your eyes."

"Maybe I needed that."

Johanna shook her head again. "Not like this. It was wrong. You have to see that."

He thought about it. "I love Corinne. I don't think the fake pregnancy really changed anything."

"But you'll never know."

"Not true," Adam said. "I've thought about this a lot."

"And you're certain you would have stayed?"

"Yes."

"For the kids?"

"In part."

"What else?"

Adam leaned forward and stared at the floor for a moment. It was a blue-and-yellow Oriental carpet he and Corinne had picked in an antiques store in Warwick. They'd gone up on an October day to pick apples, but they ended up just drinking some apple cider and buying McIntoshes and then they headed to an antiques store.

"Because whatever crap Corinne and I put each other through," he began, "whatever dissatisfaction or disappointments or resentments surface, at the end of the day, I can't imagine my life without her. I can't imagine growing old without her. I can't imagine not being part of her world."

Johanna rubbed her chin, nodding. "I get that. I do. My husband, Ricky, snores so bad it's like sleeping with a helicopter. But I feel the same."

They sat there for a moment, letting the feelings settle.

Then Johanna asked, "Why do you think the stranger told you about the fake pregnancy?"

"No clue."

"He didn't extort money?"

"No. He said he was doing it for me. He acted as

though he was on a holy crusade. How about your friend
Heidi? Did she fake a pregnancy too?"

"No."

"So I don't get it. What did the stranger tell her?"

"I don't know," Johanna said. "But whatever it was, it
got her killed."

"You have any thoughts?"

"No," Johanna said, "but now I think I might know
someone who does."

CHAPTER 45

HE KNOWS

Chris Taylor read the message and wondered yet again how and where this had all gone wrong. The Price job had been for hire. That might have been the mistake, though in most ways, the jobs for hire — and there had been only a handful — were the safest. The payments came from an emotionless third party, a top-level investigation firm. In a sense, it was more on the up-and-up, because there wasn't — and yes, Chris wasn't afraid to use the word — blackmail involved.

The normal protocol was simple: You know a terrible secret about a certain person via the Web. That person has two options. He or she can pay to have the secret kept or he can choose not to pay and have the secret revealed. Chris felt satisfied either way. The end result was either a profit (the person paid the blackmail) or cathartic (the person came clean). In a sense, they needed people to choose both. They needed the money to keep the operation going. They needed the truth to come out because that was what it was all about, what made their enterprise just and good.

A secret revealed is a secret destroyed.

Perhaps, Chris thought, that was the problem with the for-hire cases. Eduardo had pushed for those. They would, Eduardo claimed, work only with a select group of upscale security companies. There would be safety, ease, and always a profit. The way it worked was also deceptively simple: The firm would put out a name. Eduardo would check through their data banks to see if there was a hit—in this case, there was one for Corinne Price via Fake-A-Pregnancy.com. Then a figure would be paid and the secret revealed.

But that meant, of course, that Corinne Price never got the chance to choose. Yes, the secret was revealed in the end. He had told Adam Price the truth. But he had done so strictly for cash. The secret keeper had not been given the option of redemption.

That wasn't right.

Chris used the all-encompassing term *secret*, but really, they weren't just secrets. They were lies and cheats and worse. Corinne Price had lied to her husband when she faked her pregnancy. Kimberly Dann had lied to her hard-working parents about how she was earning cash for college. Kenny Molino had cheated with steroids. Michaela's fiancé, Marcus, had done worse when he set up both his roommate and eventual wife with that revenge tape.

Secrets, Chris believed, were cancers. Secrets festered. Secrets ate away at your innards, leaving behind nothing but a flimsy husk. Chris had seen up close the damage secrets could do. When Chris was sixteen years old, his beloved father, the man who had taught him how to ride a bike and walked him to school and coached his Little League team, had unearthed a terrible, long-festering secret.

He wasn't Chris's biological father.

A few weeks before their marriage, Chris's mother had one last fling with an ex-boyfriend and gotten pregnant. His mother had always suspected the truth, but it wasn't until Chris was hospitalized after a car accident and his father, his beloved father, had tried to donate blood that the truth finally came out.

"My whole life," Dad had told him, "has been one big lie."

Chris's father had tried to do the "right thing" then. He had reminded himself that a father is not merely a sperm donor. A father is there for his child, provides for his child, loves and cares and raises him. But in the end, the lie had just festered too long.

Chris hadn't seen the man in three years. That was what secrets did to people, to families, to lives.

After Chris finished college, he'd landed a job at an Internet start-up called Downing Place. He liked it there. He thought he'd found a home. But for all the company's fancy talk, it was really just a facilitator of the worst kind of secrets. Chris ended up working for one particular site called Fake-A-Pregnancy.com. The company lied, even to itself, pretending that people bought the silicone bellies as "gag" gifts or costume parties or other "novelty funsy" rationales. But they all knew the truth. Someone might, in theory, go to a party dressed as someone pregnant. But fake sonograms? Fake pregnancy tests? Who were they fooling?

It was wrong.

Chris realized right away that it would make no sense to expose the company. That was simply too big a task and, as bizarre as it seemed, Fake-A-Pregnancy had competitors. All of these sites did. And if you went after one, the others would just grow stronger. So Chris remembered a lesson that, ironically, his "father" had taught him as a young child: You do what you can. You save the world one person at a time.

He found a few like-minded people in similar businesses, all with the same access to secrets that he had. Some were much more interested in the moneymaking side of the venture. Others understood that what they were doing was right and just, and while Chris didn't want to make it into some kind of religious crusade, there was an aspect of his new operation that felt like a moral quest.

In the end, the core group had been five—Eduardo, Gabrielle, Merton, Ingrid, and Chris. Eduardo had wanted to do everything online. Make the threat online. Reveal the secret via an untraceable e-mail. Keep it completely anonymous. But Chris didn't agree. What they were doing, like it or not, was devastating people. You were changing lives in a flash. You could dress it up all you wanted, but the person was one thing before his visit, and something entirely different after. You needed to do that face-to-face. You needed to do that with compassion and with a human touch. The secret protectors were faceless websites, machines, robots.

They would be different.

Chris read Adam Price's business card and Gabrielle's short message again: HE KNOWS

In a sense, the shoe had been put on the other foot. Chris now had a secret, didn't he? But no, his was different. His secret was not for the sake of deception but protection—or was that just what he told himself? Was he, like so many of the people he encountered, simply rationalizing the secret?

Chris had known that what they were doing was dangerous, that they were making enemies, that some would not understand the good and want to retaliate or continue to live in their "secrets" bubble.

Now Ingrid was dead. Murdered.

HE KNOWS

And so the response was obvious: He had to be stopped.

CHAPTER 46

KIMBERLY Dann's dorm room was in a seemingly ultrahip section of Greenwich Village in New York City. Beachwood wasn't Hicksville, not even close. Many of their residents had migrated from New York City, wanting to escape the hustle and bustle and live a somewhat more financially comfortable life in a place with lower property values and tax rates. But Beachwood certainly wasn't Manhattan, either. Johanna had done enough traveling—this was her sixth time here—to know that there was no place like this isle. The city did indeed sleep and rest and all that, but when you are here, your senses were always alive. You were plugged in. You felt the constant surges and crackles.

The door flung open the moment Johanna knocked, as though Kimberly had been standing by the door, hand on the knob, waiting.

"Oh, Aunt Johanna!"

Tears streamed down Kimberly's face. She collapsed onto Johanna and sobbed. Johanna held her up and let her cry. She stroked her hair down to her back the way she'd seen Heidi do a dozen times, like when Kimberly fell at the zoo and scraped her knee or when that jerk

Frank Velle down the block had taken back his invitation to the prom because he was "upgrading" to Nicola Shindler.

Holding her friend's daughter, Johanna felt her own heart start to break anew. She closed her eyes and made what she hoped were comforting shushing sounds. She didn't say, "It's going to be okay," or offer false words of comfort. She just held her and let her cry. Then Johanna let herself cry too. Why not? Why the hell pretend that this wasn't crushing her too?

What Johanna needed to do would come soon enough. Let them both have their cries in the meantime.

After some time had passed, Kimberly let go and took a step back. "I got my bag," she said. "When is our flight?"

"Let's sit and talk first, okay?"

They looked for places to sit, but since this was a dorm room, Johanna took the corner of the bed while Kimberly collapsed on what looked like an upscale beanbag chair. It was true that Johanna had come on her own dime to interrogate Adam Price, but she was here for more than that. She'd promised Marty that she'd accompany Kimberly back home for Heidi's funeral. "Kimmy's so upset," Marty had said. "I don't want her traveling alone, you know?"

Johanna knew.

"I need to ask you something," Johanna said.

Kimberly was still drying her face. "Okay."

"The night before your mom was killed, you two talked on the phone, right?"

Kimberly started to cry again.

"Kimberly?"

"I miss her so much."

"I know you do, honey. We all do. But I need you to focus for a second, okay?"

Kimberly nodded through the tears.

"What did you and your mom talk about?"

"What difference does it make?"

"I'm looking into who murdered her."

Kimberly started to cry again.

"Kimberly?"

"Didn't Mom interrupt a robbery?"

That was one of the county boys' hypotheses. Drug fiends desperate for money had broken in, and before they could find anything of value, Heidi had interrupted them and gotten killed for her trouble.

"No, honey, that's not what happened."

"Then what?"

"That's what I'm trying to figure out. Kimberly, listen to me. Another woman was murdered by the same person."

Kimberly blinked like someone had whacked her with a two-by-four. "What?"

"I need you to tell me what you and your mom talked about."

Kimberly's eyes started dancing around the room. "It was nothing."

"I don't believe that, Kimberly."

Kimberly started crying again.

"I checked the phone records. You and your mom exchanged a bunch of texts, but you've only talked on the phone three times this semester. The first call lasted six minutes. The second, only four. But the night before she was murdered, the call between you two lasted more than two hours. What did you two talk about?"

"Please, Aunt Johanna, it doesn't matter anymore."

"Like hell it doesn't." There was steel in Johanna's voice now. "Tell me."

"I can't...."

Johanna dropped off the bed and knelt in front of Kimberly. She took the girl's face in her hands and forced her to look directly at her. "Look at me."

It took some time, but Kimberly did.

"Whatever happened to your mother, it's not your fault. You hear me? She loved you and she would want you to go on and live the best life you can. I'll be there for you. Always. Because that's what your mother would have wanted. Do you hear me?"

The girl nodded.

"So now," Johanna said, "I need you to tell me about her last phone call."

CHAPTER 47

ADAM watched from what he hoped was a safe distance as Gabrielle Dunbar hurriedly packed a suitcase in the trunk of her car.

A half hour ago, Adam had decided to take one more run at Gabrielle on his way to work. But as he turned down her street, Gabrielle Dunbar was throwing a suitcase in the trunk. Her two children—Adam estimated them to be about twelve and ten—lugged smaller bags. He pulled his car to the side, kept a safe distance, and watched.

So now what?

The night before, Adam had tried to reach out to the other three people Gribbel had been able to identify and locate in that photograph on Gabrielle Dunbar's page. None gave him anything useful on the stranger. No surprise. Whatever line of bull he threw at them, they were all naturally wary of a "stranger"—yep, irony strikes again—asking them in one fashion or another to identify a person, possibly a friend or coworker, from a group photograph. None of them lived close enough for Adam to chance, as he had with Gabrielle, confronting them in person.

So his mind went back to Gabrielle Dunbar.

She was hiding something. That much had been obvious to him yesterday—and suddenly she was rushing out of the house again with her third suitcase.

Coincidence?

He didn't think so. He stayed in his car and watched. Gabrielle threw the bag into the trunk and struggled to slam it closed. She swept her children into the car, both in the backseat, and made sure they were strapped in. She opened her own door, paused, and then Gabrielle looked down the street right at him.

Damn.

Adam quickly slid down in the driver's seat. Had she spotted him? He didn't think so. Or if she had, would she know who he was from this distance? And hold up, so what if she had? He had come here to confront her, right? He raised himself back up slowly, but Gabrielle wasn't looking in his direction anymore. She'd gotten into the car and had started moving.

Man, he was no good at this.

Gabrielle's car started down the block. Adam thought about his next move but not for very long. In for a penny, in for a pound. Adam shifted into drive and started to follow.

He wasn't sure how far to stay back so that she wouldn't see him and yet he wouldn't lose her. All of his knowledge on this subject had come from a lifetime of watching TV. Would anyone even know what a tail was if they hadn't watched television? She turned right. Adam followed. They started toward Route 208 and then down Interstate 287. Adam checked his gas tank. Nearly full. Okay, good. Just how long did he plan on following her anyway? And when he caught up, what exactly did he plan on doing then?

One step at a time.

His cell phone rang. He glanced down and saw the name JOHANNA pop up.

He had programmed her phone number into his smartphone after her visit last night. Did he fully trust her? Pretty much, yeah. She had a simple agenda: Find her friend's killer. As long as that wasn't Corinne, Johanna could be, he thought, an asset and even an ally. If the killer was Corinne, then he had bigger problems than trusting a cop from Ohio.

"Hello?"

"I'm about to board a plane," Johanna said.

"Heading back home?"

"I'm already back home."

"In Ohio?"

"At the Cleveland airport, yeah. I had to take Heidi's daughter home, but I'm flying back out to Newark in a few. What are you up to?"

"I'm tailing Gabrielle Dunbar."

"Tailing?"

"Isn't that what you cops call it when you follow someone?"

He quickly explained how he came to her house and saw her packing up.

"So what's your plan here, Adam?"

"I don't know. I can't just sit around and do nothing."

"Fair point."

"Why did you call?"

"I learned something last night."

"I'm listening."

"Whatever is happening here," she said, "this isn't just about one website."

"I don't understand."

"This stranger guy. He doesn't just tell his victims

about their wives faking pregnancies. He has access to other sites. Or at least one other site."

"How do you know this?"

"I talked to Heidi's daughter."

"So what was the secret?"

"I promised I wouldn't tell—and you don't need to know, trust me on that. The key thing is, your stranger may be blackmailing a whole slew of people for a variety of reasons, not just for faking a pregnancy."

"So what do we think is going on here exactly?" Adam asked. "This stranger and Ingrid were blackmailing people about what they do online?"

"Something like that, yeah."

"So why is my wife missing?"

"Don't know."

"And who killed your friend? And Ingrid?"

"Don't know and don't know. Maybe something went wrong with the blackmail. Heidi was tough. Maybe she stood up to them. Maybe the stranger and Ingrid had a falling-out."

Up ahead, Gabrielle was pulling off an exit to Route 23. Adam hit his turn signal and stayed with her.

"So what's the connection between your friend and my wife?"

"Other than the stranger, I don't see any."

"Hold up," Adam said.

"What?"

"Gabrielle's pulling into a driveway."

"Where?"

"Lockwood Avenue in Pequannock."

"That's in New Jersey?"

"Yeah."

Adam wasn't sure whether he should stay back and

stop suddenly or drive past and find a spot to pull over. He opted for the latter, cruising by the yellow split-level with the aluminum siding and red shutters. A man opened the front door, smiled, and strolled toward Gabrielle's car. Adam didn't recognize him. The car doors opened. The girl came out of the car first. The man gave her an awkward hug.

"So what's going on?" Johanna asked.

"False alarm, I guess. Looks like she's dropping her kids off at her ex's place."

"Okay, they're calling my flight. I'll call you when I land. Don't do anything stupid in the meantime."

Johanna hung up. Now Gabrielle's son got out of the car. Another awkward hug. The man who might have been the ex waved at Gabrielle. She may have waved back, but he couldn't tell from here. A woman appeared at the doorway. A younger woman. A *much* younger woman. An old story, Adam thought. Gabrielle stayed in the car as the probable ex opened the trunk. He took out one of the suitcases and closed it again. He started back toward the front of the car with a puzzled look on his face.

Gabrielle hit reverse and pulled out before he could reach her. She started driving back down the street.

With a lot of luggage still in her car.

So where was she going?

In for a penny . . .

Adam saw no reason not to keep following her.

CHAPTER 48

GABRIELLE'S car climbed up Skyline Drive into the Ramapo Mountains. The road was only forty-five minutes from Manhattan, but it might as well have been in another world. There were legends about the tribes who still lived in this area. Some called them the Ramapough Mountain Indians or the Lenape Nation or the Lunaape Delaware Nation. Some believed the people were Native American. Others claimed that they dated back to Dutch settlers. Still others thought they were Hessian soldiers who fought for the British during the American Revolution or were freed slaves who found a home in the barren woods in northern New Jersey. Many, too many, had dubbed them, perhaps derogatorily, the Jackson Whites. The origin of that name also remained a mystery but probably had something to do with their multiracial appearance.

As is always the case with such people, scary stories surrounded them. Teenagers drove up Skyline Drive and scared one another with tales of kidnappings, of being dragged into the woods, of ghosts crying out for revenge. It was all myth, of course, but myth can be a powerful thing.

Where the hell was Gabrielle going?

They were heading into the wooded areas of the mountains. The elevation was causing Adam's ears to clog up. She cut back onto Route 23. Adam followed her nearly an hour, until she crossed the narrow Dingman's Ferry Bridge into Pennsylvania. The roads were less traveled now. Adam again wondered how far to stay behind in order not to be spotted. He erred against caution, figured that it would be better to be spotted and possibly confronted than to lose Gabrielle altogether.

He checked his phone. The battery was low. Adam stuck the phone into his glove compartment charger. A mile farther up the road, Gabrielle took a right. The woods grew denser. She slowed and turned onto what looked like a dirt driveway. A faded stone sign read LAKE CHARMAINE — PRIVATE. Adam veered to the right and stopped behind an evergreen. He couldn't just pull his car into the driveway, if indeed it was a driveway.

So what was his next move?

He opened the glove compartment and checked the phone. The battery hadn't had much of a chance to charge, but it was still hovering at ten percent. That could be enough. He pocketed it and got out of his car. Now what? Just walk up to this Lake Charmaine and ring the bell?

He found an overgrown path in the woods running parallel to the driveway. That would do. The sky above him was a beautiful robin's-egg blue. Branches jutted into the pathway, but Adam pushed through them. The woods were silent, save for the sounds Adam himself was causing. He stopped every once in a while to listen for . . . for anything, but now, as he got deeper into the woods, he couldn't even hear the passing cars on the road anymore.

When Adam stepped into a clearing, he saw a buck nibbling on some leaves. The buck looked up at Adam, saw he meant no harm, went back to nibbling. Adam kept moving, and soon the lake rose before him. Under other circumstances, he would have loved being up here. The lake was as still as a mirror, reflecting the green of the trees and the robin's-egg blue of the sky. The view was intoxicating and soothing and so damned peaceful, and man oh man, would it be wonderful to just sit down and stare at it for a little while. Corinne loved lakes. The ocean scared her a bit. Waves, in her view, were often violent and unpredictable. But lakes were quiet paradise. Before the boys were born, he and Corinne had rented a lake house in northern Passaic County. He remembered lazy days, both of them sharing a humungo hammock, him with a newspaper, her with a book. He remembered watching Corinne read, the way her eyes would narrow as they crossed the page, a look of pure concentration on her face—and then, every once in a while, Corinne would look up from her book. Corinne would smile at him and he would smile back and then their gaze would drift to the lake.

A lake like this one.

He spotted a house on the right. It looked abandoned except for one car sitting in front of it.

Gabrielle's.

The house was either a log cabin or one of those snap-together facsimiles. Hard to tell from here. Adam carefully padded down the hill, ducking behind trees and shrubbery as he went. He felt foolish, like a kid playing capture the flag or paintball or something. He tried to think of another time in his life when he had done this, when he'd had to sneak up on someone, and his mind had to travel all the way back to the Y summer camp when he was eight.

Adam still wasn't sure what he'd do when he got close to the house, but for a split second, he wished he was armed. He didn't own a handgun or anything like that. Maybe that was a mistake. His uncle Greg had taken him shooting a few times when he was in his early twenties. He liked it and knew that he could handle a weapon. In hindsight, that would have been the smart play. He was dealing with dangerous people. Killers, even. He reached into his pocket and felt for his phone. Should he call someone? He didn't know who or even what to say. Johanna would still be on her flight. He could text or call Andy Gribbel or Old Man Rinsky, but what would he tell them?

Where you are, for one thing.

He was about to grab his phone and do just that when he spotted something that made him freeze.

Gabrielle Dunbar stood alone in the clearing. She was staring right at him. He felt the rage build up inside him. He took a step closer, expecting her to run off or say something. She didn't.

She just stood there and watched him.

"Where's my wife?" he shouted.

Gabrielle kept staring.

Adam took another step into the clearing. "I said—"

Something smacked him so hard in the back of the head that Adam could actually feel his brain jarring loose from its moorings. He dropped to his knees, seeing stars. Working on pure instinct, Adam somehow managed to turn and look up. A baseball bat was coming down on the top of his skull like an axe. He tried to duck or turn away or at least lift a protective arm.

But it was much too late.

The bat landed with a dull thud, and everything went dark.

CHAPTER 49

JOHANNA Griffin was a natural rule follower, so she didn't turn off the airplane mode on her smartphone until they'd stopped moving on the active runway. The flight attendant made the standard "welcome to Newark where the temperature is" announcement as Johanna's texts and e-mails loaded up.

Nothing from Adam Price.

The past twenty-four hours had been exhausting. Kimberly had been hysterical. Extracting her horrible story had been painstaking and time-consuming. Johanna had tried to be understanding, but what on God's green earth had that kid been thinking? Poor Heidi. How had she reacted to the news about her daughter and that horrible website? Johanna thought back to that videotape of Heidi in the Red Lobster parking lot. Heidi's body language made complete sense now. In a way, Johanna had been watching an assault on that tape. That guy, that goddamn stranger, was pummeling her friend with his words, breaking her heart with his revelations.

Did he comprehend the damage he was wreaking?

So Heidi had gone home after that. She had called Kimberly and gotten her daughter to tell the truth. She had stayed rational and calm, even as she withered away inside. Or maybe Heidi hadn't withered away. Maybe, because Heidi was the least judgmental person Johanna had ever known, she had dealt with the bad news and was ready to fight back. Who knew? Heidi had comforted her daughter. She had then tried to figure a way of removing her from the terrible mess she had gotten herself into.

And maybe that had gotten her killed.

Johanna still didn't know what had happened to Heidi, but clearly it was somehow connected to the revelation that her daughter had become a whore—forget the more marketable terms like *sugar baby*—for three different men. Johanna had started to dig into it, but that would take time. Kimberly didn't know the men's real names, which was another wow, but hey, there was a reason they were called johns. Johanna had spoken to the president of the sugar babies website, listened to her rationalizations, and wanted to take a long, hot shower after she hung up. She—yes, in a nice feminist touch, the site was run by a woman—defended her company's "business arrangements" and her clients' "right to privacy" and said there was no way she would reveal any information without a court order.

Since the company was located in Massachusetts, that would take time.

Then, after dealing with this crap, the annoyed county homicide cops wanted a full debriefing on Johanna's renegade trip to New Jersey. This wasn't about ego for her. She wanted the bastard who killed her friend caught. Period. So she told them everything, including what Kimberly had just told her, and now those guys were getting the court order and putting manpower toward figuring out who the stranger was and what his connection to the murders might be.

All of that was good. But it didn't mean Johanna was taking herself off the case.

Her cell phone rang. She didn't recognize the number, but the area code was 216, which meant the call was from someone close to home. She picked up and said hello.

"This is Darrow Fontera."

"Who?"

"I'm the head of security for Red Lobster. We met when you asked for surveillance footage."

"Yes, right. What can I do for you?"

"I asked you to return the DVD when you were done."

Was this guy for real? Johanna opened her mouth to tell him to go pound sand, but then she thought better of it. "We aren't done with the investigation yet."

"Could you please make a copy, then, and return the original DVD to us?"

"What's the big deal?"

"That's protocol." The tone was pure bureaucrat. "We provide one DVD copy only. If others are needed—"

"I only took one copy."

"No, no, you were the second."

"Pardon?"

"The other police officer got a copy before you."

"Wait, what other police officer?"

"We took a scan of his ID. He'd retired from New York, but he said . . . oh, wait, here it is. His name is Kuntz. John Kuntz."

CHAPTER 50

FIRST came the pain.

For a few moments, the pain shut out everything else. It was all-consuming, driving out any sort of awareness about where Adam might be or what had happened to him. His skull felt as if it'd been cracked into bone fragments, the jagged edges floating around and tearing through brain tissue. Adam kept his eyes closed and tried to ride it out.

Second came the voices.

"When's he going to wake up?" . . . *"You didn't have to hit so hard."* . . . *"I wasn't taking a chance."* . . . *"You got the gun, right?"* . . . *"Suppose he doesn't regain consciousness."* . . . *"Hey, he came here to kill us, remember?* . . . *"Hold up, I think he's moving. . . ."*

Awareness started to creep in, clawing its way past the pain and numbness. He was lying on cold ground, his right cheek on a rough, hard floor. Concrete maybe. Adam tried to open his eyes, but it felt like spiders had spun webs across them. When he blinked hard, a fresh surge of pain nearly made him gasp out loud.

When his eyes finally did open, he saw a pair of Adidas sneakers. He tried to remember what had happened.

He'd been following Gabrielle. He remembered that now. He'd been following her to a lake and then. . . .

"Adam?"

He knew that voice. He had heard it only once before, but it had echoed in his head ever since. With his cheek still on the concrete, he forced his gaze upward.

The stranger.

"Why did you do it?" the stranger asked him. "Why did you kill Ingrid?"

THOMAS Price was taking a test in AP English class when the classroom phone rang. His teacher, Mr. Ronkowitz, picked up the phone, listened for a moment, and then said, "Thomas Price, please go to the principal's office."

His classmates, like millions of classmates have done all over the world a million times over, made an "ooo, you're in trouble" noise as he grabbed his books, stuffed them in his backpack, and headed out. The corridor was empty now. That always felt odd to Thomas, an empty high school corridor, like a ghost town or haunted house. His footsteps echoed as he hurried toward the office. He had no idea what this meant, if it was good or bad, but you rarely get called down to the principal's office for nothing, and when your mom had decided to run off and your dad was coming unglued, your mind imagines all kinds of horrifying scenarios.

Thomas still couldn't figure out what had gone wrong with his parents, but he knew that it was bad. Big-time bad. He also knew that Dad hadn't told him the full truth yet. Parents always think it's best to "protect" you, even though by "protect," they mean "lie." They think they're helping by shielding you, but in the end, it makes it worse. It's like

Santa Claus. When Thomas had first realized that Santa Claus wasn't real, he didn't think, "I'm growing up" or "That stuff is for babies" or any of that. His first thought was more basic: "My parents lied to me. My mom and dad looked me in the eye, and for years and years, they lied to me."

What's that supposed to do for long-term trust?

Thomas had hated the whole idea of Santa Claus anyway. What was the point? Why do you tell kids that some weird fat guy who lives at the North Pole watches them all the time? Sorry, that's just creepy. Even as a child, Thomas remembered sitting on a mall Santa's lap and he smelled a little like piss and Thomas thought, "This guy is the one who brings me toys?" And why tell kids that anyway? Wouldn't it be nicer to think your parents, who worked hard, gave you those presents instead of some creepy stranger?

Whatever was going on now, Thomas just wished that his dad would come clean. It couldn't be worse than what Thomas and Ryan had been imagining. He and his brother weren't stupid. Thomas could see that his dad had been tense even before Mom ran off. He had no idea why, but since Mom got back from that teachers' conference, something had been really wrong. Their house was like a living thing, like one of those delicate ecosystems in science, and now something foreign was throwing off everything.

When Thomas opened the office door, that lady police officer, Johanna, was standing with the principal, Mr. Gorman. Mr. Gorman said, "Thomas, do you know this woman?"

He nodded. "She's a friend of my dad's. She's also a police officer."

"Yes, she showed me her ID. But I can't leave you alone with her."

Johanna said, "That's okay," and stepped toward him. "Thomas, do you have any idea where your father is?"

"At work, I guess."

"He didn't show today. I tried his cell phone. It's going straight to voice mail."

That little pang of panic in his chest started to grow. "It only does that if someone switches the phone off," Thomas said. "Dad never switches it off."

Johanna Griffin came closer. He could see the look of concern in her eyes. It scared him, and yet this was what he wanted, right? Honesty instead of protection? "Thomas, your dad told me about the tracker your mom put on his phone."

"It won't work if the phone is dead."

"But it shows where he last was when the phone was turned off, right?"

Thomas got it now. "Right."

"Do you need a computer to access—?"

He shook his head, reaching into his pocket. "I can look it up on my phone. Just give me two minutes."

CHAPTER 51

WHY did you kill Ingrid?"

When Adam tried to sit up, tried even to peel his face off the concrete — where was he anyway, that log cabin? — his head screamed in protest. He tried to bring his hands to his skull, but they wouldn't move. Confused, Adam tried again and heard the rattling.

His wrists were tied.

He looked behind him. A bike chain had been wrapped around his wrists and threaded behind a pipe running from the floor to the ceiling. He tried to take stock of the situation. He was in a basement. Directly in front of him, still wearing the same baseball cap, was the stranger. Gabrielle stood on the stranger's right. A young guy, not much older than Thomas probably, was on the left. The kid had a shaved head and tattoos and too many piercings.

He was holding a gun.

Behind the three of them was another man, maybe thirtyish, with long hair and the start of a beard.

"Who are you?" Adam asked.

The stranger took that one. "I told you before, didn't I?"

Adam tried again to sit up. The bolts of pain nearly paralyzed him, but he dodged past them. There was no way he could stand. Between the pain in his head and the chains on his wrists, there was nowhere to go anyway. He sat now and leaned against the pipe.

"You're the stranger," Adam said.

"Yes."

"What do you want with me?"

The kid with the gun stepped forward and aimed the weapon at Adam. He turned the gun sideways, like something he'd seen in a bad gangsta film, and said, "You don't start talking, I'm going to blow your head off."

The stranger said, "Merton."

"Nah, man. We don't have time for this. He needs to start talking."

Adam looked up at the gun. He looked into Merton's eyes. He'd do it, Adam thought. He'd fire and not think twice.

It was Gabrielle who spoke next. "Put that gun away."

Merton ignored her. He stared down at Adam. "She was my friend."

He pointed the gun at Adam's face.

"Why did you kill Ingrid?"

"I didn't kill anyone."

"Bullshit!"

Merton's hand started shaking.

Gabrielle: "Merton, don't."

With the gun still pointed at Adam's face, Merton reeled back and kicked him like he was attempting a field goal from long range. He wore steel-toed boots and the blow landed right on the delicate spot on the bottom of Adam's rib cage. He let out an *oomph* sound and slumped over.

"Stop that," the stranger snapped.

"He's gotta tell us what he knows!"

"He will."

"What are we going to do?" Gabrielle asked, her voice in full panic. "This was supposed to be easy money."

"It is. We're fine. Just calm down."

The guy with the long hair said, "I don't like this. I don't like any of it."

Gabrielle: "I didn't sign up for kidnapping."

"Will you all just stay calm?" But even the stranger now sounded on edge. "We need to find out what happened to Ingrid."

Adam winced and said, "I don't know what happened to Ingrid."

They all turned toward him.

"You're a liar," Merton said.

"You need to listen to—"

Merton cut him off with another kick to the ribs. Adam's face landed back on the hard concrete. He tried to crawl into a protective ball, tried again to free his hands so that they could cradle his aching head.

"Stop it, Merton!"

"I didn't kill anyone," Adam managed.

"Right, sure." It was Merton. Adam tried to tighten up his protective ball in case another kick was coming. "And I suppose you didn't ask Gabrielle about Chris either, right?"

Chris. He knew the man's first name.

"Back up," Chris—the stranger—said. He moved closer to Adam and said, "You started searching for Ingrid and me, right?"

Adam nodded.

"And you found Ingrid first."

"Just her name."

"What?"

"I found her name."

"How?"

"Where's my wife?"

Chris frowned. "Excuse me?"

"I said—"

"No, I heard you." He looked back toward Gabrielle. "Why would we know where your wife is?"

"You started this," Adam said. He struggled up into a sitting position. He knew that he was in deep trouble here, that his life was in danger, but he also knew that these people were amateurs. The stench of their fear was everywhere. The bike chain was loosening. He was starting to work his wrists free. That might help, if he could get Merton and his gun close. "You came at me first."

"So, what, you wanted revenge? Is that what this is about?"

"No," Adam said. "But I know what you do now."

"Oh?"

"You learn something compromising about a person. Then you blackmail them."

"You're wrong," Chris said.

"You blackmailed Suzanne Hope about her faking a pregnancy. When she didn't pay up, you told her husband, just like you told me."

"How did you know about Suzanne Hope?"

Merton, who was the most frightened and thus the most dangerous of all of them, shouted, "He's been spying on all of us!"

"She was friends with my wife," Adam said.

"Ah, I should have seen that," Chris said with a nod. "So Suzanne Hope was the one who referred Corinne to the site?"

"Yes."

"What Suzanne did—what your wife did—it's a horrible thing, don't you think? You see, the Internet makes it easy to be deceptive. The Internet makes it easy to be anonymous and to lie and to keep terrible, destructive secrets from your loved ones. We"—he opened his hand, indicated his group—"are just evening the playing field a little bit."

Adam almost smiled. "Is that what you tell yourself?"

"It's the truth. Take your wife, for example. The Fake-A-Pregnancy site, like all those sites, promises to be discreet, and she thought because it's online and makes that silly promise that no one would ever know. But do you really believe anything is truly anonymous? And I'm not talking about some kind of spooky governmental NSA thing. I'm talking about human beings. Do you really think that everything is that automated, that there aren't employees who can access your credit card information or your browsing history?" He smiled at Adam. "Do you really think anything is truly a secret?"

"Chris? That's your name, right?"

"Right."

"I don't care about any of that," Adam said. "I care about my wife."

"And I told you the truth about her. I opened your eyes. You should be grateful to me. Instead, you hunted us down. And when you found Ingrid—"

"I told you. I didn't find her. I searched for you, that's all."

"Why? Did you check the link that I gave you?"

"Yes."

"And then you checked your Visa bill. You knew that what I told you was the truth, right?"

"Right."

"So—"

"She's missing."

"Who?" Chris frowned. "Your wife?"

"Yes."

"Wait, when you say she's missing, did you confront her with what I told you?"

Adam said nothing.

"And then, what, she ran off or something?"

"Corinne didn't just run off."

Merton said, "We're wasting time. He's stalling."

Chris looked at him. "You moved his car out of sight, right?"

Merton nodded.

"And we took the battery out of his phone. Relax. There's time." He turned back toward Adam. "Don't you see, Adam? Your wife had deceived you. You had a right to know."

"Maybe," Adam said. "But not from you." He felt his right wrist start slipping through the chain. "Your friend Ingrid is dead because of you."

"You did that," Merton shouted.

"No. Someone killed her. And not just her."

"What are you talking about?"

"The same person who killed your friend also murdered Heidi Dann."

That made them all stop. Gabrielle said, "Oh my God."

Chris's eyes narrowed. "What did you say?"

"You didn't know about that, did you? Ingrid isn't the only murder victim. Heidi Dann was shot and killed too."

Gabrielle said, "Chris?"

"Let me think."

"Heidi was murdered first," Adam continued. "Then

Ingrid. And on top of that, my wife is missing. That's what your revealing of secrets got you."

"Just shut up," Chris said. "We need to figure this out."

"I think he's telling the truth," the long-haired guy added.

"He's not," Merton shouted, hoisting the gun up and pointing it back at Adam. "But even if he is, he's a threat to us. We have no choice here. He's been asking questions and searching for us."

Adam kept his voice as steady as he could. "I've been searching for my wife."

"We don't know where she is," Gabrielle said.

"So what happened, then?"

Chris stood there, still stunned. "Heidi Dann is dead?"

"Yes. And maybe my wife is next. You need to tell me what you did to her."

"We didn't do anything," Chris said.

The wrist was almost free. "Like you said before, start at the beginning," Adam said. "When you blackmailed my wife, how did she react? Did she refuse to pay?"

Chris turned and looked at the long-haired man behind him. Then he turned back to Adam and knelt down next to him. Adam was still working his wrist free. He was close. Of course, what would he do then? Merton had taken a step back. If he grabbed Chris, Merton would have plenty of time to aim the gun.

"Adam?"

"What?"

"We never blackmailed your wife. We never even spoke to her."

Adam didn't understand. "You blackmailed Suzanne."

"Yes."

"And Heidi."

"Yes. But your case was different."

"Different how?"

"We were hired to do it."

For a moment, the pain in his head was gone, pushed out by pure confusion. "Someone hired you to tell me that?"

"They hired us to find lies and secrets about your wife and then reveal them."

"Who hired you?"

"I don't know the name of the client," Chris said, "but we were hired by an investigation firm named CBW."

Adam felt something inside of him plummet.

"What is it?" Chris asked.

"Untie me."

Merton stepped forward. "No way. You ain't going—"

Then a gunfire blast shattered the room. And Merton's head exploded in blood.

CHAPTER 52

KUNTZ had gotten the address of Eduardo's garage from Ingrid.

He sat on it and waited. It didn't take long. Eduardo had driven up through the mountains and over Dingman's Ferry Bridge. Kuntz followed him. When Eduardo arrived, the skinhead wannabe was already there. That would be Merton Sules. Then the woman showed. That would be the one named Gabrielle Dunbar.

One more to go.

Kuntz stayed hidden. As he did, he spotted another man creeping through the woods. He had no idea who the man was. Had Ingrid forgotten to mention him? Not likely. By the end, Ingrid had told him everything. She had told him everything and begged for death.

So who was this guy?

Kuntz stayed still and watched the setup. He saw Merton hide behind a tree with a baseball bat. He saw Gabrielle stand in the clearing and draw the man out. He almost called out a warning when he saw Merton sneak up behind the man, the baseball bat raised. But he didn't. He needed to wait. He needed to make sure they were all here.

So he watched Merton swing the bat and connect with the back of the man's head. The man staggered and fell. Merton, probably unnecessarily, hit him again. For a moment, Kuntz thought that Merton's intent was murder. That would be strange and interesting. The group, according to Ingrid, was completely nonviolent.

This man must have been seen as a threat.

Or . . . or did they think the man was Kuntz himself?

He thought about that. Was there any chance that the group knew they were under threat? By now, they almost certainly knew Ingrid had been murdered. He had counted on that to draw them together. It'd worked. He had also counted on the fact that they were rank amateurs, all high on trying to help the world by revealing secrets or some such nonsense.

But of course, with Ingrid dead, they would know they were in danger.

Was that what this assault was about?

Didn't matter. Kuntz still had the upper hand. He would just have to be patient, that was all. So he waited. He saw them drag the man inside the house. Kuntz waited. Five minutes later, another car pulled up.

It was Chris Taylor. The leader.

They were finally all here. Kuntz considered taking Chris Taylor out then, but that would alarm the others. He needed to be patient. He needed to see if anyone else would show up. He needed to figure out why they had assaulted this other man and what they planned to do with him.

Kuntz quietly circled the house, peering in windows. Nothing. That was odd. There were at least five people inside. Had they gone upstairs or had they . . . ?

He checked a basement window in the back.

Bingo.

The assaulted man was still unconscious. He lay on the floor. Someone had wrapped a bike chain around one of his wrists, looped it around a pipe, and then wrapped the chain around the other wrist. The others—Eduardo, Gabrielle, Merton, and now Chris—paced liked caged animals waiting for slaughter, which, in a sense, they were.

An hour passed. Then two.

The guy never moved. Kuntz wondered if good ol' Merton had killed the poor guy, but eventually the man stirred. Kuntz checked his SIG Sauer P239. He was using 9mm ammunition, so the gun held eight rounds. Should be enough. He had more 9mms in his pocket, just in case.

With the weapon in hand, Kuntz crept toward the front of the cabin. He put his hand on the doorknob and tested it. Unlocked. Perfect. He pushed his way inside and tiptoed toward the basement.

He stopped at the top of the stairs and listened.

What he heard was mostly good news. In short, Chris Taylor and his colleagues had no idea who had murdered their friend Ingrid. The one negative, though it couldn't be helped, was that the assaulted man knew there was a connection between Ingrid's and Heidi's deaths. Not a big deal, though. Kuntz had figured that eventually someone might put it together, but the fact that they had learned it so quickly troubled him a bit.

It didn't matter. He would have to take them all out, including the assaulted guy. He steeled himself by thinking again of Robby in that hospital bed. That was really what it came down to for him. Did he let these people continue to break the law and blackmail people? Or did he do what a father had to in order to ease his family's suffering?

Not much of a choice, was there?

Kuntz was still crouching near the top of the steps, lost for a moment in his thoughts about Barb and Robby, when Eduardo turned and spotted him.

Kuntz didn't hesitate.

Since Merton had the gun, Kuntz took him out first with a bullet to the head. Then he swung his aim back toward Eduardo. Eduardo raised his hand, as though it could somehow stop a bullet.

It didn't.

Gabrielle was screaming. Kuntz turned the gun on her and fired a third time.

The screaming stopped.

Three down, two to go.

Kuntz hurried down the stairs to finish the job.

USING the locator app, Thomas had figured out that his dad had been on Lake Charmaine in Dingman, Pennsylvania, when his phone died. Johanna then insisted that Thomas go back to class and not worry, a position backed up by the principal, who wouldn't let her take him anyway.

After making a few calls, Johanna reached the dispatcher at Shohola Township Police Department. Dingman was in their jurisdiction. She sent him the coordinates from the GPS locator app and tried to explain the situation. The dispatcher didn't really get it or understand the urgency.

"What's the big deal?"

"Just send someone out."

"Okay, Sheriff Lowell said he'd drive by."

Johanna jumped into her car and hit the accelerator.

If a cop tried to pull her over, she had her badge at the ready. She'd signal for them to pull up alongside her and flash it. A half hour later, she got a call back from the same dispatcher. Adam's car wasn't in sight. The locator wasn't precise enough to pinpoint an exact house—they had several on the lake—and what exactly did she expect them to do about it?

"Start going door-to-door."

"I'm sorry. Under whose authority is this coming from?"

"Mine. Yours. Anyone's. Two women have already been killed. This man's wife is missing. He's trying to find her."

"We'll do our best."

CHAPTER 53

IT was amazing how many things could happen in a single moment.

When the first bullet rang out, Adam's mind and body seemed to go in a dozen different directions. He had already gotten his right hand loose from the chain. That was all he needed. With the chain attached to only his left wrist, it did no good. So when the bullet sounded, Adam rolled away, forgetting the pain in his head and ribs, and looked for cover.

Something wet splashed on his face. Adam realized through the fog that it was Merton's brains.

At the same time, various possibilities to explain the shooting ricocheted through his head. The first was a positive one: Could the gunman be a cop sent here to rescue him?

That possibility took a huge hit when the long-haired man dropped like a stone. The possibility was completely blown away a second later when Gabrielle went down too.

It was a slaughter.

Keep moving. . . .

But where? He was in a basement, for crying out loud.

There weren't a whole lot of hiding places. He commando-crawled to his right. Out of the corner of his eye, he spotted Chris Taylor leaping up toward the window. The gunman came down the stairs and took a shot. With surprising speed, Chris kicked his legs up and pushed himself through the window and out of sight.

But Adam heard Chris shout.

Had he been hit?

Maybe. It was hard to tell.

The man with the gun hurried all the way down the stairs.

Trapped.

Adam thought about surrendering. The gunman might, in a sense, be on his side. He, too, might very well have been a victim of Chris's group. But that didn't mean he was about to leave around any witnesses. This guy had, in all likelihood, been the one to kill Ingrid and Heidi. He had now killed Merton and the long-haired man. Gabrielle, he thought, was still alive. Adam could hear her moaning on the ground.

The man was at the bottom of the stairs now.

Adam rolled again to his right and found himself under the very stairs the gunman had just come down. The gunman started toward the window, probably to check on Chris Taylor, but he stopped when he heard Gabrielle groan. The man looked down at her and barely broke stride.

Gabrielle lifted a bloody hand and said, "Please."

The gunman shot her dead.

Adam almost screamed out loud. The gunman didn't hesitate. He kept walking toward the window where Chris had escaped.

That was when Adam spotted Merton's gun.

It was across the room, not far from the window. The gunman's back was turned. Adam had two options here. One, he could try to run up the stairs. But no, that would leave him too exposed for too long. He'd be a sitting duck. So two, if he could just make a sudden move toward the gun, if he could just get there in time and reach out while the man was distracted . . .

Or wait, there was a third option. Should he just stay right where he was? Should he just stay hidden under the stairwell?

Yes. That was it. Stay out of sight. Maybe the man hadn't seen him. Maybe the man didn't know he was here.

No.

The man had shot Merton first. Merton had been standing right next to Adam. There was no way he could have seen Merton and not seen him. The gunman just wanted to make sure no one escaped. He wanted them all dead.

Adam had to go for the weapon.

These calculations didn't take seconds. They didn't even take nanoseconds. All of it—the three options, the computations, the rejections, the planning—happened in no time, as though the world had been frozen just so he could sort this out.

The gun. Get the gun.

It was, he knew, his only hope. So with the man's back turned, Adam leapt from his spot toward the weapon. He stayed low, diving for it, coming closer. His hand was just inches away when a black shoe came out of nowhere and kicked the gun away.

Adam landed on the concrete with a thump. He watched helplessly as the gun skittered underneath a chest of drawers in the corner.

The gunman looked down and, just as he had done with Gabrielle, took aim.

It was over.

Adam knew that now too. His brain had gone through the various options again—roll away, grab the man's leg, try to attack—but he could see that there would not be time. He closed his eyes and winced.

And then a foot came through the window, kicking the man in the head.

Chris Taylor's foot.

The gunman stumbled to the side, but he regained his balance fast. He aimed the gun out the window and fired twice. No way to know if he had hit anything. The gunman started to turn his attention back to Adam.

But Adam was ready.

He leapt to his feet. The bike chain was still attached to his wrist. Adam used it now, swinging it blindly like a whip. It landed flush and heavy on the man's face. He cried out in pain.

Sirens. Police sirens.

Adam didn't let up. He pulled the chain back toward him as his free hand came forward in a fist. It, too, landed on the gunman's face. Blood gushed from his nose. The gunman tried to push Adam away, tried to free himself.

Uh-uh, no way.

Adam kept his body close. He wrapped the gunman up in a bear hug, his momentum still pushing him forward. They fell hard on the concrete, forcing Adam to let go. The gunman took advantage of the moment. He connected with an elbow to Adam's head.

The stars came back. So did the nearly paralyzing pain.

Nearly paralyzing.

The gunman tried to roll away, tried to put just enough space between them so he could free his gun hand. . . .

The gun, Adam thought. *Just concentrate on the gun.*

The sirens were getting closer.

If the man couldn't use his gun, Adam could survive this. Forget the pain. Forget the shots to the body or the head or anything like that. He had but one mission: Grab the man's wrist and stop him from being able to use the gun.

The man tried to kick his way free, but they were still tangled up just enough. The man kicked at him again. Adam's grip loosened. The man was almost free now. He was on his stomach, slipping out of Adam's grasp.

Just grab the wrist.

Without warning, Adam let go of everything. The man, thinking he was free, started to scoot away. But Adam was ready. He leapt toward the gun hand. He grabbed the wrist with both hands, pinning the arm to the concrete but leaving himself otherwise exposed.

The man took advantage of that.

He punched Adam hard in the kidney. The blow stole his breath. Jolts of hot pain surged through his nerve endings. But Adam didn't budge. The man punched him again, harder this time. Adam held on, but now he could feel his body start to shut down.

Another blow and he wouldn't be able to keep his grip.

No choice now. He would have to be more proactive.

Adam lowered his mouth toward the gun hand. He opened wide and bit down like a rabid dog on the inside of the man's wrist. The gunman howled. Adam held on with his teeth and twisted hard, ripping the thin skin.

The gun fell from the man's hand.

Adam dove for it like a drowning man after a life preserver. His hand clasped around the weapon as he felt the man punch him yet again.

But the punch was too little too late. The gun was Adam's now.

The gunman jumped onto Adam's back. Adam rolled backward toward him, swinging his gun in a big arc. The butt of the SIG Sauer landed on the man's already broken nose.

Adam stood up, pointed the gun down at the man, and said, "What did you do to my wife?"

CHAPTER 54

THIRTY seconds later, the cops were there.

They were local guys. Johanna wasn't far behind. She'd been the one to call them, getting the location from Thomas. Adam was proud of his son. He would call him later and explain.

But not quite yet.

Adam dealt with the police. It took some time. That was okay. He could plan as he talked to them. He kept his tone even. He answered all their questions. He answered them in his best attorney voice. He followed his own lawyerly advice: Only answer what is asked.

Nothing more, nothing less.

Johanna told him that the gunman's name was John Kuntz. He was an ex-cop forced to resign. She was still putting the pieces together, but Kuntz now worked security for yet another Internet start-up that was about to go public. Apparently, his motives were financial and involved his sick kid.

Adam nodded as she spoke. He accepted treatment from an EMT, but he refused to go to the hospital. The EMT wasn't happy about that, but there wasn't much he could do. When they were winding down, Johanna put her hand on his shoulder.

"You need to see a doctor."

"I'm fine. Really."

"The cops will want to ask you more questions in the morning."

"I know."

"There'll be a ton of media too," Johanna said. "Three dead bodies."

"Yeah, I know that too." Adam checked his watch. "I better go. I called the boys, but they'll be a wreck until I get home."

"I'll give you a ride, unless you want the police to take you."

"No, that's okay," Adam said. "My car is here."

"They won't let you take it. It's evidence."

He hadn't thought of that.

"Hop in," Johanna said. "I'll drive."

They were quiet for a while. Adam fiddled with his phone for a bit, typing out an e-mail. Then he sat back. The EMT had given him something for the pain. It was making him feel groggy. He closed his eyes.

"Just rest," Johanna said.

He would, but he knew that sleep was still a long way away. "So when are you flying back?" he asked her.

"I don't know," Johanna said. "I might stick around a few more days."

"Why?" He pried his eyes open, looked at her profile. "You got the guy who killed your friend, right?"

"Right."

"That's not enough?"

"Maybe it is, but"—Johanna tilted her head—"we aren't done yet, are we, Adam?"

"Oh, I think we are."

"Still some big loose ends left dangling."

"Like you said, it's a big story now. They'll catch the stranger."

"I'm not talking about him."

He had figured as much. "You're worried about Corinne."

"And you're not?"

"Not as much," he said.

"You want to tell me why?"

Adam took his time, considering his words carefully. "Like you said, there'll be a ton of media now. Everyone will be looking for her, so she'll probably just come home. But the more I think about it, the more I think the answer was pretty obvious right from the start."

Johanna arched an eyebrow. "Do tell."

"I kept wanting it not to be my fault, you know? Her running off had to be more than it appeared. It had to be some big conspiracy involving Chris Taylor's group or something."

"And you don't think that anymore?"

"No, I don't."

"So what do you think?"

"Chris Taylor exposed my wife's most closely held and painful secret. We all know what that does to a person."

"It messes you up," Johanna said.

"Right. But more than that, a revelation that big—it strips you bare. It tears you down and takes away how you look at your life." Adam closed his eyes again. "You need time after something like that. To rebuild. To figure out what's next."

"So you think Corinne . . . ?"

"Occam's razor," Adam said. "The simplest answer is

usually correct. Corinne texted that she needed time apart. It's still only been a few days. She'll come back when she's ready."

"You sound pretty sure."

Adam didn't respond.

Johanna hit her blinker and kept driving. "You want to stop and clean up before you get home? You still got blood on you."

"That's okay."

"You'll scare the boys."

"Nah," Adam said. "They're more resilient than you know."

A few minutes later, Johanna dropped him by his front door. Adam waved and waited until she drove off. He didn't go into his house. The boys weren't there anyway. When he was alone back at the lake, he had called Kristin Hoy. He asked if she could pick the boys up from school and keep them at her house for the night.

"Of course," Kristin Hoy said. "Are you okay, Adam?"

"I'm great. I appreciate this favor."

Corinne's minivan, the one that had been left in the hotel parking lot, was sitting in the driveway. Adam slipped into it. The driver's seat, too, smelled wonderfully of Corinne. The medication was wearing off, and the pain was flooding back in. He didn't care. He could deal with the pain. But he had to be sharp. He had his iPhone in his hand. The police had let him take it from the crime scene. He told them that he thought Chris Taylor had thrown his phone underneath the old chest of drawers. They'd let him reach under for it, but of course it wasn't there.

Merton's gun was.

Another police officer called down that he'd found Adam's phone upstairs. The battery had been removed.

Adam put the battery back and thanked him. Merton's gun was now hidden in his waistband. The police hadn't searched him again. Why would they?

The gun had dug into his side the entire ride with Johanna, but he didn't dare move it.

He needed that gun.

He sent the e-mail he'd composed during the car ride to Andy Gribbel. The subject read:

DO NOT READ UNTIL TOMORROW MORNING.

If something went wrong—and that was likely—Gribbel would read the e-mail in the morning and pass it on to both Johanna Griffin and Old Man Rinsky. He had debated telling them now, before this, but they would have stopped him. Law enforcement would have been contacted and then the suspects would circle the wagons and go silent. They'd hire attorneys like him and the truth would never come out.

He had to handle it this way.

He drove over to Beth Lutheran Church. He parked by the gymnasium exit and waited. He thought that he understood what had happened now, but something was still niggling at the base of his brain. Something still didn't feel right—hadn't felt right from the beginning.

He took out his phone, brought up Corinne's text, and read it once again:

MAYBE WE NEED SOME TIME APART. YOU TAKE CARE OF THE KIDS. DON'T TRY TO CONTACT ME. IT WILL BE OKAY.

He was about to read it again when Bob "Gaston"

Baime came sauntering out. He said good night to the other guys with high fives and knuckle pounds. He wore shorts that were too short. A towel was draped around his neck. Adam waited patiently until Bob was close to his car. Then Adam got out and said, "Hey, Bob."

Bob turned toward him. "Hey, Adam. Whoa, you startled me there. What's—?"

Adam punched him hard in the mouth, knocking the big man onto the driver's seat. Bob's eyes went wide with shock. Adam came up to his door and stuck the gun in his face.

"Don't move."

Bob's hand was on his mouth, stemming the flow of blood. Adam opened the car door behind him and slid him into the backseat. He pressed the gun against Bob's neck.

"What the hell are you doing, Adam?"

"Tell me where my wife is."

"What?"

Adam pushed the muzzle of the gun into the back of his neck. "Just give me a reason."

"I don't know where your wife is."

"CBW Inc., Bob."

Silence.

"You hired them, didn't you?"

"I don't know what—"

Adam struck him in the bony part of the shoulder with the butt of the gun.

"Ow!"

"Tell me about CBW."

"Goddamn it, that hurt. That hurt a lot."

"CBW is your cousin Daz's investigation firm. You hired him to dig up dirt on Corinne."

Bob closed his eyes and moaned.

"Didn't you?"

Adam hit him again with the gun.

"Tell me the truth or I swear I'll shoot you dead."

Bob lowered his head. "I'm sorry, Adam."

"Tell me what happened."

"I didn't mean it. It was just ... I needed something, you know?"

Adam pressed the gun against his neck. "Needed what?"

"Something on Corinne."

"Why?"

The big man went quiet.

"Why did you need something on my wife?"

"Go ahead, Adam."

"What?"

Bob turned and faced him. "Pull the trigger. I want you to. I got nothing anymore. I can't find work. Our house is in foreclosure. Melanie is going to leave me. Go ahead. Please. I bought a good insurance policy from Cal. The boys will be better off."

And then the niggling started up again.

The boys ...

Adam froze and thought about Corinne's text.

The boys ...

"Do it, Adam. Pull the trigger."

Adam shook his head. "Why did you hurt my wife?"

"Because she was trying to hurt me."

"What are you talking about?"

"The stolen money, Adam."

"What about it?"

"Corinne. She was going to pin it on me. And if she did, what chance would I have against her? I mean, come on. Corinne is this nice schoolteacher. Everyone loves her. And me, I'm the one out of a job with the house in foreclosure. Who would believe me over her?"

"So you figured, what, get her before she got you?"

"I had to fight back. So I told Daz. I asked him to look into her, that's all. He didn't find anything. Of course not, right? Corinne's Little Miss Perfect. So Daz says to me that he'd put her name out there with some of his"—he made quote marks in the air—"'unorthodox sources.' He ended up getting a hit with some weird group. But they had their own rules. They have to reveal the dirt themselves."

"Did you steal the money, Bob?"

"No. But who'd believe me? And then Tripp confided in me what Corinne was doing—that she was trying to pin the whole thing on me."

And then the niggling in Adam's brain stopped.

The boys . . .

Adam's throat went dry. "Tripp?"

"Yeah."

"Tripp said Corinne was trying to pin it on you?"

"Right. He said we needed something, that's all."

Tripp Evans. Who had five kids. Three boys. Two girls.

The kids . . .

The boys . . .

He thought about that text one more time:

MAYBE WE NEED SOME TIME APART. YOU
TAKE CARE OF THE KIDS.

Corinne never referred to Thomas and Ryan as "the kids."

She always said "the boys."

CHAPTER 55

THE agony in Adam's head had grown monstrous, grotesque.

Every step sent a fresh lightning bolt through his head. The EMT had given him a few pills to hold him over. He was tempted to take them, grogginess be damned.

But he had to hold on.

Just as he had two days before, he drove past MetLife Stadium and pulled into the low-rent office space. That awful Jersey swamp smell smacked him in the face again. The snapped-together rubberized flooring squeaked under his feet. He knocked on the same ground-level office door.

And again when Tripp opened the door, he said, "Adam?"

And again Adam said, "Why did my wife call you that morning?"

"What? Jesus, you look awful. What happened?"

"Why did Corinne call you?"

"I told you already." Tripp stepped back. "Come in and sit down. Is that blood on your shirt?"

Adam entered the office. He hadn't gotten inside before. Tripp had tried his best to keep him out. Little wonder. The office was a dump. One room. The carpet was worn. The wallpaper was peeling. The computer was dated.

Living in a town like Cedarfield cost big bucks. How had Adam not seen the truth before?

"I know, Tripp."

"Know what?" He studied Adam's face. "You need to see a doctor."

"You stole the lacrosse money, not Corinne."

"Jesus, you got blood all over you."

"Everything was the opposite of what you told me. You asked Corinne for time, not the other way around. And you used that time to set her up. I don't know how exactly. You altered the books, I guess. Hid the stolen money, whatever. You turned everyone else on the board against her. You even told Bob that she was going to pin it on him."

"Listen to me, Adam. Sit down, okay? Let's just talk this out."

"I keep thinking about Corinne's reaction when I confronted her about faking the pregnancy. She didn't bother denying it. What she really wanted to know is how I found out. She figured that you were behind it somehow. Sending her a warning. That's why she called you. To let you know she'd had enough. What did you say back to her, Tripp?"

He didn't bother replying.

"Did you beg her for one more chance? Did you ask her to meet you so you could explain?"

"You got some imagination, Adam."

Adam shook his head and tried to hold it together. "All that philosophizing to me about how the sweet old lady or sports board member rationalizes embezzling funds. How it begins small. Gas money, you said. A coffee at the diner." Adam moved a step closer. "Is that how it went for you?"

"I really have no idea what you're talking about."

Adam swallowed and felt the tears start to come. "She's dead, isn't she?"

Silence.

"You killed my wife."

"You can't really believe that."

But Adam could feel his body start to quake from the truth. "We're living the dream, right? Isn't that what you always say, Tripp? How lucky we all are, how thankful we should be. You married Becky, your high school sweetheart. You have five wonderful kids. You'd do anything to protect them, wouldn't you? What would happen to your precious dream if it got out that you're nothing but a thief?"

Tripp Evans straightened up and pointed at the door. "Get out of my office."

"It came down to you or Corinne. That's how you saw it. Your family gets destroyed. Or mine. For a guy like you, the choice was easy."

Tripp's tone was colder now. "Get out."

"That text you sent pretending to be her. I should have seen it right away."

"What are you talking about?"

"You killed her. And then, to buy time, you sent that text. I was supposed to read it and figure she was blowing off steam—and if I didn't believe that, if I thought something happened to her, the police wouldn't pay attention. They'd see the text. They'd learn we just had a giant fight. They wouldn't even bother filling out a report. You knew all that."

Tripp shook his head. "You got it wrong."

"I wish I did."

"You can't prove this. You can't prove any of this."

"Prove? Maybe not. But I know." Adam held up his cell phone. "'You take care of the kids.'"

"What?"

"That's what the text says. 'You take care of the kids.'"

"So?"

"So Corinne never called Thomas and Ryan the kids." He smiled even as his heart sank. "It was always the boys. That's what they were. Not her kids. Her boys. Corinne never wrote that text. You did. You killed her and then you sent that text so no one would start looking for her right away."

"That's your proof?" Tripp almost laughed. "You really think anyone is going to believe that crazy story?"

"Doubt it."

Adam lifted the gun out of his pocket and took aim.

Tripp's eyes went wide. "Whoa, just calm down and listen a second."

"I don't really need to hear more of your lies, Tripp."

"Just . . . Becky is meeting me here in a few minutes."

"Oh, good." Adam moved the gun closer to the man's face. "What would your little philosophizing say about that? Eye for an eye maybe?"

For the first time, Tripp Evans's mask slipped off and Adam could see the darkness beneath. "You wouldn't hurt her."

Adam just stared at him. Tripp stared back. For a second, neither of them moved. Then something changed in Tripp. Adam could see it. Tripp began to nod to himself. He leaned back and grabbed his car keys.

"Let's go," Tripp said.

"What?"

"I don't want you here when Becky arrives. Let's go."

"So where are we going?"

"You wanted the truth, right?"

"If this is some sort of trick . . ."

"It's not. You'll see the truth with your own eyes, Adam. Then you can do whatever you want. That's the deal. But we gotta go right now. I don't want Becky hurt, do you understand?"

They started out the door. Adam walked a step behind. He kept the gun on Tripp for a few seconds, but then he realized how that might look if someone walked by, so he put the gun in his jacket pocket. He still pointed it at Tripp through the pocket, like some guy in a bad movie using his finger to pretend he had a gun.

When they stepped outside, a familiar Dodge Durango pulled into the lot. Both men froze as Becky pulled in. Tripp whispered, "If you touch a hair on her head . . ."

"Just get rid of her," Adam said.

Becky Evans had the cheerful smile on her face. She waved with too much enthusiasm and pulled up next to them.

"Hey, Adam," Becky called out.

She was still so damn cheerful.

"Hey, Becky."

"What are you doing here?"

Adam looked toward Tripp. Tripp said, "Something came up with the sixth-grade boys' game."

"I thought that was tomorrow night."

"Well, that's just it. We might get kicked out of the whole tournament because of some registration problem. Adam and I are just going to take a ride over there and see if we can work it out."

"Oh, that's a shame. We were going to go out to dinner."

"We still will, hon. It shouldn't take more than an hour or two. We'll go to Baumgart's when I get home, okay? Just the two of us."

Becky nodded, but for the first time, the smile faltered. "Sure." She turned to Adam. "Take care, Adam."

"You too."

"Give my best to Corinne. We really need to go out soon, the four of us."

Adam managed to say, "I'd like that."

With another cheery wave, Becky drove off. Tripp watched her. His eyes were wet. When she was out of sight, he started walking again. Adam followed. Tripp took out his key and unlocked the car. He got in on the driver's side. Adam took the seat next to him. He pulled the gun out of his pocket and pointed it at Tripp again. Tripp seemed calmer now. He hit the accelerator and started out on Route 3.

"Where are we going?" Adam asked.

"Mahlon Dickerson Reservation."

"Near Lake Hopatcong?"

"Yes."

"Corinne's family used to have a house there," Adam said. "When she was little."

"I know. Becky went with her when they were in third grade. It's why I chose it."

Adam's adrenaline began to ebb. The dull, thudding ache in his head returned with renewed energy. Dizziness and exhaustion sapped him. Tripp veered onto Interstate 80. Adam blinked and gripped the gun tighter. He knew this ride and calculated that they were about a half hour away from the reservation. The sun had started to set, but they probably had another hour at least of daylight.

His cell phone rang. He checked the caller ID and saw it was Johanna Griffin. He didn't answer it. They drove some more in silence. When they reached the exit for Route 15, Tripp said, "Adam?"

"Yeah."

"Don't do that again."

"Don't do what?"

"Don't ever threaten my family."

"Ironic," Adam said, "coming from you."

Tripp turned, met his eye, and said it again: "Don't ever threaten my family."

His tone sent a chill down Adam's back.

Tripp Evans turned back to the road. He had both hands on the wheel. He took Weldon Road and then veered off onto a dirt road into the woods. He parked up along the trees and turned off the ignition. Adam kept his gun ready.

"Come on," Tripp said, opening the car door. "Let's get this over with."

He stepped out of the car. Adam did the same, making sure to keep the gun pointed at Tripp. If he was going to try something, here, alone in the woods, was probably his best chance. But Tripp didn't hesitate. He trekked into the woods. There was no path, but they could still make their way. Tripp walked steadily, with purpose. Adam tried to keep up, but in his condition, it was hard going. He wondered whether this would be Tripp's big move—to get farther and farther ahead of him and then make a run for it, maybe sneak up on Adam as it got darker.

"Slow down," Adam said.

"You want the truth, don't you?" Tripp's tone was almost singsong. "Keep up."

"Your office," Adam said.

"What about it? Oh, it's a shit hole, is that what you're thinking?"

"I thought you'd done well at some big Madison Avenue firm," Adam said.

"I was there for about five minutes before they laid me off. See, I always figured that I'd have a job for life with my dad's sporting goods store. Put all my eggs in that basket. When that went south, I lost everything. Yeah, I tried to put out my own shingle, but, well, you just saw the results of that."

"You were broke."

"Yep."

"And there was enough money in the lacrosse treasury."

"Way more than enough. You know Sydney Gallonde? Rich guy I went to Cedarfield High with? Sucked at lacrosse. Rode the bench. He gave us a hundred grand because I worked him. Me. There were other donors too. When I came in, the organization could barely buy a goalpost. Now we have turf fields and uniforms and . . ." Tripp stopped talking. "I guess you think I'm just rationalizing again."

"You are."

"Maybe, Adam. But you're not naïve enough to think the world is black-and-white."

"Hardly."

"It is always us against them. That's what all of life is. We fight wars for that reason. We make decisions every day to protect our own loved ones, even if it means hardships for others. You buy your boy a new pair of cleats for lacrosse. Maybe you could have used that money to save a starving child in Africa. But no, you let that child starve. Us against them. We all do this."

"Tripp?"

"What?"

"This really isn't a good time for your bullshit."

"Yeah, you're right." Tripp stopped in the middle of the woods, knelt down, and started feeling his way around on the ground. His hand pushed away the brush and leaves. Adam readied his gun and took two steps back.

"I'm not going to attack you, Adam. There's no need."

"What are you doing?"

"I'm looking for something. . . . Ah, here it is."

He stood up.

Holding a shovel.

Adam's legs went rubbery. "Oh no. . . ."

Tripp just stood there. "You were right. In the end, it came to my family or yours. Only one could survive. So let me ask you, Adam. What would you have done?"

Adam just shook his head. "No. . . ."

"You got most of it right. I did take the money, but I had every intention of paying it back. I won't go through the justification again. Corinne found out. I begged her not to say anything, that it would ruin my life. I was trying to buy time. But really, there was no way I could repay that money. Not yet. So yeah, I have a background in bookkeeping. I did it at my dad's store for years. I started to change the books so the finger pointed more at her. Corinne didn't know about it, of course. She actually listened to me and kept quiet. She didn't even tell you, did she?"

"No," Adam said. "She didn't."

"So I went to Bob and Cal and then, with great pretend regret, Len. I told all of them Corinne had stolen the lacrosse funds. Strangely enough, Bob was the one who didn't really buy it. So I told him that when I confronted Corinne, she said it was him."

"And then Bob went to his cousin."

"I didn't count on that."

"Where is Corinne now?"

"You're standing right where I buried her."

Just like that.

Adam made himself look down. Vertigo took over. He didn't bother to steady himself. The earth beneath his feet, he could see, had recently been disturbed. He collapsed to the side, leaning against a tree, his breath hitching in his chest.

"You okay, Adam?"

He swallowed and lifted the gun. *Keep it together, keep it together, keep it together....*

"Start digging," Adam said.

"What good is that going to do? I already told you she's there."

Still dizzy, Adam staggered toward him and put the gun right in his face. "Start digging now."

Tripp shrugged and walked past him. Adam kept the gun on him, trying hard to not even blink. Tripp pierced the dirt with the shovel, scooped up the dirt, tossed it to the side.

"Tell me the rest of it," Adam said.

"You know the rest of it, don't you? After you confronted her about faking the pregnancy, Corinne was furious. She'd had enough. She was going to tell what I'd done. So I told her, okay, fair enough, I'll come forward. I said, let's just meet at lunchtime and go over it, so we're on the same page. She was reluctant, but hey, I can be persuasive."

The shovel dug into the earth again. Then again.

"Where did you meet?" Adam asked.

Tripp tossed the dirt to the side. "Your place. I went in through the garage. Corinne came out and met me. She didn't want me in the actual house, you know? Like it was a place only for her family."

"So what did you do?"

"What do you think I did?"

Tripp looked down and smiled at the ground. Then he stepped back so Adam could see.

"I shot her."

Adam looked past him and down to the ground. His heart crumbled into dust. There, lying in the dirt, was Corinne.

"Oh no...."

His legs gave way. Adam dropped next to Corinne and started brushing the dirt off her face. "Oh no...." Her eyes were closed, and she was still so damn beautiful. "No ... Corinne ... Oh God, please ..."

He lost it then. He placed his cheek against her cold, lifeless one and sobbed.

A small dim part of him thought about Tripp, about him still holding the shovel and maybe attacking him. Adam looked up, gun ready.

But Tripp hadn't moved.

He stood there with a small smile on his face.

"Are you ready to go now, Adam?"

"What?"

"Are you ready to go home?"

"What the hell are you talking about?"

"It's like I promised back at the office. You know the truth now. It's over. We need to bury her again."

Adam's head started spinning again. "Are you out of your mind?"

"No, my friend, but perhaps you are."

"What the hell are you talking about?"

"I'm sorry about killing her. I really am. But I saw no other way out. Seriously. Like I said, we kill for our own, right? Your wife was threatening my family. What would you have done?"

"I wouldn't have stolen the money."

"It's done, Adam." His voice was like a steel gate slamming shut. "Now we both need to move on."

"You're insane."

"And you haven't thought this through." The smile came back to his lips. "The lacrosse books are a mess. No one will ever be able to untangle them. So what will the police know? You found out Corinne tricked you by faking a pregnancy. You two had a huge fight about it. The next day, she was shot in your garage. I cleaned up the blood a bit, but so what? The police will find traces of it. I used the cleaner under your sink. I threw out the bloody rags in your garbage can. Are you starting to see, Adam?"

He looked back down at Corinne's beautiful face.

"I put her body in the trunk of her own car. The shovel in my hand—doesn't it look familiar? It should. I took it from your garage."

Adam just stared down at his beautiful wife.

"And if that's not enough, the security cameras in my office corridor will show you forcing me into my car with a gun. If any of my fibers or DNA are found on the body now, well, you forced me to dig her up. You killed her, you buried her here, you parked her car near an airport, but you stayed away from an actual airport lot because everyone knows they have a ton of security cameras. Then you bought time by sending yourself a text about her running off. Then, to confuse matters more, you probably, oh, I don't know, tossed her cell phone in the back of a delivery truck at, say, a Best Buy store. If anyone searched for it, they'd think she was driving somewhere, at least as long as the battery lasted. That would cause more confusion."

Adam just shook his head. "They're never going to buy that."

"Sure they will. And if not, let's be honest. You're the husband. It's a lot more logical than claiming I killed her, don't you think?"

Adam turned back to his wife. Her lips were purple. Corinne didn't look peaceful in death. She looked lost and scared and alone. He stroked her face with his hand. In one way, Tripp Evans was right. It was over, no matter what happened now. Corinne was dead. His life partner had been taken away from him forever. His sons, Ryan and Thomas, would never be the same. His boys—no, *her* boys—would never know the comfort and love of their mother again.

"What's done is done, Adam. It's détente now. Don't make something bad even worse."

And then Adam saw one more thing that broke his heart all over again.

Her earlobes.

Her earlobes . . . they were empty. He flashed back to that Forty-Seventh Street jewelry store, the Chinese restaurant, the waiter delivering them on the plate, the smile on her face, the way Corinne carefully took them off and left them on the night table before going to bed.

Tripp hadn't just killed her. He had stolen the diamond studs off her dead body.

"And one more thing," Tripp said.

Adam looked up at him.

"If you ever go near my family or threaten them," he said, "well, I've already shown you what I will do."

"Yes, you have."

And then Adam lifted the gun, aimed it at the center of Tripp's chest, and squeezed the trigger three times.

CHAPTER 56

THE lacrosse game took place in the optimistically dubbed SuperDome, an air-inflated sports facility made from some sort of pliable material. Thomas was playing in an indoor league for the winter season. Ryan had come along too. He half watched his brother, half played catch in the corner with a couple of other kids. Ryan also kept looking over at his father. He did that a lot now, looked for his father, as though Adam might suddenly vanish into thin air. Adam got it, of course. He tried to reassure him, but what could he really say?

He didn't want to lie to the boys. But he wanted them to feel happy and safe.

Every parent has to deal with that balance. That hadn't changed with Corinne's death, but maybe you learn that happiness based on untruths is, at best, fleeting.

Adam watched as Johanna Griffin pushed through the glass door. She came across the back of the goal and stood alongside him facing the field.

"Thomas is number eleven, right?"

"Right," Adam said.

"How's he been playing?"

"Great. The coach of Bowdoin wants him to commit."

"Wow. Good school. He going to do it?"

Adam shrugged. "It's a six-hour drive. Before all this, yeah. But now . . ."

"He wants to stay closer to home."

"Right. Of course, we can move too. There's nothing left for us in this town."

"Why are you staying?"

"I don't know. The boys lost enough already. They grew up here. They have their school, their friends." On the field, Thomas scooped up a loose ball and started down the field. "Their mom is here too. In that house. In this town."

Johanna nodded.

Adam turned to her. "It's so great to see you."

"Same."

"When did you get in?"

"A few hours ago," Johanna said. "They're sentencing Kuntz tomorrow."

"You already know he's getting life."

"Yeah," she said. "But I want to see it happen. And I also wanted to make sure that you were officially exonerated."

"I was. I got word last week."

"I know. But I still wanted to see it for myself."

Adam nodded. Johanna looked over toward where Bob Baime and other parents sat.

"You always stand alone on the sidelines?"

"I do now," Adam said. "But I don't take it personally. You know how I told you that whole thing about living the dream?"

"Yeah."

"I'm living proof that the dream is flimsy stuff. They all know it's flimsy, of course, but no one wants to hang around a constant reminder."

They watched the game some more.

"They have nothing new on Chris Taylor," she said. "He's still on the run. But in the end, he's not exactly Public Enemy Number One. All he did was blackmail some people who don't want to press charges because their secrets will be revealed. I doubt he'd get more than probation, even if he was caught. Would you be okay with that?"

Adam shrugged. "I go round and round with it."

"How so?"

"If he'd let Corinne keep her secret, this may have never happened. So I ask myself: Did the stranger kill my wife? Or did her own decision about faking the pregnancy? Or did I, by not realizing how insecure I'd made her? You can drive yourself crazy with that kind of thinking. You can go back and look at the ripples forever. But in the end, there is only one person to blame. And that person is dead. I killed him."

Thomas passed the ball and ran to the area behind the goal known in lacrosse jargon as X. According to the medical examiner's report, the first bullet had been enough. It had pierced Tripp Evans's heart, killing him instantly. Adam could still feel the gun in his hand. He could still feel the retort when he pulled the trigger. He could still see Tripp Evans's body collapse and hear the long echoes of the gunshots in the quiet forest.

For a few seconds after the shooting, Adam had done nothing. He had sat there, numb. He hadn't thought about the repercussions. He had just wanted to stay with his wife. He had lowered his head back to his Corinne.

He had kissed her cheek and closed his eyes and let himself cry.

Then a moment later, he heard Johanna say, "Adam, we need to move fast."

She had been following him. She slowly pried the gun from Adam's hand and placed it in Tripp Evans's. She looped her finger over his and fired off three shots, so that there would be gun residue on Tripp's hand. She picked up Tripp's other hand and used it to scratch Adam, making sure that DNA got beneath his fingernails. Adam just followed her orders in a daze. They came up with a story of self-defense. It wasn't perfect. There were holes and plenty of skepticism, but in the end, the physical evidence, along with Johanna's own testimony of overhearing Tripp Evans's confession, made it impossible to get an indictment.

Adam was free.

Still, you live with what you've done. He had killed a man. You don't get a free pass on something like that. It haunted him at night, robbed him of sleep. He understood that he had had no choice. As long as Tripp Evans was alive, he was a threat to Adam's family. And something primitive in him even took satisfaction in what he'd done, in avenging his wife, in protecting his boys.

"Can I ask you something?" he said.

"Sure."

"Do you sleep okay?"

Johanna Griffin smiled. "No, not really."

"I'm sorry."

She shrugged. "I may not sleep well, but I would sleep a lot worse if you spent the rest of your life in prison. I made a choice when I saw you in the woods. I think I made the choice that lets me sleep best."

"Thank you," he said.

"Don't worry about it."

There was something else that had always bothered Adam, but he never spoke about it. Tripp Evans in the end—did he really think his plan would work? Did he really think Adam would simply let him get away with killing his wife? Did he really think it was wise to threaten his family like that when Adam was kneeling beside his dead wife with a gun in his hand?

After his death, Tripp's family had been on the receiving end of a huge death-benefit payout. The Evans family stayed in town. They got support. Everyone in Cedarfield, even those who believed Tripp was a murderer, rallied around Becky and the kids.

Had Tripp known that would happen?

Had Tripp, in the end, wanted Adam to kill him?

The game was tied with a minute left.

Johanna Griffin said, "Funny, though."

"What?"

"It was all about secrets. That was the whole thing with Chris Taylor and his group. They wanted to rid the world of secrets. And now you and I have been forced to keep the biggest secret of all."

They both stood and watched the time ticking down. With thirty seconds to go, Thomas scored a goal to break the tie. The crowd erupted. Adam didn't leap for joy. But he did smile. He turned toward Ryan. Ryan was smiling too. So, he bet, under the helmet, was Thomas.

"Maybe that's what I really came for," Johanna said.

"What's that?"

"To see you all smile."

Adam nodded. "Maybe."

"Are you a religious man, Adam?"

"Not really."

"Doesn't matter. You don't have to believe that she actually sees her boys smile." Johanna kissed his cheek and started to walk away. "You just have to believe that she'd want to."

ACKNOWLEDGMENTS

The author wishes to acknowledge the following in no particular order because he can't remember exactly who helped with what: Anthony Dellapelle, Tom Gorman, Kristi Szudlo, Joe and Nancy Scanlon, Ben Sevier, Brian Tart, Christine Ball, Jamie Knapp, Diane Discepolo, Lisa Erbach Vance, and Rita Wilson. As always, any mistakes are theirs. Hey, they're the experts. Why should I take all the heat?

I'd also like to give a quick shout-out to John Bonner, Freddie Friednash, Leonard Gilman, Andy Gribbel, Johanna Griffin, Rick Gusherowski, Heather and Charles Howell III, Kristin Hoy, John Kuntz, Norbert Pendergast, Sally Perryman, and Paul Williams, JP. These people (or their loved ones) made generous contributions to charities of my choosing in return for having their names appear in this novel. If you'd like to participate in the future, visit HarlanCoben.com or e-mail giving@harlancoben.com for details.

ABOUT THE AUTHOR

Harlan Coben is the international bestselling author of more than twenty previous novels, including the #1 *New York Times* bestsellers *Missing You*, *Six Years*, *Stay Close*, *Live Wire*, *Caught*, *Long Lost*, and *Hold Tight*, as well as the popular Myron Bolitar series and, more recently, a series aimed at young adults featuring Myron's nephew, Mickey Bolitar. The winner of the Edgar®, Shamus, and Anthony awards, he lives in New Jersey.

CONNECT ONLINE

harlancoben.com
facebook.com/harlancobenbooks
twitter.com/harlancoben